Praise for Mary Daheim and her Emma Lord mysteries

THE ALPINE ADVOCATE

"In THE ALPINE ADVOCATE the lively ferment of a life in a small Pacific Northwest town, with its convoluted genealogies and loyalties [and] its authentically quirky characters, combines with a baffling murder for an intriguing mystery novel."
—M. K. WREN

THE ALPINE BETRAYAL

"Editor-publisher Emma Lord finds out that running a small-town newspaper is worse than nutty—it's downright dangerous. Readers will take great pleasure in Mary Daheim's new mystery."
—CAROLYN G. HART

THE ALPINE CHRISTMAS

"If you like cozy mysteries, you need to try Daheim's Alpine series. . . . Recommended."
—*The Snooper*

By Mary Daheim
Published by Ballantine Books:

THE
ALPINE
ESCAPE

Mary Daheim

BALLANTINE BOOKS • NEW YORK

A Ballantine Book
Published by The Random House Publishing Group

Published in the United States by Ballantine Books, an imprint of The Random House Publishing Group, a division of Random House, Inc., New York, and simultaneously in Canada by Random House of Canada Limited, Toronto.

BALLANTINE and colophon are registered trademarks of Random House, Inc.

www.ballantinebooks.com

ISBN-13: 978-0-345-38842-1

Printed in the United States of America

First Edition: April 1995

19 18 17 16 15 14

Chapter One

I HAD BEEN warned. Sooner or later, it was bound to happen. My beautiful secondhand Jaguar would develop mechanical problems. Apparently, it finally had. It wouldn't start. To me, that's a mechanical problem.

I'd parked the Jag at the end of a long row of cars in the lot reserved for the Three Crabs Restaurant & Lounge near Dungeness Spit. On an overcast July day the Strait of Juan de Fuca looked gray and dull, as if it were bored with its endless passage between the Olympic Peninsula and Vancouver Island.

I, however, was not bored but agitated. And confused.

My car wasn't my only problem. With great reluctance I'd abandoned my duties as editor and publisher of *The Alpine Advocate* in an attempt to reassess my life. Maybe it's naive to think that forty-two years of eluding reality can be rectified in three days, but I had to start somewhere. The Olympic Peninsula seemed like a good place for soul-searching.

Now my priority was a tow truck. I marched back inside the restaurant, found the pay phone, and scanned the local directory. The towing service in Sequim would be out in an hour. Where did I want to go?

That was a good question. I had no idea who could handle Jaguar XJ6 repairs on the Olympic Peninsula. I was just off Highway 101, so I wasn't exactly stranded

in the middle of nowhere. The town of Sequim was a
bustling place, chock-full of dissatisfied and retired Californians who had found an authentic Sunbelt in the Pacific Northwest. A few miles to the west lay Port
Angeles, with a population of 18,000. Surely one or two
of these people owned a Jaguar. Surely someone could
do the repairs.

"Gee," said the friendly voice at the other end of the
line, "I don't know who fixes those things around here.
There used to be a bunch of hippies at Happy Valley
who worked on foreign cars. Good mechanics, too."

"It might be something simple," I said, sensing the
onslaught of a panic attack. "The Jag's green. My name
is Emma Lord. How about taking me to a Chevron or
a BP station here in Sequim?" I had plastic for the two
oil companies. My budget for the three-day trip was
two hundred and fifty dollars. If the repair was over
fifty bucks—and when was it ever under?—I'd have to
charge it.

"We'd better haul you into Port Angeles," said the
man at the other end. "You'll have better luck there
with that Jag. See you around two. More or less."

Back outside, I prowled the sands, feeling a cool
breeze on my face and hearing the tide slap against the
shore. Dungeness Spit snakes five miles out into the
strait, with one of the last two manned lighthouses in
the continental United States. Recently, I'd heard it was
scheduled for conversion to a computerized operation.
So much for romance. But I, too, was trying to convert.
Outmoded romantic notions were impeding my personal
progress as well.

Some seventeen miles across the strait, I could make
out the cluster of buildings that was Victoria, British
Columbia. I hadn't been to Victoria in twenty years. Indeed, I hadn't been on the Olympic Peninsula since
then, either. My plan to drive around the loop was hit-

ting a snag. Trying to avoid added pressure on myself, I'd resolved not to make reservations. I dealt with deadlines every day on the job in Alpine. But the ferry from Edmonds to Kingston had been full; traffic heading across the Hood Canal Floating Bridge had been heavy. Maybe I should go back to the restaurant and call ahead to book a motel room. If nothing else, it would help kill time while I waited for the tow truck.

With my short brown hair tousled by the wind—and sand in my open-toed shoes—I trudged the long, narrow spit, my eyes straying to the rugged bulk of the Olympic Mountains that seemed to rise almost directly above the highway. I was accustomed to mountains. In Alpine I live among them, eight miles west of the Cascade summit, in a town built into the rocky face of Tonga Ridge. Fleetingly, I thought of my little log house. Already I missed it. But, as my House & Home editor, Vida Runkel, had advised, I needed to get away. Alone. I went back into the restaurant, which was still busy. Judging from the license plates in the parking lot, most of the lunch crowd were tourists like me.

The motels were also doing a brisk business. They were all booked except for the ones that were out of my price range. The bed and breakfast establishments were full, too. Discouraged, I went into the bar and ordered a Pepsi, then felt my mouth twist with irony. Here I was, Emma Lord, forty-two years old, mother of a twenty-one-year-old son, never married, university graduate, newspaper owner, fairly bright, reasonably attractive, and sitting alone at a bar on a Tuesday afternoon drinking soda pop. No wonder I needed time to reflect. I felt like a real loser.

The woman tending bar was younger than I, but not by much. She was pretty, her makeup carefully if generously applied to hide a sallow complexion. At the moment I was her only customer.

"Where you from?" she asked after giving me my Pepsi.

I told her. She looked vague. "Idaho?"

"No." I explained where Alpine was located. It didn't surprise me that she hadn't heard of my hometown. With only four thousand residents living in relative isolation off the Stevens Pass highway, Alpine isn't exactly a Washington State hub.

"Traveling alone?" she asked, trying to sound casual. I nodded.

She looked vaguely shocked. "That takes guts these days. Too many creeps out there." Using her white ceramic coffee mug, she gestured in the general direction of the entrance. "You're not camping, I hope?"

It was my turn to look shocked. "Oh, no!" I've always felt that if I had a sudden urge to sleep outdoors, I'd join the army and get paid for it. On the off chance that the bartender might have a brother or a friend in the hostelry business, I told her of my dilemma.

The best she could do was suggest places I'd already called. Frowning into her coffee mug, she shook her head. "You don't know anybody around here?" Apparently, it seemed inconceivable that a stranger should have no local connections. As a small-town dweller I understood her thinking. Everyone knows everyone else, and half of them are somehow related. It was no different in Clallam County than it was in Skykomish County.

The bartender's question jolted my memory. "As a matter of fact, I do. Sort of," I added lamely. Before buying *The Advocate* and moving to Alpine, I had toiled for seventeen years on *The Oregonian* in Portland. My best friend on the paper was Mavis Marley Fulkerston, now retired and living in Tigard, Oregon. But Mavis's daughter, Jackie, had gotten married on St. Valentine's Day and moved to Port Angeles. I hadn't attended the wedding, but I'd received an invitation. I racked my brain trying to remember her husband's name. With a dawning sense of doom I decided that I could hardly barge in on someone whose last name I didn't know. On the other hand, I'd sent Jackie and her groom a toaster oven.

The tow truck arrived just as I was finishing my drink. Overtipping the sympathetic bartender, I hurried outside. After checking the battery and finding it wasn't the cause of my trouble, we hit the road to Port Angeles. My gloomy mood persisted all the way past Morse Creek and into town. Things weren't looking up half an hour later when the mechanic at the Chevron station announced that he couldn't find the trouble. Could I wait for Jake? He knew a little something about foreign cars.

I didn't have any choice, but since Jake and his knowledge were off somewhere in the mysterious West End, I resumed cudgeling my brain for Jackie Fulkerston's married name. I went halfway through the alphabet in my mind and stopped at *M*. With my eyes locked on the Jag, which was up on the hoist, I snapped my fingers. One of the mechanics darted me a curious look.

"Melcher," I said firmly. "Do you know a young couple named Melcher? They moved here late last winter."

The mechanic, who was young and needed a shave, closed one eye and wrinkled his thin nose. "Melcher. 'Ninety-two Wrangler. 'Eighty-nine Honda Accord. Yeah, they come in here. She had a lube job on the Honda last week."

Figuring that the newlywed Melchers wouldn't have made it into the current Port Angeles phone book, I trotted over to the corner booth and dialed directory assistance. Jackie's husband was named Paul. Their phone was answered on the second ring.

"Emma!" shrieked Jackie Fulkerston Melcher. "How *funny!*" To my dismay she began to sob.

"Jackie, what's wrong?" I asked, alarmed.

Two gulps later she replied, "I'm pregnant! Isn't it wonderful?" She sobbed some more.

"Well . . . it sure is." I frowned into the stainless-steel pay-phone panel. "I . . . uh . . . just thought I'd call and say hi since I'm passing through."

Jackie sniffed loudly before speaking again. "You've got to stop in and have a drink or something. Where are you?"

I told her, then added that my car was temporarily out of commission. I was beginning to feel embarrassed.

Jackie, however, was a font of sympathy. "Oh, how awful when you're on a trip! I *hate* it when that happens! Remember the time Mom had to drive down to Coos Bay and her wheels fell off?"

I did, but my version wasn't quite the same. Mavis had hit a deep rut while trying to turn around off the highway and had jarred her axle. I'd forgotten that Jackie was inclined to dramatic exaggeration.

"Cars are such a *pain*," Jackie was saying, and I could envision her wide mouth turning down at the corners and her gray eyes rolling heavenward. "Listen, I'll be down to get you in five minutes. We're right up here on Lincoln Hill. Oh, I'm so *glad* you called! It's like the answer to a prayer!"

I was properly surprised. "It is?" Not having seen Jackie since her mother's retirement party two years ago, I couldn't imagine why she'd been invoking divine intervention to hear my voice.

"Yes! It's incredible, the next best thing to having Mom show up. Paul and I need an inquiring mind."

I was beginning to think that Jackie could use any

kind of a mind that operated on a more even keel than her own. "Oh? How come?" My tone was neutral.

Jackie lowered her voice, and instead of a tearful vibrato, she giggled. "It's so *weird,* Emma. You won't believe this!" She tittered, she gasped, she let out an odd howling sound. "We found a body! In our basement! Isn't that *great?*" Jackie burst into fresh sobs.

There was a bit of comfort in finding someone whose mental state was more unstable than my own. Or so I mused as I leaned against a lamppost at the corner of Ninth and Lincoln, waiting for Jackie Melcher to pick me up.

I wasn't alarmed. The alleged body could be anything, including a dog, a squirrel, or a gopher. Jackie's sense of high drama was probably exacerbated by pregnancy. She'd always been a volatile girl, full of energy one minute, given to morose moodiness the next. She would often exasperate her mother but never her father, who doted on his daughter.

Fortunately for the Fulkerstons, their two sons were rock-solid specimens. One was an oceanographer in California; the other produced films for the city of Portland. Jackie, as I recalled, had majored in French at the University of Oregon, where I'd finished my senior year.

But, I reminded myself, while Jackie was young and pregnant, I had no such excuses for capricious behavior. After twenty-two years of waiting for the father of my son to get up the nerve to leave his wife, I'd come to the realization that while Tom Cavanaugh might care for me as much as I cared for him, he put duty above love. Of course he'd call it *honor,* as men often do, but it boiled down to the same thing. Sandra Cavanaugh was the mother of his other two children, and when it came to mental instability, I couldn't hold a candle to her. But then neither could Napoleon. Sandra suffered from a variety of emotional problems, all no doubt caused by the fact that she was born rich. Or so I'd always told myself.

Tom and I had met when I interned on *The Seattle Times*. Sandra's mental disorders were only beginning to surface then, but living with her had become sufficiently difficult that Tom had sought comfort in my arms. He'd also apparently sought something in Sandra's because we both got pregnant about the same time. Not without regret, Tom had chosen to stay with his wife. I had chosen to leave Seattle and have my baby in Mississippi, where my brother, Ben, was serving as a priest in the home missions. I had also chosen—fiercely and proudly—to raise Adam alone. If Tom wouldn't give me his name, he wasn't going to give me any help, by God. For almost twenty years I had shut him out of my life. And out of Adam's, which wasn't entirely fair to either of them.

In the past two years I'd relented. Tom had shown up in Alpine, and I'd succumbed to his entreaties to let him meet Adam. Father and son had gotten along very well. Father and Mother had, too, so much so that when I'd attended a weekly newspaper conference at Lake Chelan in June, Tom and I had ended up in bed.

For three days and three nights we pretended it was forever. We knew better, though. Tom no longer needed Sandra's fortune as a base for his newspaper ventures, but Sandra needed Tom. He wouldn't forsake her, and I would have loved him less if he had. Tom neither loved nor lived lightly, which I suppose is why I could never quite let go. We are too much alike.

But there was no future in it. If I wanted to marry, maybe even have another child, I had to put the past aside. "Keep your options open," Vida Runkel had counseled. "You've put up a barrier to everyone but Tommy."

Only Vida could get away with calling Tom *Tommy*. And only Vida could speak so frankly to me. Even my brother, in his kind but indecisive manner, wouldn't take such a resolute stand. Ben not only sees both sides of every issue, he considers all the angles and contours. I am prone to do the same. Ben vacillates; I'm objective. Either way, the result is that it's very hard for both of us to make crucial decisions.

Thus Vida was right. I needed a shove in order to get going. Over the years there had been a few other men in my life, but never one I really loved. I wouldn't let myself love them, asserted Vida. I had built a dream house on sand and the tide was coming in fast.

Watching traffic pass by, half of which bore out-of-county license plates, I thought of Sheriff Milo Dodge. Like me, Milo was afraid of letting go. Divorced for the past six years, Milo refused to commit himself to his current ladylove, Honoria Whitman. Honoria was getting impatient. I didn't blame her. But I didn't blame Milo, either. Like me, he was afraid. Sometimes I wondered if Milo and I were afraid of each other. We spent quite a bit of time together but had only kissed once, which had been sort of an accident. Or so I had thought in the heat of the moment.

A white Honda Accord pulled up to the curb. Behind the wheel Jackie Melcher waved frantically, her heart-shaped face wreathed in smiles. I jumped in and we shot across the intersection before I could fasten my seat belt.

"Emma, you look great! You got your hair cut!"

I laughed, patting the gamine style I'd acquired not long before going off to Chelan. "It's nice and cool for summer," I said noncommittally.

Jackie was heading through the main part of town,

past the handsome old redbrick courthouse I remembered from my last visit. A large, new modern building stood next door. Apparently it now housed the county offices.

"The old courthouse is a museum," Jackie said, following my gaze as she stopped at a traffic light.

"How do you like Port Angeles?" I inquired, having decided to hold off asking Jackie about her alleged body in the basement. It was the sort of question best discussed over strong coffee or weak drink.

Jackie wrinkled her button nose. "It's okay. The setting's great. But I miss Portland."

"Me, too," I replied. After four years in Alpine I still missed the vitality and variety of the city. My plans to spend as many weekends as possible in my native Seattle had never quite worked out. I was lucky to get into the city once every couple of months.

But Jackie was right about her surroundings. Port Angeles was nestled at the base of Mount Angeles, which seemed to glower over the town like a sullen guardian angel. The outskirts were dense with evergreens, signaling the start of the vast Olympic National Park. While new businesses seemed to abound on the long stretch of highway that led into the heart of Port Angeles, the mountains to the south and the strait on the north were a reminder that residents lived close to nature.

We turned on First Street, which is also Highway 101. The houses were sturdy and old, though none reached quite as far back as the Victorian era. Like Alpine, Port Angeles was built into the foothills of the mountains. Unlike Alpine, the ascent was more gradual, starting at sea level.

Jackie pulled into a paved driveway that led to a detached garage that couldn't have held more than one modern car. I stared. The house, which was set back among the Douglas firs, was huge. The style suggested a Spanish mission reinterpreted by a late-Victorian mentality. A giant monkey tree stood in the middle of the front lawn, with a smaller, less imposing oak near the corner of the house. A concrete retaining wall separated the newlyweds' house from a two-story ramshackle edifice that looked deserted. Jackie followed my gaze and emitted a little snort of disgust.

"That was the old livery stable that served the whole neighborhood. It's a *wreck*. I don't know why it doesn't fall down in a strong wind." She led me back onto the sidewalk so that I could get a better view of the house from the front.

Several of the camellia bushes appeared to be at death's door. The magnolias didn't look much better, and even the peonies seemed lifeless. Three stories of faded amber paint, a wraparound porch with peeling Moorish arches, a big lawn choked by weeds, a scarred river-rock foundation, and a roof with missing shingles all combined to validate Jackie's description.

"You must have gotten a real deal on this place," I said.

Jackie laughed immoderately. "We sure did. It was free." She started back toward the driveway. "Paul inherited it from his uncle," she explained, leading the way to the back door. "Uncle Arthur lived here until about fifteen years ago when he got Alzheimer's and had to go into a nursing home. Uncle Arthur died last year. Aunt Wilma bought a condo in Sequim, but she died before he did. We decided to move here and fix the place up. That's how we found the body."

The interior of the house appeared to be in much better shape than the exterior. We were in the kitchen, which had been renovated and enlarged. I guessed that Jackie and her groom had enclosed the back porch. Gleaming black appliances were set off by red and white accents. A white-tiled island stood in the middle, with a rack of stainless-steel cookware suspended overhead. The basic design was orderly, but the counters were cluttered with pizza boxes, old newspapers, grocery bags, and empty bottled-water containers. My toaster oven was all but hidden by a half-dozen cookbooks that looked as if they'd never been used. Jackie headed straight for the refrigerator and pulled out a jug of white wine.

"I can't drink but you can," she said, waving the bottle at me. "I'll have some mineral water."

I didn't question her abstinence, though I recalled downing reasonable quantities of Canadian whiskey with Ben while I awaited the birth of Adam. Neither Ben nor I ever got seriously drunk, and my son seemed sober enough when he finally arrived. But it was over twenty years later, and perhaps medical knowledge had made progress. Then again, doctors were still practicing. They probably never would get it perfect.

Carrying a delicate, long-stemmed glass, I followed Jackie into what she called the den but what I suspected had once been a library. This space was also littered with magazines, videocassettes, tapes, CDs, and more newspapers. It appeared that Jackie didn't spend her spare time cleaning house.

The room was freshly painted in a soft shade of green. A tiled fireplace was flanked by glass-fronted bookcases that contained mostly paperbacks. Along the middle molding were the brass heads of monks, at least a dozen of them, their expressions ranging from puckish to surly. The furnishings were sparse, befitting a monk's cell. The absence of more than a small sofa, a huge cushiony footstool, and a TV set didn't bespeak a disdain for worldly goods but rather a credit limit on a charge card.

Jackie collapsed onto the footstool, which seemed to

devour her small frame. The flannel shirt she wore over her jeans concealed any signs of pregnancy. Running a hand through the natural waves of her taffy-colored hair, she sighed.

"It's going to take forever. I hope we get the roof replaced before winter sets in. The baby's due at the end of December." Jackie had turned pensive. The topsy-turvy emotions she'd displayed earlier over the phone seemed in abeyance. "We've already spent a fortune on making the house livable. Paul can do some of the work himself, but not the major stuff."

I tried to remember what Mavis had told me about Paul Melcher. She and Roy liked their son-in-law, I knew that much. It seemed to me that Paul was some sort of engineer. I fished a little, hoping not to show my ignorance.

"Paul was lucky to get a job here," I remarked, thinking that the bare green walls cried out for a framed print or two.

Jackie nodded enthusiastically. "It was a near thing. We thought we'd have to move here and wait it out for a while, but then that opening came along at Rayonier. In fact, he actually started work right after New Year's, before we got married. That's why we couldn't go on a honeymoon. He didn't have any vacation yet."

ITT Rayonier was the big pulp plant down on the water. I'd seen its billows of smoke from the tow truck. Like Alpine, Port Angeles was still dependent on the timber industry, though it had been able to diversify over the years. Fishing and tourism also contributed to the town's economic base.

"He gets off at four," she said, glancing at her watch. I did the same. It was just three fifty-five. I postponed asking the inevitable and switched to baby-related inquiries instead. Jackie beamed and glowed, discussing plans for the nursery upstairs and promising to take me on a tour of the house when I finished my wine.

The phone rang as she was listing potential names for both a girl and a boy. Jackie heaved herself out of the cushioned footstool and left the den. A moment later she shouted for me. It was the Chevron station. Jake had finally returned from the West End. He didn't have the foggiest notion what was wrong with my car. Could I have it towed over to Dusty's Foreign Auto Repair?

I could, of course. I'd have to. I wondered if my towing insurance covered two trips in one day. I sought the Yellow Pages and called a local tow company. Then I turned glum.

"They can't possibly fix it before evening," I moaned out loud.

"Big deal." Jackie shrugged and led us back into the kitchen. "Have some more wine. We've got tons of room. Six bedrooms, take your pick. Except ours." She showed me her dimples.

I started to make the usual demurs about not wanting to impose, but Jackie ran right over me. "Hey, why not? I haven't told you about our body yet. I'll send out for pizza." The light behind her eyes went out. "I usually do lately. I get sick every time I look at the stove."

She was pouring me a second glass of wine when Paul Melcher came home. A stocky young man in his early thirties, he sported a neatly trimmed blond mustache and a faintly receding hairline. His handshake was firm and sincere.

"I've heard Mama Mavis talk about you," he said with a diffident grin. "You two used to get into a lot of trouble at *The Oregonian*, right?"

If trouble was sneaking out for a beer and a burger while working after hours, then I guess we qualified. But I merely laughed and tossed my head as if Mavis and I were indeed a couple of scamps.

Jackie poured wine for Paul, another mineral water for herself, and then we adjourned to the den. Paul seemed mesmerized by the sad story of my Jaguar. He speculated on its problems.

"Those Jags—they're a wonderful piece of automobile," he said with a serious expression on his face, "but they didn't used to call the head of their engineering department Dr. Demento for nothing."

"Really?" I winced. But I had been warned. In fact, it was Mavis who had told me that if I couldn't afford the price of a new Jag—and I couldn't, not even with my unexpected inheritance, which had also allowed me to buy *The Advocate*—then I probably couldn't afford the repairs. It appeared that I'd been lucky. So far.

My eyes glazed over as Paul presented a litany of possible causes. The starter. The stick shift. The electrical system. I wondered what kind of pizza Jackie would order. Pastrami sounded good to me.

". . . with parts. Now over in Victoria they'd probably be able to get . . ." Paul seemed unusually talkative for an engineer, rambling on while carefully piling the magazines and stacking the videocassettes. He finally shut up. Jackie was weeping. "Sweets, what's wrong now?" He reached over from his place next to me on the small sofa and patted her knee.

Jackie wiped her eyes and sighed. "All this talk of fancy cars. How many people live in an old beat-up Volkswagen van? It made me think of the homeless. Why do they have to sleep under bridges? Do you think anybody is sleeping under a bridge in Port Angeles? We have so many of them, with all these gullies."

Gently, Paul soothed her. There weren't that many homeless people in town. It was July, and while the summer weather had been cool and uncertain, nobody would take cold even if they had to sleep under a bridge. Shelters were provided. The churches were helping out. The United Way was doing its best. Jackie shouldn't worry. The baby would get upset. Paul's arguments were logical, orderly.

Wanly, Jackie smiled at her husband. "You're right, Lamb-love. Let's talk about something cheerful. Like the body."

Paul rubbed her knee. "That's my Sweets." He gave me another big grin. "Emma would like to hear about that. It's pretty interesting."

"I'll bet it is," I said, bracing myself. "When did you find this ... ah ... body?"

Paul's grin faded only a mite. "Yesterday." He stood up. "We're keeping it in the basement. Want to see it? Afterward, we can order pizza."

Chapter Two

THE ROWLEY-MELCHER HOUSE was huge. The builder was Cornelius Rowley, some distant connection of Paul's and a local timber baron who had hailed from Saginaw, Michigan. Cornelius had built on a grand scale. The paneled entry hall was half the size of my little log home. An inglenook curved out on each side of the fireplace. Fir wainscoting, rose wall sconces, and a wrought-iron chandelier reminded me more of a hotel lobby than a honeymoon cottage. The handsome, if uncarpeted, staircase led up to the second floor. The music parlor and the living room were sparsely furnished, and the bare maple floors looked as if they had sustained some water damage.

"The flooring guy is coming next week," Jackie said, her voice echoing off the living-room walls. "Then the rug man. We're going green. Dark." She gave her husband an arch glance. "Paul wanted white. Does that make any sense with kids?"

"It'd brighten up the place," he replied with a frown. "All those big trees outside make it kind of gloomy."

Jackie shrugged as she led us into the formal dining room. "If I didn't know better, I'd think you believed those ghost stories."

Paul rolled his eyes. "I'm being practical, that's all. And might I point out that you're the one who brought up the subject of ghosts when we found the body."

Jackie seemed unfazed by the remark. So far, I still hadn't seen the remains. Clearly, there was no urgency in the Melchers' manner. My host and hostess had decided to show me through the house before venturing into the basement. We'd already trekked around the second floor, where I'd put my meager belongings into a bedroom that faced the mountains. A small fireplace was closed off, and its dark blue tiles needed cleaning. Jackie had furnished the room with a bleached maple suite she'd had in her Portland apartment. The master bedroom, which looked out over the strait, was beautifully done in Amish style, complete with a quilt on the king-size bed and a large oval braided rug. The other four bedrooms, including two on the third floor, were all but empty.

"The dining-room set is the original," Jackie noted. "We had it refinished."

I didn't blame her. The long oak table and eight matching chairs were perfect for the room with its plate rail and boxed beam ceiling. The buffet was built into the wall, its leaded-glass doors etched with a delicate spiderweb pattern. Through a Tiffany window the late-afternoon sun caught the gleam of the newly polished table.

"What's this about a ghost?" I asked as we headed for the basement stairs.

Jackie was fumbling for a light switch, or so I thought. Actually, the basement lights were turned on with a cord that was next to the top step. As we descended, the air smelled musty, with the trace of fruit that often permeates the wooden counters of old cellars and kitchens.

"You tell her," Jackie said to Paul as we reached the bottom of the stairs. "It's your ghost."

"I never paid much attention," Paul responded with a grim little smile. We were standing in what I assumed had been a ballroom or, more recently, a rec room. Paneled in birch, the room's focal point was a handsome stone fireplace. We moved on, passing a laundry room, a big furnace that looked like an octopus, a storage area, and a workshop. A glance at the latter showed that it was Paul's domain: Shelves neatly lined with jars and cans, shiny tools hanging from carefully placed nails, renovation manuals filed between sturdy bookends all attested to my host's love of order.

"My dad told me about the ghost," Paul said, resting his hand on the doorknob that, I presumed, led to the unfinished part of the basement. "He didn't believe it, of course, but he'd tell it to me as a bedtime story. It was about a woman in a big cloak who showed up outside the house—this house—whenever there was a storm. She'd wail and shriek and carry on." He lifted one shoulder. "Typical stuff you'd expect with a place like this."

I nodded. "Most of the older houses in Port Angeles probably have a ghost or two."

"I don't know," Paul answered, opening the door. "There aren't that many big old houses here. Port Angeles was kind of a latecomer in terms of settlement."

The dank smell was almost overpowering. Paul pulled yet another cord to light up the unfinished section of the basement. There were no stairs leading from the door, though a stepladder rested against the wall. I peered at bare timbers and mounds of dirt. Then I saw the skeleton.

Grabbing Jackie's arm, I let out a small shriek. "Sorry, I didn't mean to scare you and the baby. I guess I hadn't expected to see ... *that*." My free hand fluttered in the direction of the skeleton. I wasn't about to admit that I'd expected a dead mouse or a stray cat.

Paul regarded me with a tight smile. "*Body* sounds

more dramatic than *bones*." His gaze locked with Jackie's innocent stare. "My bride is a real thrill-seeker."

"I am not!" Jackie asserted as I let go of her arm. "If I were, I'd have gone with the white carpets!" She burst into tears.

Absently, Paul patted her shoulder, then frowned at the skeleton. "I still think we should compromise on a lighter shade of green. What do you think, Emma?"

"I like green—all shades, except for the institutional kind." The truth was I felt a little green around the gills myself.

"No, no," Paul said quickly, still patting Jackie, whose sobs were subsiding. "I mean, about this guy. A workman, maybe? Heart attack, got trapped, something like that?"

I summoned up my journalistic aplomb. The skeleton was in remarkably good condition. "He looks small. Did you measure him?"

Paul shook his head. "No. But I called the sheriff and the police. They're too busy to bother with a bunch of old bones. Besides, the sheriff's department is facing some big cuts. Both the police and the sheriff's people told us to get ahold of the prosecutor's office and go through channels. Maybe we should contact Jackie's doctor, too."

But Jackie, who had recovered from her latest attack of weeping, gave a vigorous shake of her head. "Dr. Carlisle has his hands full with live patients. Anyway, he's an ob-gyn. I think we should get an anthropologist or somebody who teaches anatomy at Peninsula College."

The idea seemed sound to me. "How'd you find this in the first place?" I asked.

Paul indicated that we should move away from the door with its precarious ledge. "The electricians were here yesterday. We've rewired everything except for the basement, four hundred amps, with a new breaker box. I did most of that myself, but I wanted a final runthrough by experts. The workmen were rooting around in here and found the skeleton. They practically quit on the spot."

We were heading back to the main floor. It was after five and time for Jackie to order the pizza. I wondered if I'd hear anything from Dusty's about my Jaguar.

"What's so scary about a skeleton?" Jackie demanded, apparently dialing the phone number from memory. "It must have been there for years and years. I mean, it's kind of creepy in a way, but Paul's right—the guy probably had a heart attack. Or maybe he was a crook and hid out in the basement. How can we know why he died? There might have been a hermit in the— *Oh!* Hi! We want a large double cheese, Canadian bacon, mushrooms, and green pepper with three small salads. . . . That's right, you know my voice! Thanks much." Jackie replaced the receiver and beamed. "I've called so often lately that they don't even have to ask for our address."

"Great," Paul said with forced enthusiasm. "But how come you didn't get Italian sausage this time?"

Jackie clutched her stomach and made retching noises. "Don't even think about it! Sausage! Yuck!" Reeling around the kitchen, she finally landed next to her husband. "Hey—don't you know somebody at the college? Rand or Randolph or something like that?"

Paul put an arm around Jackie. "Mike Randall. But he's a biologist. I could call him and see who he'd recommend, though." Paul's expression was thoughtful as he studied the telephone. It rang even as I followed his gaze.

The news was not good. For me. Dusty—or his mechanics—couldn't get to my Jag until morning. Offhand, they'd guess it was an electrical problem. It often was, with the XJ6 model. How many times had the car done this before? It hadn't, I replied. The man at the other end of the line laughed incredulously and told me I was certainly a lucky person.

I didn't feel so lucky when I hung up. "You're stuck with me, at least for the night," I said in a humble voice. "Let me buy the pizza."

Jackie wouldn't hear of it. Indeed, she seemed excited about having a houseguest. She urged Paul to telephone Mike Randall.

"It's perfect," she enthused, "just like I told Emma on the phone. We've got somebody with an inquiring mind. Let's start our investigation. It'll be like a game, only with a real body!"

Paul winced and I blanched. Over the years my job had brought me into contact with too many dead bodies. It wasn't a parlor game. It was real life and often tough to accept. But Jackie's high spirits couldn't be dampened. Five minutes later Paul was on the line with Mike Randall of Peninsula College. Mike volunteered; he'd taught anatomy at the high school level before coming from Tacoma to the two-year community college in Port Angeles.

"Mike was my high school biology teacher," Paul explained while we waited for the pizza at the breakfast counter in the kitchen. Paul busied himself with clearing off the space, neatly placing the paper products in one recycling container, the plastic items in another. "Mike and his wife were divorced a couple of years ago, so he wanted a change of scene. I didn't realize he was in P.A. until I ran into him having breakfast at Landing's Restaurant last winter."

Jackie perched on her stool and tickled Paul under the chin. "Lamb-love! You were still a carefree bachelor then! Both of you! Now you've got me—and baby makes three! But poor Mike . . . he's all alone. Think of

it, parted from his family, forced to start over in an un-
familiar place, leaning on strangers for emotional support. It's so sad. Have I met him?"

"No," Paul replied firmly. "And it's not sad, Sweets.
His brother works here for the Fish and Game Department. Mike and Janice didn't have any kids, and she
drinks like a fish. He's well out of it. Mike spent over
ten years in living hell. As he says, he's no quitter, but
he's also a survivor."

"Oh." Jackie seemed taken aback, then she stared at
me, her gray eyes sparkling. "Well, now! How would
you like to meet an eligible bachelor, Emma? He'll be
here any minute!"

Paul sighed. "He'll be here at seven. I couldn't ask
him for dinner. We don't have enough pizza to go
around, and"——he added with a dark look for Jackie——
"this house really needs to be cleaned before we invite
more company."

Jackie tossed her hair. "Oh, pooh! Why bother when
we're in the middle of renovating it? You get too
worked up over being tidy. Why can't you be like other
husbands and leave a trail of socks and shorts and stuff
all over the place? Then I could nag *you*." Jackie's eyes
snapped at her mate.

Paul's small sigh of resignation was almost inaudible.
But he didn't argue. The domestic diversion had, however, let me off the hook. The last thing I needed just
now was another man to confuse my already chaotic
life. I hoped that Mike Randall was a wart-covered
gnome, with hair growing out of his nose.

He wasn't. Mike Randall was six foot one, middle
forties, with broad shoulders, a full head of wavy brown
hair, and deep blue eyes. If he wasn't handsome, he
came dangerously close. Involuntarily, I fluffed up my
bangs as he strolled through the back door.

Introductions were made, pleasantries exchanged, and

then Paul and Mike went down to the basement. Jackie and I stayed behind in the kitchen.

"Isn't he *darling*?" Jackie squirmed on the tall stool by the dining counter. "I'll bet every single woman under fifty is chasing him all over town."

"I hope he knows his anatomy," I remarked dryly, then heard Jackie giggle and wished I'd said something else. "Look, Jackie, I'm not on a hunting expedition. If you were your mother, I'd unload my sad story. In fact, she's heard it a million times. I don't need any more complications in my life."

Jackie grew somber. "Oh. You mean His Royal Pain in the Ass as my mother always calls him. She thinks you're nuts."

"Swell." Mavis had always seemed sympathetic, but I knew she thought I was carrying the all-time flaming torch. She'd never met Tom Cavanaugh, so she had no right to judge him. Still, it comes as a blow to learn that one of your closest friends thinks you're an idiot.

"Mom introduced you to a bunch of guys while you worked together," Jackie reminded me in a reproachful tone. "One of them played for the Trailblazers."

I gave her a quizzical look. "So who needs to feed a man who's seven feet tall? Who wants to talk to his belt buckle? Your mother meant well, Jackie, but I never dated any of her potential suitors more than twice. My least favorite was the stockbroker who's doing five-to-ten in some federal guesthouse for using his elderly clients' funds to keep his assorted girlfriends in riverfront condos by the Burnside Bridge."

"Oh, *him*!" Jackie dismissed the dishonest broker with a wave of her hand. "What about the senator?"

I all but fell off the kitchen stool. "His wife couldn't stand me," I finally replied with a grim set to my lips. I'd almost forgotten how desperate Mavis had become on my behalf. Having been fortunate enough to find lifelong happiness with the man of her dreams, Mavis was determined to see me married, too. I hadn't been so lucky.

I was spared further meanderings down memory lane by the return of Paul and Mike Randall. Paul wore a worried look; Mike seemed invigorated.

"It's incredible," Mike declared, accepting Jackie's offer of a beer before we returned to the den. "That skeleton's almost in mint condition. We covered it with plastic drop cloths. More respectful, you know. It's too bad we don't have carbon-dating equipment at the college. Still, we can come close, just because of the house."

"How close?" I inquired, deciding I might as well fling myself into the spirit of the thing. I couldn't do much else, given my car problems.

Mike sat down on the small sofa. "No more than a forty-year span." He saw my dismay and shook his head. "Frankly, carbon dating wouldn't bring you much closer. We know that construction on the house began in 1904 and ended about 1908, so it has to be after that. Given the humidity in that unfinished basement and the fact that Paul says his uncle never mentioned any major work being done after World War II, we could narrow it down to between 1908 and 1945. That's not bad, scientifically speaking."

Jackie didn't agree. "You're taking all the fun out of it." Noticing Mike Randall's face fall, she gave him an encouraging smile. "Sorry, Mike—may I call you Mike, even if you were Paul's teacher a zillion years ago? You sure don't look that old—does he, Emma? Anyway, we've got to be more precise if we're going to solve this mystery."

Jackie's rapid-fire delivery was making me dizzy. Or perhaps it was the third glass of wine. I was sitting on the floor, having been careful to avoid the small sofa where I figured I might wind up hip-to-hip with Mike Randall.

Mike was now looking at Paul, who was seated next to him. "If we can't rely on science, we'll have to go with history. This was your family's house, Paul. What do you know about a recluse or an accident or anything that might account for somebody being left in an unfinished basement? Don't be embarrassed. Everyone has family secrets. It's best to bring them out into the light of day and be open about things." His tone was confidential, very like that of a professional counselor.

But Paul's recollections didn't include any startling revelations. In fact, the account of his Port Angeles forebears was strictly factual.

"My grandfather lived in this house before and after he was married," Paul said, rubbing at his forehead as if to stimulate his memory. "It was sort of complicated. His mother, Lena, had been married before, to a man named Melcher, my grandfather's real dad. The second time around, she married Edmund Rowley—Eddie, they called him, I think. Eddie was several years younger than Lena. They didn't have any children of their own. The son—stepson, to Eddie—married my grandmother, Rose. They had five kids. The oldest was Uncle Arthur and the youngest was my dad. Uncle Arthur died in a nursing home last year, Uncle Henry's been dead about fifteen years, and Uncle John was killed in World War II. My dad and Aunt Sara are still around. But they were all Melchers, like me. I'm not a Rowley at all."

Jackie was nodding vigorously. "This is good, very good. I'm learning something about my baby's ancestors. The only other Melchers I ever heard of until now were Paul's folks, Aunt Sara, and Uncle Arthur. I never met him, though," she added, suddenly sad. "He was bats by the time I started going with Paul."

Her husband flinched slightly. "We should make a

family tree. I'll get some graph paper and a ruler and a pen and . . ." He paused, fingering his sandy mustache. "Maybe we should do this on the computer. There are programs for family histories."

Jackie jumped up and rummaged around in the glass-fronted bookcases. "Never mind, we don't have forever. Emma's only going to be here overnight. By the time you get everything organized, we'll all be dead, too. Here," she said, dropping back onto the footstool and opening a steno pad on her knees. "let's start with Eddie Rowley and Lena."

Paul grimaced slightly. "We'd better start with the man who built the house—Cornelius Rowley. He was Eddie's father. Eddie married Lena Stillman Melcher. I showed you her statue in the D.A.R. Park, remember? She was a suffragette."

"Oh!" Jackie clamped a hand over her bosom. "Old Hatchet Face! Talk about grim!" She wiggled her eyebrows at me. "Honestly, Emma, that woman could have cut cake with her face! Eeeek!" With an agonized expression Jackie sank deeper into the cushioned footstool, as if she were trying to hide. "I shouldn't say that! I could mark the baby! That old bag is actually related to you, isn't she, Paul?"

"I told you," Paul explained patiently, "she was my great-grandmother. A very forceful woman, I've heard. Temperance, women's suffrage, a big mover and shaker in civic reform. That's why they put up that statute."

Jackie sighed and sat up straighter. Mike Randall had shot me a sympathetic glance. I meant to smile but smirked instead. Sometimes my social graces seem to have been arrested at about age twelve.

"Okay," Jackie agreed, "we put Eddie and Lena at the top." She started to write with a bright pink marking pen.

"No, no." Paul protested. "It'll make things easier if

you start with Eddie's father, Cornelius Rowley. He's the one who built the house circa 1904 to 1908. Got that?"

"Oh, poopy!" But Jackie did as she was told.

Paul continued with the rest of his family lore. Cornelius Rowley had been a timber cruiser, originally from Saginaw, Michigan. He'd been widowed and left with two grown children, the aforementioned Eddie and Caroline, who was known as Carrie. Cornelius remarried a much younger woman from France, but they had no kids of their own. Carrie had become the wife of an Irish logger named Malone. They'd had several children but had moved away early on.

"The only one who stayed in Port Angeles was Uncle Arthur," Paul said after he'd fetched more beer for Mike and himself. I declined a refill on the wine. "As I mentioned, he was the eldest of Sanford and Rose's five kids, so I guess he got the house. He married, but his only son was drowned in a boating accident when he was just a kid. My dad and the other children were born in P.A., but they all moved away. After Dad got out of college, he went to work for the port of Tacoma. He retired last year. That's why he and Mom are touring the Orient right now. They waited to go until after Jackie and I got married and were settled in here."

The statement seemed to sum up Paul's history of the Rowleys and the Melchers. Jackie was still writing names on the pad, but she had a lot of blanks.

"None of this is very interesting," she remarked, squinting up as a shaft of light from the setting sun penetrated the den. "I don't see how a ghost ties in, let alone a body."

Mike leaned forward on the sofa. "A ghost?"

Paul repeated the story he'd told me earlier. Mike appeared intrigued. "A female ghost. Well, now. I don't want to dismiss such apparitions out of hand. It's highly suggestive, though, isn't it?"

"What do you mean?" Paul regarded his former high school teacher curiously.

"If I had to guess," Mike replied, eyeing each of us in turn, "I'd say that skeleton was a woman."

Chapter Three

IN LAYMAN'S TERMS Mike explained how he'd used Paul's ordinary steel tape measure to determine height and, in a more sophisticated way, sex. As he spoke, I watched Jackie carefully for signs of an emotional outburst. To my relief, she reacted with more fascination than alarm.

". . . right around five foot two," Mike was saying, "which could mean it was a man, but I doubt it. The pelvic configuration suggests a female. So do the breast and collarbones. The skull has deteriorated some, but again, I'd guess we've got a Caucasian here. An anthropologist might narrow it down to certain ethnicities. Slav, Scandinavian, Mediterranean, for example." He raised his hands in a helpless gesture. They were nice hands, big, strong, clean. I was trying to keep an open mind. "Does that sound like anybody you know? Or knew?"

Paul laughed apologetically. "I was born in 1961. We've already figured out that that skeleton has been down there since long before then. Like most kids I never paid a lot of attention to family history. I wouldn't know as much as I do if it weren't for my ending up with this house. My dad filled me in on the background."

Mike acknowledged Paul's response with a thoughtful nod. "Your information is exceptionally solid. It shows a real concern for family. In today's mobile, disconnected society, it's a marvel when people can be sure who their parents were, let alone grandparents and beyond."

Paul looked faintly embarrassed, presumably at the praise from his former teacher. "But I don't know enough," he protested. "I can't say for certain that this is so-and-so. We definitely are faced with a dilemma. From a practical point of view, we should call a funeral home and have them handle the matter. They'd know what to do."

Mike stood up and put a compassionate hand on Paul's shoulder. "You're right, of course. This skeleton has nothing to do with you in your new life. We all have to move on. Your main goal is to finish wiring the house. Often, it's best to bury the past."

"But we got it unburied!" Jackie's big gray eyes appealed to me. "Emma? What do you think?"

I took my time in replying, and when I did, it was with reluctance. "As soon as you call the funeral home, the story will be all over town. The local paper—*The Peninsula Daily News?*—will run it, and every person in Port Angeles who has had a disappearance in the family, no matter how long ago, will be on your front porch. There'll be dozens of people claiming that poor skeleton and fighting over the remains. It might be better to get someone from out of town—say, a funeral parlor in Bremerton or Aberdeen."

Mike sat back down, but it was a temporary perch on the arm of the sofa. "That's a good point." He eyed me with approval. "On the other hand, if you really want to discover the skeleton's identity, you might get some answers if *The News* ran the story. It's up to you, Paul, naturally. You must do whatever would be easiest to live with."

I was beginning to lose patience with the insoluble

debate. Or maybe I was tired. I shook my head at the others. My audience was composed of three people who had been born and raised in relatively large cities. They had the wrong kind of mentality to deal with small-town oddities. "A newspaper story at this point will get you too many answers. It'll raise more questions than it'll resolve. Believe me, I live in a small town, even smaller than this one, and I know how people fixate on stuff like this. They take everything much more personally, as if they're trying to establish their own identity with every event that's ever happened within their own narrow boundaries."

My little speech had a sobering effect on my listeners. Paul, in particular, wore an air of defeat. "The best thing, I guess, is to call the prosecutor tomorrow and do whatever he advises."

But Jackie wasn't giving up the chase. "That's tomorrow. For today, it's still up to us," she declared, gazing from her husband to their male guest. "Why don't you two guys go back down to the basement and search for clues?"

"Jackie . . . !" Paul clapped a hand to his forehead. "What do you expect to find? A suicide note?"

"Of course not," Jackie replied haughtily. "Despite the damp, there has to be some remnants where those workmen found the body. Or do you think this poor woman walked into the basement stark naked?"

A grisly idea occurred to me, but I didn't want to mention it, lest Jackie start to cry, pass out, or, worse yet, get the giggles.

Mike Randall, however, felt compelled to be candid.

"Sexual violence isn't confined to our own era," he said, his broad forehead creasing. "Sad to say, we might have a victim of rape and murder here. She might have been carried into the basement. Going back to the early part of the century, there was a great deal of sexual repression. These people were all basically Victorians, and the crimes committed in prudish societies are often excessive."

"Wow!" Jackie scrambled to her feet. "This is really getting interesting!" She made a shooing gesture at the men. "Go on, dig. Emma and I will go upstairs and get the family albums."

A battered steamer trunk in one of the third-floor bedrooms held a fair share of the Rowley-Melcher memorabilia. Judging from the stacks of albums, photograph folders, and old candy boxes filled with snapshots, several generations were represented. I wasn't surprised to see Paul Melcher's high school graduation picture on top. It was over a decade old and showed his face as rounder, his hair more plentiful, and with no hint of a mustache.

"I've been meaning to go through this stuff," Jackie said as she tried to determine if there was any order to the piles of pictorial history. "It's the kind of thing I can do just before the baby comes. You know, when I can't do much else."

There were high school and college yearbooks, engagement and wedding announcements, birth and death notices, newspaper clippings, and report cards. Jackie dug down to the bottom, finally pulling out a half-dozen albums bound with silk and cotton ribbons.

"Let's start with these," she said, handing me three and keeping the rest for herself.

We returned to the empty den. Obviously, Paul and Mike were still looking for what Jackie hopefully referred to as *clues*. I was now seated in a folding chair Jackie had brought out from a storage closet. With a brown imitation-leather album on my lap, I tried to work up some enthusiasm for my task. A brief perusal showed me wallet-sized photographs of grim-faced men and overweight women in 1880s' finery. There was no identification of the subjects. However, a Saginaw, Michigan, portrait studio's name was printed in elegant script on virtually every photo.

"This must be Cornelius Rowley's family," I noted. "There're quite a few pictures of little kids. Who would they be?"

Jackie checked her family tree. "What year?"

I studied the styles in a family grouping: mother, father, a boy about ten, and a girl who wasn't much more than a toddler. They all looked overdressed and under-happy. "Bustles. Deerstalkers. Post–Civil War, but before the so-called Gay Nineties."

Jackie was scowling at her bright pink printing. "That's the trouble, Paul didn't give me any dates. Maybe it's Mr. and Mrs. Cornelius Rowley and their two kids." She leaned over on the footstool to look at the photo. "Yes, that would figure. Eddie, Paul's great-grandfather, and Great-Aunt Carrie, wasn't it?"

I shook my head. "No, they'd be steprelatives, remember? Paul's not related on the Rowley side. Carrie married Malone, the Irish logger. For the time being, we'll call this foursome the Rowleys."

Jackie flipped through another album, from the same period but with posed photographs that had been taken in several different cities: Boston, Philadelphia, Chicago, Minneapolis, Denver, and San Francisco. Suddenly, she let out a little shriek.

"It's her! Hatchet Face! Look!"

The woman who peered out at me from the sepia-tinted photograph did indeed possess a severe mien. Her features were even, her mouth finely molded, and if she hadn't had her hair pulled back so tightly that it looked as if her eyes might pop, she could have been handsome. The tailored shirtwaist's stiff collar reached to her chin; Lena's only adornment was a simple cross on a chain and small dark buttons that began at the base of her throat. I tried to picture her with flowing locks, a smile, and a relaxed expression.

"Makeover City," murmured Jackie. "Think what they could do with her at the Estée Lauder counter!"

"Lena Stillman Melcher Rowley?" I saw Jackie nod solemnly. "Where's her second husband, Eddie, grown up? Maybe Lena was good in bed."

Jackie was aghast. "Did people in those days even *care*? About sex, I mean. You know what Mike said about those priggish Victorians. Didn't they just . . . do it to have kids?"

I couldn't help grinning. "I kind of think they had a good time, too. People are people, after all."

Jackie scrutinized Lena's portrait again. "Except they didn't. Have kids, I mean—her and Eddie. I'll bet they had separate bedrooms. They could, you know. This house is so big."

For the first time I began to sense the presence of the people who had posed so stiffly for these photographs. Lena Stillman Melcher Rowley had lived in this house. She had sat in this very room, probably writing her suffragette tracts and planning political strategy. Edmund Rowley had lived here, too, and his father, Cornelius, had built the place. The senior Rowley had chosen the river-rock foundation and the tiled fireplace and the wrought-iron chandelier in the entry hall. Carrie Rowley Malone had been married out of this house, no doubt sweeping down the main staircase in her wedding dress.

The century-old faces took on a spark of life. In the next album I spotted Carrie Rowley in sprigged gingham and her brother, Eddie, in a straw boater. He carried a cane and was actually smiling. Cornelius grew broader, his aspect more expansive with age and wealth. His wife seemed relegated to the background, literally. Mrs. Rowley stood in the shadows behind her husband. In the only family grouping she bowed her head, a wide-brimmed felt hat covering her face. I saw her as a downtrodden figure, a nineteenth-century wife and mother held back by social custom and an overbearing mate.

"A Bible," I said. "There must be a family Bible that would give us birth, death, and marriage dates."

Jackie was already on her feet, manning the light switches. The sun had set out over the strait. It was after eight-thirty, and the skies had finally cleared just before dusk. The weather was typical of this Northwest summer, with clouds hovering until late in the day, and then clearing as evening set in. I didn't mind; I preferred it to the previous hot, dry years of drought that had made the forests a tinderbox and soured my mood.

Jackie had removed a black Bible from the bookcase. "Here," she said excitedly. "This belonged to the family. Paul showed it to me a while ago, but I went to sleep."

Jackie and I ended up on the sofa. It was easier to go through the albums and other memorabilia while sitting side by side. When the men returned, they could fend for themselves.

"The men," I said in sudden wonder. "They've been gone for almost an hour. What do you suppose they're doing?"

Jackie shrugged. "Finding clues, I suppose. Look." She tapped a page with handwritten entries.

Cornelius Rowley had been born in 1840; he had died in 1908. The birth and death dates for his wife, Olive, were 1847 to 1898. He had remarried four years later, but there were no vital statistics for his second wife, Simone. Edmund, or Eddie, Rowley was born in 1870, died in 1930. Caroline—or Carrie—entered this world in 1877, but her date of death wasn't recorded. She had married James Malone in 1903, with their children following in rapid succession: Julia, 1904; Walter,

1906; Claudia, 1907. The only other entry was for Eddie's marriage in 1901 to Lena Stillman Melcher.

"It looks as if nobody bothered to keep this up after Cornelius Rowley died," I said, skimming through the rest of the thick Bible to see if we'd missed anything.

Jackie pursed her lips. "That's odd, isn't it? I mean, old Lena seems like the type who would have been very meticulous about record-keeping."

"But it wasn't her family," I pointed out. "Maybe she had a different Bible for the Melchers."

"If she did, it's not here." Jackie opened another photo album. "Whoa! Look at this one! She's a real babe!"

"She" took up a full page at the beginning of the third album. The eight-by-ten photograph showed a dazzlingly beautiful woman by the standards of any era. Dark hair, luminous eyes, a full, faintly pouty mouth, and a sensational if tightly corseted figure were set off against a backdrop of weeping-willow branches. The woman's gown was probably silk, her parasol ruffled, the big hat adorned with ostrich feathers. She didn't look as if she belonged in Port Angeles—not at the turn of the century, not even today.

Jackie slipped the photograph out of the triangular holders that secured it to the album page. "No name," she said with a sigh, turning the picture over. "It's not Carrie—she was blonde. So was Grandma Rose, Grandpa Sanford's wife. I know, I've seen pictures of them. There was a big one in the music parlor before we painted it."

I glanced over at the steno pad, which was lying on the footstool. "Simone, Cornelius's second wife?"

Jackie beamed at me. "Sure! She's definitely French!" She gazed anew at the portrait. "I'd swear to it. I majored in French, you know. She has the style, the *élan.*"

She did, indeed. It wasn't hard to see why a middle-aged widower like Cornelius Rowley had fallen for La Belle Simone. It was just as easy to conclude that she had married him for his money.

"I wonder what happened to her?" I mused, turning more pages and finding Simone in satin, in dimity, in gauzy chiffon. "I take it she was vain."

"Well, why not? She was gorgeous." Jackie tore her admiring gaze away as Paul and Mike finally reappeared, dirty and disheveled. Patches of sweat could be seen under the arms of both men.

"You win," Paul said in a weary voice. He presented Jackie with a chipped enamel vegetable dish.

Jackie looked at the contents and screamed.

The only thing that would preserve Jackie Melcher's sanity was another pizza. Despite Paul's efforts to soothe her with words and gestures, his pregnant wife insisted that we all hop into the Wrangler and head for Gordy's on East First Street.

"Domino's is great, but I need a change," Jackie informed us as we trudged out to the driveway, where Paul had parked his vehicle behind his wife's Honda. As we pulled into the street, I noticed a black Corvette parked at the curb. I hadn't seen it when Jackie and I arrived. I wondered if Mike Randall was in his second childhood and how he could afford to indulge himself on a college instructor's salary. But of course if Mike saw my Jag, he'd wonder the same thing about me.

Paul volunteered to detour three blocks east to D Street in order to show me the statue of Lena Stillman Melcher Rowley in the D.A.R. Park. "Lena probably was an actual Daughter of the American Revolution," he informed us as we drove along Sixth Street with its old homes and tall trees. "Now that I start thinking about it, I recall that her family came from Massachusetts."

He slowed at the corner where a parcel of land no bigger than a double lot was neatly landscaped. A streetlight illuminated the little park. We all got out of the Wrangler, though Jackie showed reluctance.

"I've seen Lena's statue a zillion times." She sighed. "Maybe she'll look better in the dark."

The grassy area was ringed by hemlock and Douglas fir trees. A granite rockery set off rhododendrons, azaleas, Oregon grape, and mountain laurel. At the center of the semicircle Lena was immortalized in bronze, life-size, with a plaque at her feet. I took a small emergency flashlight out of my handbag. The inscription read: LENA STILLMAN MELCHER ROWLEY. 1860–1944. A DEDICATED CRUSADER FOR JUSTICE, TEMPERANCE, AND EQUALITY. *FINIS CORONAT OPUS.*

"What's that?" Jackie inquired, wrinkling her button nose. "Latin?"

"Right." By the time I got to Blanchet High School in the Sixties, Latin was no longer a requirement for Catholic students. "I wonder what it means?"

Paul and Mike didn't know, either. Jackie was meandering back to the Wrangler. Paul was studying the streetlight. Mike was examining some of the rockery plants. I gazed up at Lena on her pedestal, taking in the sharp features, the severely cut suit of the post–World War I era, and the dead eyes that forever looked out in the direction of the setting sun. The sailor hat was not tipped at a rakish angle but sat squarely on the upswept hair. She wore no jewelry, though I supposed that in life there had been a wedding ring under the gloved hands. The sepia tones of the photograph I'd seen earlier had given the suggestion of a handsome woman. Bronze didn't suit her. The jutting chin, the determined set of the mouth, and the hawkish nose made me feel as if I wouldn't have wanted to do lunch with Lena. On the other hand, she certainly looked like a woman who could get things done.

Back in the Wrangler, Mike Randall gave his assessment of Lena Rowley: "A true American heroine. Difficult, perhaps, because she was a perfectionist and single-minded. I'd guess that she never expected more of others than she did of herself. But of course that was a great deal. You ought to be proud to have her on your family tree, Paul."

Paul inclined his head. "Yeah, I guess. I'll bet she wasn't easy to live with. My dad called her the Grim Reaper."

Gordy's was located on the commercial strip that formed Highway 101's eastbound route through town. The restaurant featured not only pizza but pasta, and a lively crowd of Tuesday-night diners, most of whom I judged to be college students. Mike exchanged cordial greetings with several customers as a ponytailed waitress led us to a rear booth.

"Anchovies," Jackie declared without so much as picking up a menu. "And tons of onions."

The rest of us declined food, though Paul and Mike ordered a pitcher of beer. I decided to switch to Pepsi. Then I weakened and asked for some garlic bread. If Jackie intended to be miserable, maybe she'd like some company.

"Those old relics are just too weird," Jackie said, sighing, after our order had been taken. "Stuff like that makes me shiver."

I gave a faint nod. The contents of the enamel dish had upset me, too: a garnet earring, the sole and heel of a woman's shoe, a strip of leather that might have been a belt, a silver bracelet engraved with tiny elephants, and a small gold cross. Those bits and pieces had evoked a real person, someone long dead, yet who had once worn stylish clothes and jewelry and shoes. All that remained was a pitiful skeleton, left to molder in the damp earth of an unfinished basement.

"The garnet's real." Paul noted, perhaps hoping to divert his wife with solid facts. "The silver bracelet may have come from India. There used to be an umbrella stand in the entry hall that somebody brought from there way back."

I hated to bring up the subject, but it had to be done and pre-anchovies seemed like the best time. "We shouldn't jump to conclusions. We have no proof that the jewelry and the piece of shoe belonged to the ... skeleton." I grimaced in apology.

Jackie, however, gave me a wide-eyed look. "Wow, Emma, you sound like a real detective. Or a lawyer or something. Mom never covered crime. She was Special Editions."

"I know." I smiled at Jackie, and at the memory of Mavis, always a sea of calm in a whirlwind of activity. "I often contributed articles to whichever special she was putting out. But never on crime. That was always strictly news stuff."

Mike was fingering his chin and looking pensive. "You're right about proof, Emma. But the shoe would fit the foot bones. I'll admit, it's hard to tell because of the high heel and raised arch. Still, it's a very small size, and the skeleton has very small feet."

Jackie all but jumped out of the wooden booth. "I know!" she cried, waving her arms. "We can go through the picture albums! Maybe we can find one of the women wearing the earring or the cross. Or even the bracelet."

The ponytailed waitress brought our beverages, which included an iced tea for Jackie. Paul waited until we were alone again before he spoke. "This is really kind of weird." He gave a self-deprecating laugh.

"When those workmen found the bones yesterday, I was surprised, of course. But I figured it was just some kind of freaky thing, an accident of some sort. I didn't identify with it at all. But now, when we're talking about somebody whose picture might be in the family albums—maybe a relative, for God's sake—it's *strange*." He took one of Jackie's hands in both of his and sighed. "You're right, Sweets—this isn't good for you and the baby. Let's call it quits right now before we all get the creeps."

Jackie was gazing earnestly at Paul. "I don't think we can. Not now." Her voice was hushed. "That skeleton is in our house. We're starting our life together, beginning a family. We've got to do right by . . . whoever it was. What if it *is* somebody who's related to you? Don't we have to find out who and give her a decent burial? If we don't do what's right, we may be cursed or something."

Paul studied his bride's concerned face. Out of the corner of my eye, I tried to gauge Mike Randall's reaction. In my undergraduate days at the University of Washington, we had divided people into two separate categories: the humanities majors and the science majors. History, English, foreign languages, communications—all were taught on what was known as Upper Campus. Biology, botany, oceanography, engineering, medicine et al. were Lower Campus offerings. They were two separate worlds as far as most of us were concerned. The men I now observed—a science teacher and an engineer—belonged to the Lower Campus group. They didn't think like the rest of us. Their minds were orderly and unimaginative. They were given to cold, hard facts. When they ventured into the abstract, they spoke of theories. There was no room in their logical thinking processes for fancy or superstition. I waited anxiously, if sanguinely, for their response.

"You're right," Paul declared, kissing Jackie's fingertips. "It would be terrible to ship my ancestor's remains off to somebody in Bremerton. For all we know, they'd go into a Dumpster. That'd be real disturbing."

Mike was nodding in sympathy. "You've got to at least give it a try. Identifying the poor creature, I mean. Besides, it's curious. How did she get there? A history lesson in human behavior, as it were."

History lesson notwithstanding, it was more than curious to me. If I'd been asked, I'd have said it was just plain fascinating. Still, the men of science had surprised me. I wouldn't have expected them to show the spirit and verve of Vida Runkel in tackling the antique mystery, but they certainly hadn't pooh-poohed the concept.

Jackie's pizza and my garlic bread arrived. I found myself sharing the hot slices of fresh Italian bread with Mike Randall. Paul helped Jackie eat her pizza.

With the food's arrival the conversation turned to lighter topics. Paul talked about his job at Rayonier. Mike expounded on how college students lacked self-esteem. Jackie wondered about wallpapering the downstairs rooms. I recounted my Jaguar's troubles but not the reason for making the trip in the first place. Mike accepted another chunk of garlic bread, his deep blue eyes straying in my direction. Feeling uneasy, I engaged in a drawn-out monologue about publishing *The Alpine Advocate*. By some miracle my audience was still awake when I finally wound down.

It was after ten-thirty when we got back to the Rowley-Melcher house. Mike made polite noises about not coming back inside, but Jackie insisted, at least until we finished going through the photo albums.

"It shouldn't be too hard," she assured us as we trooped into the den. "Emma says that the shoe is from around the turn of the century."

"I'm guessing, I'm guessing," I put in hastily, waving a hand at Jackie. "I did some fashion features on *The*

Oregonian for your mother's special editions. This heel
is stacked, a style that women adapted from men after
1900. It's straight, not curved, which is unusual for a
woman's shoe in the late nineteenth and early twentieth
centuries. If I have to stick my neck out further, I'd
guess that whoever wore that shoe wasn't on her way to
the opera or a ball."

Jackie giggled. "In Port Angeles? I'll bet she wasn't,
either!"

With an air of apology, Mike corrected Jackie. "Actually, there *was* an opera house in town at the time. I
understand it was the center of most social activities. I
read up on local history before I moved here."

"Neat," Jackie remarked without enthusiasm. Suddenly, she sobered and tears welled up in her eyes.
"Poor thing! The dead woman, I mean. But what was
she doing, wearing her jewelry while she was cleaning
house?"

Paul, who was now sitting next to Jackie on the sofa,
patted her knee. "They had servants, Sweets. They had
to, with this big place."

"Well, we don't!" Jackie pulled away and shot her
husband an accusing look. "That's the trouble with this
modern age, you men expect us to be superwomen!"

I had resumed my place on the floor while Mike tried
not to sink into the footstool. Jackie had a point. When
the house was finally renovated, it would be a wonderful place to live. But not to clean. Since Jackie showed
no interest in housekeeping, I felt for her. And for Paul.

"Women wore jewelry much more in those days than
we do now," I remarked, trying to steer the conversation
away from controversy. "Everyone dressed more for-
mally, even in small towns like Port Angeles."

The atmosphere perked up as quickly as it had run
down. I was trying to get used to Jackie's mercurial
temperament, but it wasn't easy. My sole reporter on

The Advocate, Carla Steinmetz, was also given to un-predictable mood swings. But Carla was inherently en-thusiastic if basically addled. She rarely resorted to tears and seldom complained. I found myself overcome with appreciation for what seemed like comparative sta-bility. Competence was another matter.

Each of us was perusing one of the old albums. We were silent for several moments, with only the sound of pages turning and a faint breeze stirring the evergreens in the spacious yard. The street was quiet, probably be-cause most traffic used the truck route a couple of blocks away.

Jackie finished her album first. "I wish that earring was bigger. With some of these pictures I can't see much. The women are looking straight at the camera."

I was the one to spot the garnet earrings, though I'd had to use a magnifying glass Paul had found in a drawer. The woman was wearing a high-necked dress with a lace yoke. Under a broad-brimmed hat her fair hair was coiffed into a pompadour. She had tilted her head just enough to permit a full view of the left ear-ring.

"That's Carrie Rowley Malone!" Paul exclaimed in an excited voice. "My God!" He began to pace around the small room, his hands clasping and unclasping be-hind his back.

The full impact of the discovery had not yet hit Jackie, who was gazing in a bemused fashion at the photograph. "She was sort of pretty, in her way. Do you suppose that's really her in the basement?"

Paul stopped abruptly in front of the bookcase. His expression was faintly appalled. "All we can do is guess from the evidence. I'd have to say so. My God, Jackie, she was part of the family! This is terrible!"

But Jackie didn't agree. "She wasn't family. She was a Rowley. You're a Melcher. She might as well be a stranger." Jackie paused, shuddered, and slumped against the sofa. "You're right, it *is* awful. But what about serial killers? All those victims who are never found? What do their parents and children and friends think? Do you realize that at this very minute someone is waiting for a loved one who isn't ever coming home?"

Incredulously, Paul stared at his wife; I looked away; Mike seemed ill at ease. "That's exactly what we're talking about, Jackie," Paul finally said in a stern voice. "Not serial killers, maybe, but somebody who disappeared and was left in the basement."

Jackie's eyes grew very wide. She put a hand over her mouth and bolted from the room. Paul hesitated, then rushed after her. I was left alone with Mike.

He got to his feet, hovering over me. "Is she ill?" he inquired in a worried voice.

I recalled that Mike and his ex-wife had had no children. "Probably," I replied. "No cause for alarm. Morning sickness doesn't always happen in the morning. It's normal, especially after all those anchovies." Feeling a trifle silly kneeling at Mike's feet, I also stood up.

"Mmmmm." Mike nodded absently. "I haven't been through the wonder of childbirth. It's a privilege to share even in a small way."

My smile was feeble. "Well, certainly," I temporized, "it's a ... marvel." The real marvel was that having once done it, anyone would do it again. Throwing up, being clumsy, having no energy, and going into labor weren't among my favorite memories. Yet I knew that if I'd had the chance, I would have given birth to more than one child. Not expecting Mike to understand, I didn't elaborate.

An awkward silence grew between us. We stood an arm's length apart, he looking vaguely embarrassed, I feeling a flush on my cheeks. Mike Randall was undeniably good-looking and apparently eligible. He was educated, employed, and in my age group. Why wasn't I warming to the man? Why did I feel that I ought to? After tonight I'd probably never see him again.

"What should we do next?" he asked, sounding vaguely helpless. But at least he broke the tension.

I checked my watch. It was almost eleven. "We can't do much. Not this late. I realize there's no way to be sure that it's Carrie Rowley Malone's remains, but it's a logical conclusion. I suppose I'd have her buried in the family plot and try to forget about it."

Mike agreed, adding that Jackie and Paul might want to have a graveside service. "I'm not a member of any formal religion myself, though we all have our spiritual side. I can't speak for Paul and his wife, but getting a minister to say a few words often makes people feel better. You know, a sense of closure."

I wasn't about to go into my own philosophy of the soul. "Jackie's parents are Episcopalian," I noted, recalling the mutual needling Mavis and I had indulged in over the years. She'd tease me about Episcopalians having purified the existing Roman Catholic Church; I'd retaliate by asking her how she could belong to a religious group founded by a king whose midlife crisis demanded that he marry a younger woman. We both took our faiths seriously but never the arguments. I had a sneaking suspicion that Mike Randall wouldn't understand that, either. Or, worse yet, that he'd try.

Paul returned without Jackie, who had gone to bed. "She's worn out from all this," he said by way of apologizing for his wife. "Jackie takes things too hard."

Mike Randall took his leave, but not before offering his suggestion about disposing of the unfortunate body. Paul seemed receptive, but after Mike had left, he shook his head.

"Jackie won't let go so easy," he declared, helping

me put the old photo albums in a temporary resting place on the bottom shelf of the bookcase. "Now that she thinks she knows who, she'll want to know why."

I couldn't blame her. So did I. If the bones in the basement belonged to Caroline Rowley Malone, if there was no record of her death in the family Bible, if the remnants of apparel could be dated to the first decade of the century, then she couldn't have been more than thirty when she died. And how had Carrie Malone, wife and mother of three, ended up in an unfinished basement?

It seemed to me that her story was also unfinished.

Chapter Four

ALL WAS NOT well in Alpine. While I had not yet heard back from Dusty's Foreign Auto Repair, I felt I should touch base with *The Advocate*. It was Wednesday, publication day. When I left the office early Monday evening, everything had seemed to be under control. If there were any last-minute crises—and there often were, even on a weekly paper—the capable Vida Runkel could handle them.

But even Vida couldn't make miracles. Carla had come down with the flu the previous morning and was still at home in bed. Her current boyfriend, Peyton Flake, M.D., couldn't make miracles, either. My ad manager, Ed Bronsky, had suddenly lost the steam he'd finally acquired in the spring.

"Ed lost two half-page ads besides," Vida fumed at the other end of the telephone line. "Flat out *lost* them! Barton's Bootery and Harvey's Hardware! The bootery was having a summer sale to unload all of the sandals nobody's wearing because it's too cold, and Harvey Adcock had a special purchase of lumber for Fixer-Upper Week. I don't want to think about what Ed's doing with that special section!"

I could almost hear Vida rubbing her eyes, a habit she has when she's agitated. In my mind I pictured my House & Home editor, the receiver propped between one ear and a wide, rayon-clad shoulder, the unruly gray curls bobbing on her head, tortoiseshell glasses sitting on the desk, fists grinding away.

The Fixer-Upper issue was due out the following week, and I'd hoped it would run at least twelve pages, bringing the paper's total to thirty-six. The present edition was set for the usual twenty-four, but with a full page of missing ads, I had to ask the dreaded question: "Have we come up short?"

"Of course," Vida responded promptly. "We're going twenty. Carla didn't finish her story on the proposed swimming-pool bond issue or the Bible school feature. And she didn't get those pictures taken of the new picnic tables up at the Icicle Creek Campground. That would have filled a page in itself—if there'd been any campers. The tourist count is way down. I did three inches on the Chamber of Commerce's lament about the downtrend in visitors. I also—God help me—relented and wrote that piece on Crazy Eights Neffel playing board games with a bear."

"Oh. Oh, no." I groaned. Crazy Eights Neffel was Alpine's resident lunatic, a seventy-five-year-old cuckoo who may or may not have been senile but who had always been insane. Roughly every six months Crazy Eights would wander into the editorial offices and demand that Vida or Carla or the hatrack—whichever he found most responsive—write a story about his latest adventures. Some of them were true; all of them were bizarre. The board games with the bear could fall into both categories.

"How long?" I asked, holding my breath and clutching the Melchers' cordless phone.

"Four inches," Vida replied. "I used one inch to describe the cave."

I nodded absently, my mind preoccupied with how we could make up for the loss of the two ads to Barton's Bootery and Harvey's Hardware. "Has the paper actually gone off to be printed yet?" It was shortly after eight A.M., and under ordinary circumstances Kip MacDuff would have left Alpine between seven and seven-thirty.

"No. I forgot to tell you that part. Kip broke his arm playing soccer."

Hearing Jackie rustle about in the kitchen, I suppressed several four-letter words. "So who's driving the paper down to Monroe?" I asked, hearing my voice rasp.

"I am," snapped Vida. "Who else is there?"

"Ed?"

"Oooooooh! Emma! I tried to tell you, Ed suffered a relapse! He has again become completely feckless. It happened overnight, from when he left early for his stupid appointment Monday afternoon and when he strolled into work yesterday around nine-thirty. I think he's on drugs."

I reeled at the idea. Ed didn't have enough imagination or daring to become involved in anything that couldn't be covered with gravy. I said as much to Vida.

"Yes, yes," she answered impatiently. "But all the same, Ed's acting very peculiar, even for Ed."

I could hear bacon sizzling in the microwave. "Morose as well as lazy, I suppose."

"No, actually." Vida's tone conveyed bafflement. "Ed seemed very chipper yesterday. He hummed."

It was my turn to be mystified. Until Ed had undergone his previous metamorphosis, he had suffered from severe gloominess as well as inertia. "One day does not a lifetime make," I noted, attempting to lift my spirits and maybe Vida's, too. "I take it he hasn't come in yet this morning?"

"That's right." Vida sounded annoyed.

My mind was wrestling with the problem of the missing ads. I hated to ask Vida to do more work than she'd already been saddled with, but I had no choice. I suggested that she use Ed's tired clip-art file and try to salvage the lost ads.

"We could go twenty-two pages," I continued. "There must be news filler or handouts to cover each of the half-pages." I hated to publish a paper with a single sheet; it cost extra because the printer had to stuff the odd page.

"I was planning to leave in five minutes," Vida said sharply. "Ginny is holding down the fort."

The reference to Ginny Burmeister, our young but efficient office manager, calmed me a bit. As of July first I'd given her a promotion and a raise. Ginny had proven her mettle during the past three years by not only excelling at her own job but by helping Ed with the advertising side of the shop. Maybe she could bail us out of the current mess.

"I hope Ginny doesn't catch whatever Carla's got," I said with fervor. Ginny and Carla were chums. I had visions of them passing the flu bug back and forth between them like a tennis ball. "It's too bad Ginny didn't handle those ads in the first place. I hate like hell to leave them out."

"We'll make it up to Barton's and Harvey Adcock next week," Vida said, still sounding testy. "There's no time to waste now. Ginny and I've already spent over an hour looking for the blasted dummies. The press is already off schedule. That'll cost you something, too."

I hardly needed the reminder. Surrendering, I gave up and told Vida to drive safely. She harumphed in my ear, asking if I thought she would otherwise drive carelessly. A hundred miles away, the receiver banged.

I wandered back into the kitchen, still holding the cordless phone. There had been no chance to tell Vida about my car troubles. Or, as a side issue, the body in the Melchers' basement. I felt a real sense of letdown.

Not only was my staff falling apart on me, so was *The Advocate* itself. And Vida, whom I sometimes thought of as my second mother, hadn't offered her broad shoulder for sympathy.

"Not that I blame her." Jackie jumped, and I realized I had spoken aloud.

"Blame her? Who, me?" She was draining three slices of bacon on paper towels.

I shook my head and gave Jackie an apologetic smile, then tried to explain the predicament with the paper. Jackie put two slices of bread in the toaster.

"Most newspapers have too many ads anyway," she asserted, sounding as if she and Ed would get along famously. "I always used to argue with Mom about that before she retired from *The Oregonian*. Who wants to look at all that stuff? Especially the electronics ads. They're so *ugly*. Paul's the only one I know who ever reads them."

If Mavis hadn't been able to convince her daughter that advertising revenue paid the bills, then I wasn't about to try. I accepted a cup of coffee and arranged myself at the breakfast counter on one of the kitchen stools. Paul had left for work before I got up. Jackie's breakfast had consisted of soda crackers and coffee. She insisted on fixing toast and bacon for me.

"I can't do eggs, though," she said, putting my plate in front of me. "The yolks—they're like big yellow eyes staring up at me. And soft-boiled—all I can think of is what's going on inside the shell. Isn't it gruesome?"

Never having considered the inner workings of an egg, I was at a loss for words. Bacon and toast would do nicely. There were many mornings when I didn't eat anything for breakfast unless somebody on the staff stopped off at the Upper Crust Bakery.

Jackie joined me on one of the other stools. "I've

been planning our day," she announced. "We'll start with the museum."

"Good," I said, assuming she meant we were going sightseeing. "We'll have to wait until Dusty's calls, though. I'd like to go out on Ediz Hook, too." The Hook was a topographical companion to Dungeness Spit. It curved out into the strait like a big scimitar, forming the city's natural harbor.

Jackie, however, was shaking her head and blowing on her coffee. "We don't need to do that. The museum, the newspaper, maybe the city and county libraries—that's where the information will be."

I blinked at Jackie. "Oh! You mean ... research on the family?"

"Right." Jackie sipped her coffee and made a face. "Uhg, needs more sugar." She scooped two heaping teaspoons out of a red ceramic bowl.

My first reaction was to discourage Jackie in her attempt to delve deeper into the mystery of the basement. But I was curious, too. If I helped her with the task, I wouldn't feel like such a freeloader. My car might not be ready until late afternoon.

A moment later I discovered I was being optimistic. Dusty's informed me that I needed a new fuel pump. The estimate was somewhere between two and three hundred dollars for parts and labor. The fuel pump would have to be ordered from Victoria, but the ferry that would bring it across the strait probably wouldn't arrive until three o'clock. I'd be lucky to have the Jag back by noon on Thursday.

I groaned, but Jackie clapped. "You see! It was meant to be! I should call Mom and tell her you're here. Except that she and Dad are in Santa Fe."

We left the house shortly after nine. I wondered if Vida had arrived in Monroe yet. I wondered if Carla was recovering. I wondered if Ed was still doing nothing except humming.

On the short drive to the museum Jackie asked me what I thought of Mike Randall. I told her that he seemed nice. The comment was, I hoped, ambivalent.

"Good," Jackie responded, angling her Honda into a parking place on Lincoln Street. "Sexy, too, huh?"

Jackie ran one wheel up onto the curb, which was lucky for me because she became distracted. She also had to feed the parking meter and needed to borrow a dime. I didn't want to tell her that despite Mike's good looks and obvious intelligence, I hadn't found him sexy. He struck me as utterly humorless, a sin far worse than blowing broccoli out one's nose. But maybe I hadn't given him a fair chance.

The museum was housed in the old redbrick courthouse. The lobby was finished in classic marble, with a sweeping staircase at each side of the rotunda. Since Jackie seemed as confused as I was, I guessed she hadn't been inside before.

"We'll get somebody to help us," she whispered, then marched up to the main desk. A plump woman with graying red hair offered us a pleasant smile.

A few minutes later we were trudging through the standing exhibits, which depicted the history of Port Angeles. I knew that the area had been staked out some four hundred years ago by Juan de Fuca, a Greek pilot sailing under the Spanish flag and a Spanish name. Two centuries later Spain had been joined by England and the United States in making claims along the strait named for de Fuca. By the mid-nineteenth century the Americans had persevered. But the English and Spanish place-names endured. Captain George Vancouver had gone on a spree: Mount Rainier, Mount Baker, Whidbey Island, Bainbridge Island, Vashon Island, Puget Sound—they were but a few of the places Vancouver had named for crew and friends. Port Angeles, however, had originally been called Puerto de Nuestra Señora de los Angeles. The natives couldn't pronounce it and neither could the early settlers who started arriving at the outbreak of the Civil War. It was easier to call the fledgling town Port Angeles.

And for a brief period during the Civil War, Abraham Lincoln had designated the frontier settlement as the second national city. Had the Confederacy captured Washington, D.C., President Lincoln planned to move the capital to this tiny, rugged outpost. The concept caused me to smile. But it wasn't much help in solving the Melchers' mystery.

We quickly moved through the conflict between Native Americans and white pioneers. We scarcely paused at the mock-up of the failed Puget Sound Co-operative Colony, which had stood on the site of ITT Rayonier. We merely smiled at the account of how vigilantes stole the county records from Dungeness and moved them to Port Angeles to change the seat of Clallam County. We skipped over the squatters who had jump-claimed government reserve lands in the 1890s. It was only when we reached the turn of the century that we began to slow down and study the past.

On the edge of the Olympic Peninsula, Port Angeles was isolated, more so than Alpine. The Great Northern Railroad had helped give birth to the mining town on Stevens Pass. It had linked Seattle and Minneapolis in 1893, though in the beginning the name had been Nippon and the inhabitants had been either railroad men or Japanese miners. The real settlement hadn't begun until 1910 when Carl Clemans came up from Snohomish, built a sawmill, and renamed the town Alpine.

But Port Angeles had no such early bond with larger cities. Except for rough overland travel or going by ship, the struggling county seat had been cut off from the rest of the world. During the last decade of the nine-teenth century the town had not only failed to thrive but had actually shriveled. The future had looked bleak.

The West had been built by men of vision, also known as gamblers. Port Angeles had had its share, from Judge George Venable Smith and his Utopian colony to banker Thomas T. Aldwell, who brought hydro-electric power to the Olympic Peninsula. They, along with a number of other expansionists, had also hopped on those homesteads. So had Cornelius Rowley, Michi-gan timber cruiser, whose claim had included a tract of virgin timber on Lincoln Hill.

"Here he is!" Jackie cried, though she tried to lower her voice while pointing to a mounted photograph of a bearded, burly man in a three-piece suit and a derby hat. According to the lengthy cutline, Rowley had come to Port Angeles in 1892 and worked for the Filion brothers, who had also hailed from Michigan. Eventu-ally, Rowley had bought up some five thousand acres of his own in the Little River Valley outside of town. In 1896 he had brought his family west to homestead.

Sure enough, there was the Rowley house in a photo-graph that had been blown up and mounted on posterboard. The graininess of the enlargement made it impossible to identify the four people who stood under the Moorish arches of the front porch.

"Two men and two women," I noted, squinting at the exhibit. "Cornelius and Mrs. Rowley and the two grown kids?"

Jackie ran a hand through her taffy-colored hair. "Carrie and Eddie? Maybe. Isn't one of the women holding something?"

Trying for a closer look, I practically fell into the dis-play. At least no one else was going through the mu-seum this early in the day. "A baby, I think." My eyes traveled down to the fifth and last of the arches that fronted the big house. "There's someone else, almost hidden behind the corner pillar. A man or a woman? I can't tell."

Jackie frowned. "I can't, either." She gazed at the wide expanse of front lawn that ran all the way down to the unpaved street. "Hey, look! They hadn't put the rockery in yet. I could have sworn it was a million years old!"

It didn't take long to finish our tour. Jackie suggested we try the genealogy room, but I figured it was more for general-interest ancestor seekers than for those looking for historical specifics. If Paul's memory had served him well, we had a firm grip on the family tree. Thus, we polished off the rest of the museum, quickly passing by the arrival of the railroad, the opening of the Elwha River Dam, the introduction of electricity, and the patriotic fervor of World War I. We lingered, however, at the tribute to Lena Stillman Melcher Rowley, who looked as if she could have eaten steel girders for lunch. Lena's accomplishments were many, including a hatchet job on a couple of local taverns, one of which still stood on East First Street. Her husband, Edmund Rowley, was mentioned in a footnote. In 1898 he had served under Teddy Roosevelt in the Spanish-American War and been wounded in the charge up San Juan Hill.

"Eddie," murmured Jackie as we moved through Port Angeles's bootlegging days in the Roaring Twenties and on up through the doleful Great Depression. "That's Paul's stepgreat-grandfather, isn't it?"

"It is if he was Sanford Melcher's stepdad," I replied. "And Eddie was Carrie's brother."

We had reached World War II. "Weird," Jackie remarked. "Eddie's sister may be in the basement under a plastic drop cloth. I wonder if we should put her in a box."

I concentrated on the bunkers that had been built outside of town to help protect Port Angeles from a possible Japanese invasion. "I think it's called a coffin," I said lightly.

Jackie didn't see the humor in my remark. "We'll do that after we make sure it's Carrie. And find out what happened to her. Paul was going to phone the prosecutor's office from work this morning. I hope he doesn't press them to act. We need time to solve this on our own. Officials tend to meddle and muddle."

I glanced at the mock-up of Peninsula College, then moved on past Modern Fishing Methods and Global Industry for Tomorrow. Port Angeles and Alpine had many things in common, including their semi-isolation. But my present hometown wasn't as diversified. We had no window on the sea. Timber and tourism were the mainstays of Alpine's economy. The logging business was as endangered as the spotted owl, and due to the cool summer the tourists weren't flocking through town. I foresaw a winter with no snow, thus ruining business at the ski lodge. A vague sense of depression began to envelop me again.

Jackie was enveloped by another hunger attack. It so happened that Gordy's had a second restaurant on Lincoln Street, two blocks from the museum and a stone's throw from the public library. While Jackie ordered three slices of green pepper, black olives, and pineapple on double cheese, I browsed through the collection of memorabilia housed at the rear of the restaurant. Among the items on display was a woman's tan felt hat faced with emerald velvet and decorated with a bright green bird. It was said to be from Paris, circa 1905. I was charmed, and also curious. If Cornelius Rowley's second wife was French, had the chic *chapeau* belonged to her? But the busy waitress who was putting Jackie's pizza in a cardboard box had no idea where or how the exhibits had been acquired.

"You can't eat that in the library," I cautioned Jackie as we emerged back on the street.

"I know," she mumbled, gulping down the pizza. "You go ahead without me."

I started to demur, then shrugged and went into the library. At the rate Jackie was devouring her eleven A.M. snack, she wouldn't be far behind. I headed for the periodical section to go through old newspapers. I expected them to be on microfiche, but some were still in bound volumes. Almost immediately I became confused.

Before the turn of the century it seemed that newspapers had broken out all over the Olympic Peninsula like an epidemic. The simplest method would be to trace the history of the current paper, *The Peninsula Daily News,* but its origins only went back to 1916. I was running an agitated hand through my short brown hair when Jackie wandered up to the table where I was seated.

"Do you ever worry about women who live alone?" she asked in a whisper. Her chair scraped on the floor. "Especially when they get old. They're so vulnerable, and often frail and handicapped. What happens when it snows?"

Trying to sort out *The Democrat-Leader* from *The People* from *The Herald* from *The Beacon* from *The Daily Pop* from *The Simoon,* I wasn't ready to cope with lonely elderly women. At the rate I was going, I would become one of them. I couldn't even figure out what the hell a *simoon* was.

"I live alone," I said in a voice that made a middle-aged man at the next table jump.

Jackie brushed pizza-crust crumbs off her oversized Reebok T-shirt. "I remember how the old men used to come into the downtown library in Portland and sit all day and read the papers. . . . It was so sad. But I hardly ever saw old women there. Where were they? Afraid to go outside? Shut in, needing food and medical attention, waiting for a neighbor to come . . ."

"Jackie." I smiled kindly and patted her arm. "Why don't you volunteer? As long as you're not working and you're feeling good, check in with some of the service centers. They're crying for helpers, I'll bet."

Her heart-shaped face was bewildered. "I wouldn't know where to start."

Neither did I, but a sudden inspiration struck. I got out of my chair and went over to a computer terminal. Keying in ROWLEY, CORNELIUS under subject heading, the screen showed me a list of four articles. One was entitled "Tireless Tycoon Ushers in Gracious New Era—The House That Rowley Built." A second appeared to be about a hunting trip in eastern Washington, a third featured Mrs. Rowley, and the fourth—and final—was an obituary. I started to rejoin Jackie when the middle-aged man at the next table swiveled around and gave me a cockeyed grin.

"I can't imagine why you're living alone," he said in a hoarse whisper. "You're too damned cute."

With that, he fell facedown on the front page of *The New York Times.*

Chapter Five

ONE OF THE librarians called for the medics, but I could tell from the reek of whiskey that the man was drunk. With a mixture of pity and revulsion I studied his profile, which rested on a story about Croatia. The features were regular except for the nose, which probably had been broken in a fight. The dark red hair was plentiful but graying. In repose, the man looked pale, almost ashen, but I suspected his complexion was usually flushed with broken capillaries caused by boozing. He wore tan pants, a denim shirt, and loafers that looked as if they had originally cost a bundle.

Jackie was shivering beside me, clutching at my arm. "Is he dead?"

I shook my head. "He's drunk. He'll probably end up in jail." I sighed. "Maybe we should check his pockets and get some ID. He's probably got a wife someplace who's tearing her hair."

The man didn't stir as I reached into the back pocket of his slacks. The wallet, like the loafers, was well worn, but made of real leather. I flipped through it, finding a California driver's license issued to Leo Fulton Walsh of Culver City.

"He's a tourist," I said in a low voice. Jackie and I had been joined by three librarians, four patrons, and the mailman.

"There's an old beat-up car from California parked a

couple of places down the street," volunteered the mail-man. He was young, with fuzzy side whiskers and a rabbitlike expression. "I keep track of out-of-state cars. I've got thirty-nine states, five Canadian provinces, and the Canal Zone so far this summer."

"Wonderful," I responded. One of the librarians asked the postman if he thought the people from the Ca-nal Zone had driven all the way to Port Angeles. Before he could answer, the medics arrived. Leaving the open wallet on the table next to the man's outstretched hand, Jackie and I backed off.

"Now what do we do?" Jackie asked in a worried voice.

I shrugged. "Go about our business. We've got four articles on Cornelius Rowley. You can start with the one about the building of the house. You might get some decorating tips."

But Jackie seemed fascinated by Leo Fulton Walsh. The medics were not. Mr. Walsh was just another boozer who had interrupted their gin rummy game. Still unconscious, the man from Culver City was whisked away. I could have sworn that his mouth curved into a smile.

The hunting-trip story, dated September 2, 1906, wasn't very enlightening. Presented in the fulsome style of the early 1900s, the writer waxed on about Cornelius Rowley's prowess as a hunter, particularly with moose. Mr. Rowley, "one of this city's most prominent and suc-cessful businessmen, has used his manly skills and na-tive cunning to triumph over all manner of game, from the lowly chukar to the fierce black bear. His palatial home on Lincoln Hill is filled with trophies. . . ."

I rolled my eyes. Ninety years ago there had been enough wildlife in the Pacific Northwest that a hunter could have herded it into his dining room with a broom. Cornelius Rowley hadn't needed a gun to bag those trophies. I sensed that his expertise had been highly exaggerated.

"Hey," I said, giving Jackie a poke, "what happened to the mounted heads and stuffed birds?"

Jackie's expression was blank. "Huh? Like antlers, you mean?"

I showed her the hunting piece. "Somebody must have redecorated since Cornelius Rowley died. Lena, maybe? Or Grandma Rose?"

Jackie shook her head. "Don't ask me. I never saw the house until this winter. Emma, look." She pointed to a paragraph midway down in the Rowley house story. "It says here that Cornelius hired an architect from Seattle to design the house. Two architects, I should say—Kerr and Rogers. Then he had his own mill build the place. Mrs. Rowley added her special decorative touches. Listen to this: 'Like all Frenchwomen, Simone Dupre Rowley possesses an inherent ability to make her home a tasteful showcase for entertaining. Mr. and Mrs. Rowley expect to launch many gala evenings for the city's social elite.' "

I gaped. "In Port Angeles? I mean, *then,* in Port Angeles? The town sounds too rough-and-ready for top hats and diamond tiaras." But Mike had mentioned an opera house. Port Angeles hadn't been as primitive as I'd envisioned it."

Jackie was wearing a dreamy expression. "Think of it! A small orchestra, servants with silver trays, women wearing jewels and long white gloves and gowns with tiers of lace! It must have been wonderful!" She swayed on the stiff wooden chair as if she could hear the strains of a Strauss waltz.

I confiscated the article. Jackie's quote was accurate and perhaps the glowing prophecy had come true. But I wanted to see the rest of the story for myself. The writer was obviously impressed by the grandeur of Rowley

House, calling it the "finest residence yet in Port Angeles, surpassing even the Van Kuren, Filion, and Grable homes. Construction is expected to take a full two years, with yet another year to finish the interior craftsmanship." Several paragraphs were lavished on the architecture and embellishments; more were devoted to the sheer number of rooms. "When completed, the basement will be no dreary dungeon for laundry, storage, and furnace, but will include a sewing room, furnished with all the latest dressmaking accessories from Paris, and the first private billiards room in the city, with a hand-carved table made of teak from Ceylon."

The article was accompanied by sketches of the house and a plan of the main floor. Except for the recent enlargement of the kitchen, it appeared that the architects had stuck by their original renderings.

I moved on to Cornelius Rowley's obit, which had rated a full fourteen-column inches. Born in Saginaw, he had served under Major General John Sedgwick at Antietam and Chancellorsville. His postwar exploits were condensed until he moved west. Upon arriving in Port Angeles, Rowley had been a comet of activity. His job as a timber cruiser had encouraged him to strike out on his own, to build a mill, to purchase more and more tracts of virgin forest. At last he moved his family to the farthest corner of the country and erected his gracious home. His success was lauded by his peers and his hearty manner "was an uplifting source to all who knew him. Ever a generous man, Mr. Rowley's employees revered him for his many kindnesses, particularly to those in need."

Funeral services were held on May 14, 1908, at the parlors of the Lyden Company, with burial in Ocean View Cemetery. His survivors were listed as his widow, Simone; his son, Edmund; his daughter, Caroline; and three grandchildren, all of Port Angeles.

Jackie was absorbed in the Simone Rowley article. A two-column photo showed Mrs. Rowley in a box-pleated bolero jacket and long skirt, tailored shirtwaist, and a straw hat with flowers. She balanced gracefully on a parasol. A second smaller picture was primarily a headshot. A wave of dark hair fell seductively over her forehead. Simone wore a thick, pearl dog collar at her throat and showed off what I assumed to be a milky-white bosom and shoulders. All I could see of her dress were black ribbons and the top of a lace big-bertha collar.

"She got all her clothes in Paris!" Jackie exclaimed in awe. "Dishes and upholstery fabric and lace, too! Wasn't she a lucky woman?"

Jackie handed me the bound volume, and I scanned the story. It was not about Simone Rowley but about the things that belonged to her. Simone's sulky mouth seemed to mock me and the rest of the world; the faintly hooded eyes held sensual secrets. I didn't think I'd want to do lunch with her, either.

"Mrs. Rowley isn't given to philosophizing," the writer concluded. "Of her Paris origins, her move to this country, and the journey to its most distant corner, Mrs. Rowley says little, except to shrug and murmur, 'C'est la vie.'"

"Mme. Cliché," I remarked, hoping that Simone had been beautiful but dumb. "We haven't raked up any scandal so far."

Jackie slumped in the chair, her toes pointing at one another. She looked very young and quite ungainly. "It's hopeless, isn't it? How can we find answers to questions that are ninety years old? I feel like giving up."

"Courage," I said, ready to try for clippings on Edmund Rowley. "This is like an in-depth reporting

job. We have to keep digging. What we've found at this
point is all surface material. Background, as it were."

Jackie looked dubious, then brightened. "Hey, it's
lunchtime. Let's go to Drake's for pizza. It's a U-bake
place. We can fix our own toppings."

I didn't think I could bear the sight of another pizza.
I was trying to figure out a tactful way to say so when
a wiry little woman with tight blue curls hurried over to
our table. Behind outsized spectacles her lively eyes almost matched her hair.

"You were in the museum," she said in a husky voice
that didn't go along with her sprightly style. "Researching the Rowleys, I heard. I'm Tessie Roo, genealogist."

We shook hands. Tessie's collection of dangling
chains jingled on her flat breast. "I was afraid I'd lost
track of you," she continued, her chipper smile in place.
"The library turned out to be a good guess, eh?"

My own guess was that Tessie originally hailed from
Canada. Her pronunciation of *out* as *oot* gave her away.
I couldn't help but ask.

Tessie's blue eyes widened in surprise. "How clever
of you! Such an ear! I was born in Nanaimo, but I married one of your Yanks. A very long time ago, I must
say, and he's been dead for ten years now, but I've
stayed here. It's home. And genealogy can be done anywhere. You must come back to the museum."

Jackie demurred, but I saw an opportunity to escape
another pizza binge. Urging Jackie to follow her whim,
I sent her along to Drake's while I accompanied Tessie
Roo back to the old courthouse. Along the way I explained Paul Melcher's connection to the Rowleys but
refrained from mentioning the skeleton. I might as well
have saved my breath.

"Yes, I heard about that this morning," Tessie replied,
no longer smiling but nodding gravely. "Such a shock

for everyone! My son-in-law installs hot-water heaters. One of the electricians who found the skeleton told him about it."

I should have known. Port Angeles wasn't as small as Alpine, but the grapevine seemed to be just as effective. "I don't suppose you've heard anyone speculate about the person's identity?"

Tessie shook her blue curls. "Not yet. There will be plenty of ideas, of course. Especially among the old folks. They do love to dwell on the macabre, eh?"

Announcing to the woman behind the front desk that her search was a success, Tessie whisked me upstairs to the cubbyhole that served as her office next to the genealogy room. Tessie worked among chaos, it seemed, and the clutter reached from floor to ceiling. She cleared off a spare chair and we both sat down.

"Newspaper clippings," she mused, pulling out the drawer of a steel file cabinet. "They're all well and good, but not as comprehensive as we are." A stiff brown folder tied with string thudded onto the desk. Tessie opened a second drawer, produced a similar folder, and then a third and a fourth. Folding her hands in front of her, she gave me her infectious smile. "Computers are fine, too, but I prefer material I can feel. Old-fashioned files bring me closer to my subjects. Now. Where shall we begin?"

I told her that we seemed to have covered Cornelius Rowley and his daughter-in-law Lena from birth to death. We hadn't gotten to Edmund yet, who was the next logical choice.

"Melcher, Edmund." Tessie untied one of the folders. "Yes. Edmund, called Eddie, born 1870, died 1930. Partly crippled in the Spanish-American War. Tried to run the Rowley Mill, but ran it into the ground." The blue eyes twinkled. "Naughty of me, but it's true. Eddie had no head for business. The mill went bankrupt in

1913. Eddie opened a haberdashery, but that lasted only three years. He invented things, most of which didn't work very well. His attempt to put in a staircase lift came a cropper when the chair fell off and he flew out. Eddie broke his neck and died. Poor man, not a success, at least not when it came to commerce."

"Alas, poor Eddie," I murmured. "Did he get involved in Lena's politics?"

Tessie talked as she flipped through the file. It was clear that she knew most of Eddie's history by heart but was refreshing her memory. "He gave lip service to her. Or so I've gathered. Lena tended to rely more on her son, Sanford, who fancied himself a writer, particularly of poems. He did some speeches for his mother, though."

I reflected on Sanford Melcher's limb of the family tree. Who was his father, the man who had been Paul Melcher's great-grandfather? Where had Lena come from, other than a Revolutionary War family in Massachusetts? I posed these questions to Tessie Roo.

"Excellent." Tessie beamed as if she were a veteran teacher encouraging an inquiring young mind. Paging through sheets of foolscap, she pounced on the desired dates. "Lena Stillman, born 1860 to Ebenezer and Clara Stillman of Quincy, Massachusetts, which makes Lena ten years older than her second husband, Eddie Rowley. Ebenezer Stillman was a Congregational minister, as was his father before him. Great-grandfather Stillman fought in the Revolutionary War. On the wrong side, from my point of view." Tessie winked. "Are you interested in going back any further?"

I shook my head. Lena's parents were as far as I needed to go. Besides, I didn't know if I could take in two generations of nineteenth-century Congregational ministers on an empty stomach. "Was it her father who was the ardent abolitionist?"

"That's right." Tessie's eyes scanned the page, then she continued in a brisk voice: "A great friend and ally of Henry Ward Beecher. Much pounding of pulpits and beating of breasts. Lena married Ferris Melcher in 1878. He came from solid New England stock but had a yen to see the world. Their son, Sanford, was born in Philadelphia in 1879. The family kept moving, apparently seeking some elusive star that only Ferris glimpsed. He was tubercular and died on the way to Arizona in 1901." Tessie moved on to another piece of paper while I tried to envision Paul's great-grandfather coughing up his lungs somewhere in the Midwest. Tessie, however, wasted no sympathy on dead men who had never reached Port Angeles: "Ferris Melcher's widow and their twenty-two-year-old son had to make a major choice. Here, read it for yourself. It's an excerpt from one of Lena's speeches."

I accepted the sheet of foolscap from Tessie. Yellowed newspaper articles were pasted on it, all relating to the suffragette movement. With a blunt fingernail, Tessie tapped the second paragraph of the upper-left-hand clipping. The quote read:

As a helpless widow, I was faced with a grave decision. I could return to Massachusetts, where I could rely on the grudging generosity of relatives and friends. Or, I could boldly strike out on my own and make a new life for myself. I chose the latter. Guided by Destiny, I came to Seattle, where I met my second husband. His need of me was far greater than mine for him, which is as it should be when it comes to the married state. But I do not regret for one moment moving to Port Angeles, for this is where my work lies. Never harbor regrets. Such useless emotions detract from an avowed purpose. Spare neither tears nor sentiment, which sap strength and energy. Rather, shake the dust of encumbering people and places from your feet and march bravely into the future. We are the women of the world, and we will not be denied.

"Wow." I smiled wryly. "Not exactly a soft touch. But you have to admire her spirit."

Tessie nodded, though without great enthusiasm. "Yes, and you have to put that speech into historical context. It was 1917, you'll note. At that point Lena had been remarried for some fifteen years and deeply involved in her social causes. Most widows with a twenty-two-year-old son would have sat at home and let the young man support them. Lena doesn't even mention his name."

I considered my own almost twenty-two-year-old son. Adam was about as likely to support me as a chicken was to sing "The Star-Spangled Banner" at an upcoming Mariners' game. After almost four years of attending two different colleges, Adam was still drifting. Currently, his hazy focus was on archaeology, but only because he was spending part of the summer with my brother on an Anasazi dig in Arizona. Silently, I marveled at how independent we women had become in the last eighty years. We were now able to stand alone so that everybody else could lean on us until we collapsed.

"What became of Sanford Melcher?" I asked, thrusting aside my mingled self-adulation and self-pity.

Tessie dug into another file. "He married a local girl, Rose Felder, in 1909, and had five children, one of whom was your friend Paul's father. Sanford and Rose lived with Lena and Edmund Rowley. Sanford never was much of a provider. A poet, as I mentioned."

It occurred to me that Sanford had inherited the pursuit of the elusive star from his father, Ferris Melcher.

Neither of them had been ambitious. As for Sanford's offspring, I recalled Paul's account. Two of them, including Paul's dad, were still around, but I'd forgotten who the other one was. "Is it the daughter who survived along with . . . Mr. Melcher?" I'd forgotten the name of Paul's father.

"Samuel Melcher, the youngest, born, 1927. He lives in Tacoma, but you know that." Tessie consulted the family tree, which she had spread out on a big crate next to her chair. "The other surviving child is Sara Melcher Beales, born 1922. She's seventy-one and lives in Seattle, with her husband, Verne. You want the address? It's on Lake Washington Boulevard."

I knew the name and I recognized the street. Vernon Beales was a retired Boeing executive. Lake Washington Boulevard was home to many of Seattle's well-to-do families. Dutifully I jotted the house address down in my notebook. It might not hurt for Paul to contract his aunt Sara.

It was time to turn my attention to Carrie Rowley. Expecting another detailed account, I tried to settle back into my uncomfortable chair. But Tessie held up a sheet of paper and frowned.

"Caroline Rowley Malone and her husband, James, moved away shortly after Cornelius Rowley died in 1908. The articles here are on her wedding and the birth announcements of her children. There's nothing else."

I studied the glowing account of Carrie's wedding in June 1903. The dress, the flowers, the music, and the attendants were all recorded in faithful, fulsome detail. The maid of honor and the bridesmaids wore crepe de chine trimmed with silk. The bride's damask gown was edged with tiers of Belgian lace. She carried white roses, lilies of the valley, and baby's breath. Her ten-foot veil and train swept down the newly laid carpet in the Methodist church. The groom, James Malone, seemed to be a footnote.

"He was a logger, originally from Armagh," Tessie explained. "You have to wonder, eh?"

I gave her a quizzical look. "About . . . social standing?"

Tessie nodded solemnly. "Oh, yes. Cornelius Rowley started out as a timber cruiser, but he was a self-made man. His success story was the sort that was much admired in the early part of the century. Carrie was twenty-six when she married. I daresay she was afraid of being a spinster. Perhaps she took potluck. James Malone was known as Jimmy, but he was also called Smooth-Bore." A mischievous smile spread across Tessie's face. "Note the birth announcements and you'll see why."

There they were, the three little Malones, Julia, Walter, and Claudia, all born in less than four years. "My, my," I responded. "I guess he kissed more than the Blarney Stone."

Tessie laughed richly. "So he did, eh? I'm sorry we have nothing else on that branch of the family." Her merriment faded, replaced by professional chagrin.

"That's okay," I assured her, though I couldn't help but wonder if the reason for the dead end lay in the Melchers' basement. "How about Simone, the second Mrs. Rowley?"

Tessie's chagrin deepened into outright annoyance. "That's another void. As soon as Cornelius was in his grave, his young widow left town. All we have is an unauthenticated birth year of 1874 or maybe 1878, take your choice. She was supposedly born in Paris but went to New York in 1901. How she got out west isn't explained. She married Cornelius Rowley in 1902 here in Port Angeles. Six years later she was gone." With an irritated gesture, Tessie closed one of the files. "I detest vagueness in record keeping. It's a genealogist's curse."

I had to agree. It was a problem for journalists, too. Thanking Tessie profusely, I went off to find my hostess. It didn't take long. Jackie was leaning against her car, clutching a parking ticket with one hand and her stomach with the other.

"Oh, poopy! Those stupid cops! I was only twenty minutes over! I feel awful. We'd better go home." Clumsily, Jackie got into the driver's side of the Honda.

Not having wolfed down a couple of pounds of pizza, I was suffering from hunger rather than excess. I was about to suggest stopping at a takeout place so I could grab a burger when Jackie doubled over the wheel. Unfortunately, she had braked in the middle of Laurel Street just before it turned onto Eighth, the main east-west artery through town. A van with Montana plates almost rear-ended us. The driver, who looked as if he'd just emerged from a bar in Butte, began to honk.

"You drive," Jackie said in a breathless voice. She all but fell over in the direction of the passenger's seat.

Frantically, I got out of the car and ran around to the other side, making apologetic hand motions at the furious Montanan. There were now a half-dozen other vehicles lined up behind the van.

"What's wrong?" I asked with alarm as I turned onto Eighth Street. Mercifully, the van kept going up Laurel.

Jackie merely shook her head, the taffy-colored hair swinging listlessly. Getting my bearings, I crossed the bridge over the gully and turned on A Street. Two minutes later we were in the Melcher driveway. Helping Jackie out of the car, I half carried, half dragged her to the back door. She fumbled with the keys, then staggered through the kitchen and on into the den, where she collapsed on the small sofa.

"It's pains," she finally said, still breathless. "Here." She rested a trembling hand on her upper abdomen.

"Like cramps?" I asked anxiously. My pregnancy

with Adam had been relatively routine, but I knew the signs of a threatened miscarriage when I heard them.

Jackie's forehead furrowed. "Like . . . sort of, yes. I guess." She closed her eyes and leaned her head against the back of the sofa.

I volunteered to call Dr. Carlisle. It was noon straight up, and I wondered if the staff might be out to lunch. Luckily they weren't. Even more luckily Dr. Carlisle was heading home to eat. The reassuringly calm voice of his nurse informed me that he would swing by the Melcher house on his way.

By the time I got off the phone, Jackie had opened her eyes and was sitting up straight. Her first reaction was to call Dr. Carlisle back and tell him not to bother. She was being a *nuisance*. My response was firm: Either she let the doctor come by or else I was taking her to Olympic Memorial Hospital. I also asked if I should phone Paul.

"No!" Jackie exclaimed. "He'd worry. And make a big fuss and be a bigger nuisance than I am. Men are such goofs about babies. He's too big a wienie to go to the childbirth classes." She winced with pain and closed her eyes again.

Dr. Norman Carlisle arrived five minutes later. His solid, homely presence instilled immediate confidence. Tactfully, I withdrew from the den and foraged in the refrigerator. The pickings were slim, but there was enough bacon left for a BLT. Or just a plain B, I decided, discovering there was neither lettuce nor tomato. The crisper drawer contained only half an onion, a couple of garlic cloves, and a wilted celery stalk.

I was munching on the last of my meager sandwich when Dr. Carlisle came into the kitchen. To my relief, he was smiling. "Jackie tells me you're an old family friend," he said, eyeing the empty coffeemaker a bit wistfully. "Have you got any clout with the little mother?"

Briefly, I explained my tenuous relationship to Jackie. "I can call Mavis and ask her to do the meddling. What's the problem?"

Leaning against the kitchen counter, Dr. Carlisle sighed. "We caution pregnant women about alcohol, smoking, drugs, even over-the-counter remedies, but we can't seem to get nutrition into their heads. It's the cravings and the morning sickness and all the hormonal changes, of course, but that's where most of them go off the deep end. In Jackie's case it's all that blasted pizza. The tomato sauce, of course. It's highly acidic. She's got heartburn."

I slumped a bit on the kitchen stool. "I should have known. In fact, I wondered. But she seemed to be in such agony."

Dr. Carlisle shrugged. "She's healthy as a horse. I don't imagine she's ever had heartburn before. It scared her. Try to steer her away from that pizza. I'll talk to Paul about it, too."

"Good," I said, then, in a burst of gratitude, offered to make a pot of coffee. To my surprise, Dr. Carlisle accepted. My appreciation for his concern spilled over. House calls in Alpine were not unheard of, but Drs. Gerald Dewey and Peyton Flake never had far to go. Port Angeles was five times the size, in population and area.

Dr. Carlisle chuckled at my effusiveness. "No big deal." He settled his bulk onto one of the stools. "Every other week I take Wednesday afternoons off. I was going to go fishing off the Hook, but those killer whales have been through here this morning. The folks coming across on the Victoria ferry think they're great, but for us fishermen it means there aren't any salmon. I guess I'll have to kill weeds instead."

Pouring out the first cup of coffee, I commiserated. In Alpine it was the dearth of trout and steelhead. The rivers hadn't been planted, they were off-color, they were too high, they were too low, it was too warm, it was too cold, it had rained too much, it hadn't rained enough. Whatever the reason, the fishing was lousy. I hadn't heard from a happy fisherman since I'd read Hemingway's *The Old Man and the Sea*. And if *he* could be called happy, that shows what a bunch of whiners the rest of them are.

Dr. Carlisle sipped his coffee, then rubbed at his graying crew cut. "Say, Jackie was telling me about that skeleton she and Paul have down in the basement. I think she was hinting I might want to take a look. Can you lead the way?"

I could, but I didn't have to. Jackie appeared just then, looking a trifle wan. Or perhaps merely foolish.

"I feel better," she announced, propping herself up against the door frame. "Do you really think it's all right for me to take Tums?"

Dr. Carlisle nodded. "Loaded with calcium. The important thing is for you to lay off the pizza." He downed the rest of his coffee. "Speaking of bones—in a way, of course—why don't you show me your skeleton? Interesting, that. I've been here almost twenty years and I've never heard of such a thing before. Not a complete set of bones, anyway."

Having finished my sandwich, I trudged along after Jackie and the doctor. The unfinished basement still smelled damp. The flashlight wavered in the darkened area, and the pitiful skeleton was now resting on an old army blanket.

"You know," Dr. Carlisle began after making his careful way down the stepladder apparently left by Paul, "I began my practice in eastern Oregon. I'm from Pendleton originally. Anyway, I was the only doctor for miles around in Wallowa County, so I had to be the coroner, too. Tough duty for a young practitioner, especially a guy whose specialty is ob-gyn work. Fortunately, I didn't have to do a lot of autopsies, but . . ." He paused, carefully removing the drop cloth and examining the skeleton. "Female, I'd say. Youngish." He paused again. "Cracks in the right tibia and left fibula. Ankle bones to you. Never mended. Hmmmm."

I glanced at Jackie, who was staring at the doctor with rapt attention. Gently, she burped. "What does that mean, Dr. Carlisle?" Jackie asked, either out of genuine curiosity or to cover her embarrassment.

The doctor didn't look up. He seemed fascinated by the skeleton. "Remarkably well preserved, considering the damp down here. The house is well insulated, I imagine." Abruptly he turned, craning his neck to gaze up at us. "What was that? The ankle bones? Hard to say, really. The poor thing may have fallen." He made a sweeping gesture with one hand, from the edge of the basement floor to the dirt-covered cavern, where he stood. "A ten-, fifteen-foot drop? That would do it."

I frowned. "You mean she fell off the . . . Wait, I don't get it."

Dr. Carlisle was now examining the skull. I held my breath; Jackie didn't blink. The basement had suddenly become too warm. Fleetingly, I wondered if summer had finally arrived or if we were feeling a sense of oppression.

"Well." Dr. Carlisle rearranged the drop cloth, covering the skeleton as gently as if it had been a sleeping baby. He dusted off his hands and climbed up the step-ladder. Rubbing one eye, he shook his head. "That's odd. More than odd. The skull has been badly damaged. It looks to me as if there'd been a blow to the head. But then it's been a long time since I was a coroner. I'll stick to babies. They're much nicer."

Chapter Six

DR. CARLISLE WAS right. Murder wasn't nice, and it seemed that was how the Melchers' skeleton had met her end. It could have been an accident, the doctor had pointed out, a fall from the finished ledge of the basement floor. Perhaps the poor woman had hit her head on the way down. But why hadn't she been found? According to everything Jackie and I had learned so far, the Rowley house had been a hub of activity in the first decade of the twentieth century. A missing woman, especially a family member, would certainly have caused a stir. I was convinced that the body had never been found because somebody had wanted it that way. And that somebody had probably been the killer. A practical man, Dr. Carlisle didn't try to dissuade me.

Jackie took to her bed. The doctor's revelation hadn't upset her as much as it had me. She exhibited natural curiosity but was more concerned with her recovery from the overdose of pizza. I resisted the temptation to call Dusty's Foreign Auto Repair and wondered how to fill the early-afternoon void.

I started by going back to the third floor to see if we'd missed any items of interest. There were more picture albums, but all of relatively recent vintage. There were also two scrapbooks, though one contained souvenirs from the Thirties and Forties and the other was devoted solely to movie stars of the silent-film era.

Buster Keaton and Theda Bara seemed unlikely to throw any light on the Melchers' mystery.

At last I poked inside a sturdy cardboard tube. The contents revealed the floor plan of the Melcher house. At a glance it seemed to be the same rendering Jackie and I had seen in the library archives. The precise draftsman's lines revealed nothing new.

I searched the nooks and crannies. But there were no scented letters tied with ribbon, no locked diaries, no postcards from traveling friends or relations. Discouraged, I knelt by the dormer window that looked out toward Pine Hill.

Jackie might be right. What was the point of trying to solve a mystery that was over eighty years old? It wouldn't help Carrie Rowley Malone—or whoever she was. If she had met a violent end, her killer was also dead by now. Why rake up an old scandal?

Why ever search for truth? Because it's there, somewhere, obscured by human frailty, delusion, intention, deception, rationalization—and time. I liked to ennoble my profession by calling myself a seeker of truth. But when *I* am being truthful, I admit that most journalists are part-snoop, party-voyeur. We are eternal observers, distancing ourselves from events, sparing ourselves from direct involvement.

The gray clouds were moving slowly across Pine Hill. It was a typical day of this strange summer, with cool temperatures, morning drizzle, and the sky not clearing until late afternoon. Only a native Pacific Northwesterner like me could love the cloudy weather.

And as I searched my soul, I knew that I was allowing myself to get deeper into the Melcher mystery because it diverted me from my own problems. It was easier to try to solve the riddle of a turn-of-the-century skeleton than it was to concentrate on Emma Lord's contemporary problems. I could face up to the murder of a young woman some eighty-plus years ago, but I didn't want to look in the mirror. The truth stops at my own doorstep.

Taking the floor plan with me, I headed back downstairs just as the phone rang. With mixed emotions I wondered if it was Dusty's, telling me my Jag was ready.

It wasn't. Tessie Roo's husky, cheerful voice was on the line.

"You got me intrigued," she said, sounding pleased with herself. "I've researched the Rowleys and the Melchers before, of course, but with that skeleton there's much more to it than just documenting the lineage of Port Angeles's early residents. Right after you left I called one of my fellow genealogists in Seattle to check on Carrie Rowley Malone and her husband, Jimmy. I heard back just now."

I smiled into the phone. Tessie's enthusiasm warmed me. "And?"

"Interesting," she said as a preface. "Jimmy Malone died in 1953. His survivors included six children, nine grandchildren, two great-grandchildren, and his wife, Minnie." Tessie paused for effect.

"*Minnie?* Maybe," I added quickly, "it's a misprint."

"No," Tessie replied with conviction. "Minnie died two years later, in 1955. She was born a Burke in Ireland, from Londonderry."

I made a murmuring sound. "A second marriage. But nothing on Carrie?"

"Nothing." Tessie's voice conveyed excitement rather than dismay. "Oh, the obituary may be there somewhere, especially if she died much earlier on. But I tried to give my colleague some parameters, figuring Jimmy Malone lived a normal life span. I had her concentrate on 1940 to 1955. He died at eighty-one; Minnie was seventy-two. But the fascinating part is that my source also found a piece about the Malones' golden wedding anniversary. They celebrated it in 1953, four months before Jimmy Malone died."

My mind tripped over the impossibility. "That's wrong," I declared. "Jimmy Malone married Carrie Rowley in 1903. The newspaper must have made a mistake." It could happen, as I knew only too well.

"No, they couldn't," Tessie replied with equal fervor. "People have to submit this sort of thing. It would be the couple who made the mistake, not the paper. And I doubt very much that Mr. and Mrs. Malone forgot the year they were married. Well, Mr. Malone, perhaps. But not his wife. Women don't do that sort of thing, eh?"

"Maybe Minnie was senile by then," I muttered, unwilling to own up to the fact that I should know more about newsgathering than even the estimable Tessie Roo.

"Yes, certainly, I understand your point of view," Tessie said in her amiable manner. "And it might have happened that way. It's harrowing, all these discrepancies we come across, just because somebody got mixed up about Grandma's birthplace or Cousin Fiona's first marriage. But we must stay with the *facts*. We *know* Jimmy Malone married Carrie Rowley in 1903. Either he was a bigamist or the golden wedding anniversary story is in error."

Tessie was right. "Did the anniversary article say where Jimmy and Minnie were married?"

"Seattle," Tessie replied promptly. "So it *is* possible he married both of them in the same year. But next we must account for the children. Three of the six seem to be the ones he had by Carrie—Julia, Walter, and Claudia. Daniel, Joseph, and Mary Ann must have belonged to Minnie."

I was lost in a sea of progeny. "Prolific," I murmured. "I wonder if any of them are still around."

"Shall I check?" Tessie sounded eager.

"Sure, why not?"

"I'll call Seattle back. We have an eight hundred number," Tessie added ingenuously.

I put the phone down just as Jackie came into the kitchen. "I couldn't sleep," she announced with a yawn. "I'm hungry. What should I eat?"

Having assessed the contents—or lack of them—in the Melcher refrigerator, I suggested a trip to the grocery store. But Jackie didn't feel up to it.

"Every time I go there, I run into all these women who want to tell me their war stories about having babies. Nineteen hours of labor, a last-minute C-section, breech births, postpartum depression, the dog got jealous—I'm sick of them! What do you suppose happened to Mr. Walsh?"

I was taken aback. "Mr. Walsh? I've been concentrating on Mr. Malone."

Jackie shook her head. "No. His name was Walsh. Do you suppose he's in jail?"

"Oh!" I'd already forgotten about the drunk from Culver City. "It depends on how tough the local police are when it comes to DIPs."

It was Jackie's turn to look puzzled. "DIPs?"

"Drunk in public." Port Angeles must have a bigger jail than Alpine. Sheriff Milo Dodge was inclined to hold drunks only until they sobered up. Skykomish County's facilities were lamentably limited.

"I don't know much about the jail here," Jackie admitted. "We haven't lived in Port Angeles very long. They're sure tough on parking-meter infractions." Her heart-shaped face grew sad. "I kept thinking about Mr. Walsh the whole time I was trying to nap. Why is he so far from home? Why is he alone? Why is he *drunk*? And in the morning! His life must be full of unbearable tragedy. A wife dying young, teenage children lost to drugs, aged parents helplessly crippled, fired from his job, evicted from his house, hounded by creditors—"

"Stop!" I held up a hand though I couldn't refrain from laughing. "He's probably a carefree sightseer who partied too much last night. Let's concentrate on feeding you. I'll go to the store alone, if you don't mind me driving your Honda."

Jackie had no objections, but before I could get out of the house, Mike Randall showed up. His last class had been at one o'clock, and he didn't keep office hours on Wednesdays.

"My summer quarter schedule isn't as demanding as the rest of the year," Mike explained. "The students need an extra sense of freedom. Hopefully, it will help them expand their minds."

The last college professor I'd dated in Portland had dreaded office confrontations with his students because, as he put it, "the little shits only come in to bitch about their grades." Thus, I should have found Mike Randall's attitude refreshing. Instead, I thought of Carla Steinmetz and wondered how many teachers she'd driven to the window ledge.

"I hear you two have been doing your homework," Mike said, discreetly clearing off one of the kitchen stools. "The city librarian called the college librarian. Is there anything new?"

I was prepared to let Jackie fill Mike in, but she seemed lethargic, toying with her hair and staring at the refrigerator. The burden fell on me. As concisely as possible I recounted the pertinent information we had unearthed.

Mike was impressed. "You've been very busy. That's astounding about the smashed skull. I should have spotted it myself. Has Paul heard any of this?"

Paul hadn't, of course. I made my excuses about going to the store, but Mike insisted on accompanying me.

"You're a visitor and all these gullies and dead ends and one-way streets are terribly confusing. Come on, I'll give you a lift in my car."

I feigned enthusiasm for Mike's offer. The black Corvette was a handsome automobile, though I felt it didn't measure up to my green Jag. Except that the 'Vette started and kept going. I wondered what was happening at Dusty's. If my car was ready by the end of the afternoon, I'd feel compelled to leave Port Angeles. But I hated to give up on the Melcher mystery. I also hated the idea of being alone with my thoughts.

We weren't taking the route to the Safeway I'd seen near the courthouse. Instead, we were driving west, away from the business district and along the water where huge freighters lay at anchor. Gulls swarmed on the ships' pilothouses; longshoremen readied big crates for loading; forklifts rumbled over the docks. Mike explained the town's importance as a Pacific Rim port. Currently, pulp and paper were being shipped to Japan. The looming presence of a Daishowa America mill confirmed the connection.

"There's been a lot of change here in the past few years," Mike informed me as he turned the car around. "The timber industry's been hit hard by the environmental concerns. There's a rumor that ITT Rayonier may close. Poor Paul—he just got here."

I knew all about the decline in forest products. In the past logging had been the lifeblood of Alpine. Now the economy was so depressed that the town seemed to be existing on an IV. Too many loggers were out of work. Like doctors or actors or priests, most seemed unable to find another calling.

But it appeared that Port Angeles was more diversified. Along with the port and the paper and the pulp, there was a helicopter manufacturer, commercial fishing, tourism, a two-year college, and the fallout from a burgeoning retired population. There was also the U.S. Coast Guard, and Mike insisted on taking me out to Ediz Hook to admire the installation.

The Hook is so narrow in places that the road feels more like a bridge. I tried to relax and enjoy the view, which was spectacular. To the north, the waters of the strait were ruffled but not choppy. On the south, the town sprawled at sea level, then climbed up into the foothills of the Olympics. Smoke poured from the tall stacks on the Daishowa and Rayonier mills. I suspected there had been great struggles over pollution, but so far I hadn't noticed that Port Angeles smelled bad.

"Most of downtown is fill," Mike explained as we paused in front of the Coast Guard station's gates. "Originally, there wasn't enough solid, level land for building, so the early settlers hauled in dirt to create what's now the business district." He nodded at the harbor, where the *Coho* ferry was pulling into its slip. Maybe the Jaguar part was on board.

Mike was turning the car around again. Civilians weren't allowed on the Coast Guard base. We headed back along the Hook, past the empty fishing-boat ramps and a picnic area. Another big freighter was moored in the harbor, awaiting space at the docks. Closer in were the logjams, evidence that somebody was still cutting trees on the Olympic Peninsula.

Back in town, we passed the marina with its proud cluster of pleasurecraft. Mike frowned as we paused at an intersection on the edge of downtown.

"I was going to show you the Arthur D. Feiro Marine Lab and the city pier's viewing tower, but the Victoria ferry just got in. Traffic downtown will be tied up."

From what I could see so far, that statement was relative. There were more cars in Port Angeles than in Alpine, but compared to Seattle and Portland the local congestion was a long way from gridlock.

"That's okay," I said. "I really should get some food to bring back to Jackie." I explained that she'd been ill earlier in the day.

"So that's how Dr. Carlisle ended up at the house," Mike mused. "That's very odd about the skull. I can't get over it. Do you suppose it was a blunt instrument?" Before I could speculate, he turned left, not right, on Lincoln Street. Safeway was a reflection in the rearview mirror. "Would you care for a quick drink? The Greenery is right off the alley. We'll miss the ferry traffic altogether."

My patience was growing thin. I tried not to sound waspish. "Look, Mike, I really have to go to the store. If Paul gets home before I do, he'll think I'm a lousy guest. Jackie's starving. So's the baby."

Mike glanced at the digital clock on the dashboard that read two fifty-eight. "Paul gets off at four, which gives us ample time." He had turned toward me in the bucket seat, resting his jaw on his hand. The smile he gave me might have melted the heart of a nineteen-year-old coed, but not a fortyish newspaper publisher with a pregnant mother to feed. "I'm enjoying your company," Mike said, his other hand gripping the steering wheel. "This skeleton situation is intriguing, and I've been admiring your input. You've got an excellent mind." He slipped the key out of the ignition. "Ten minutes, that's all I ask. I'll be candid. Life's too short not to seize opportunities. Tomorrow you'll be on your way and we may never see each other again. I'd hate to look back at this interval and feel regret. Come, they make a fine tequila sunrise in here."

Wearily, I got out of the Corvette. I began to wonder who had been the real alcoholic in his family. But maybe that wasn't fair. I pictured thirty Carlas in a classroom and understood his need for a pick-me-up.

All the same, I didn't see the necessity for me to join him.

But across the alley Mike was giving me a sheepish look. "They're closed," he said, returning to the car. "I forgot, they shut down between lunch and dinner. Oh, well." He slid behind the wheel before I could decide whether or not he was a complete boob or just another pathetically flawed human being like the rest of us.

Mike reversed out of the alley and headed for Safeway. "You must think I'm a fool," he remarked, not looking in my direction.

"Nonsense," I replied, hoping I sounded sincere. "I appreciate your . . ." I faltered, searching for the right word.

"Openness," Mike said. "I'm reaching out, and the best way to do that is to be up-front. No games, just two people trying to . . ." It was his turn to pause.

"Reach out?" I felt my mouth twist with irony, then immediately berated myself for being crass. "Look, Mike, I'm all for honesty. I'm not good at games. But let's face it, we don't know each other. You're right, after tomorrow I'll be gone." Seeing his face tighten, I softened. "That doesn't mean I'll be out of touch. I mean, if we wanted to be friends, that would be wonderful. But at this point in time we're barely acquainted."

Pulling into the Safeway parking lot, Mike's blue eyes were sorrowful. "It's not easy meeting women who are intellectually stimulating as well as physically attractive. Oh, you'd think there would be plenty of them at the college, but either they're married or living with someone or they're . . . uh . . ." Again Mike stumbled.

"Repulsive?" I couldn't keep from laughing. Mike, however, remained serious, merely nodding as he eased the 'Vette between a pickup truck filled with scrap metal and a gleaming-white Chrysler Imperial. I sobered, wishing I could do more for Mike than offer flippant remarks. "You aren't used to being on your own," I said, hoping to strike a compassionate note. "It's a tough world out there in Singleland. For one thing, the rules have changed."

Mike sighed as he leaned back in the bucket seat. "They certainly have. When did flirtation become harassment? Where did gallantry go? What has become of romance?"

The man of science was more fanciful than I'd guessed. I hadn't heard anybody talk like this since going with a guy who wrote freelance verse for a greeting-card company. Even he usually had to smoke a lot of pot before he got the hang of it. No wonder his specialty had been sympathy cards.

But Mike had hit a raw nerve. I wagged a finger at him. "You got it. Those things are all still there, though under a different guise. The key is taking the time to build friendship. What I just said. Friendship creates trust. Women are scared, Mike."

"So are men."

He was right, of course. I gave him a sad smile and got out of the car. So did he, following me like a pet pup. Maybe I could lose Mike in produce, with the rest of the rutabagas. Or, better yet, the cold-storage locker. I drove my grocery cart as if it were an entry in the Indy 500. Two young mothers, four senior citizens, and a man in a clerical collar were scattered in my wake. Ten minutes later I checked out of the store with fifty dollars' worth of groceries. If Jackie didn't reimburse me, I'd have to eat cat tuna for the rest of the trip. On the other hand, I was her guest and I shouldn't press for payment. Maybe cat tuna wouldn't taste as bad as it sounded.

Mike was waiting at the magazine rack, still looking

miserable. Somewhat diffidently, he offered to carry two of my four grocery bags. I figured that that was his way of showing me that we were equal. I made sure I gave him the two that were the heaviest.

Determined to pass the five-minute drive in a lighter vein, I asked Mike questions about the college and his classes. He answered in a polite but strained manner. I barely heard him; I was too busy asking myself why I was being so perverse. Mike's candor was admirable; he had exhibited nothing but kindness and courtesy; his eagerness for companionship should have been endearing, not annoying. So what if he didn't have a sense of humor? Maybe he did. I'd said it myself, I didn't know him well enough to judge. The real Mike Randall was still a stranger.

Unless the open, earnest, sensitive, caring man beside me *was* the real thing. To further prove my perverse nature, I gathered up all the grocery bags and carried them into the house myself.

Chapter Seven

I WAS SORELY tempted to tell Vida about the possibility of a murdered woman in the Melcher basement. But I never got the chance. When I called *The Advocate* at ten to four, my House & Home editor was full of her own problems, which, of course, were mine as well.

"Ginny and I patched something together for Barton's Bootery and Harvey's Hardware. It isn't fancy, but it carries the message and takes up space. As long as we were late getting to the printer anyway, I figured we might as well try to salvage the ads and stretch the paper to twenty-four pages. That would save you the charge for the single-sheet insert."

"Bless you, Vida," I breathed into the phone. Mike had joined Jackie in the den for a quick meal I'd prepared of boneless chicken breasts, white rice, and carrot sticks. I had the feeling that Mike's bachelor eating habits might be as unwholesome as Jackie's.

"Don't bless me," Vida snapped. "With all this extra work I didn't have a chance to proofread the paper thoroughly. I'm vexed with myself, and you will be, too."

My face fell. "Oh." I hate typos. I hate sloppy work of any kind. I'm not a perfectionist, but there's no excuse for a lack of professionalism. "Like ... what?"

"The paper delivery was forty-five minutes late, which means it hit the mailboxes around ten minutes ago. I'm already *getting calls*." Vida sniffed into the receiver. It was hard to tell if she was more angry with herself or our readers.

I teetered on the kitchen stool, waiting for the worst. There was a stream of invective about the print job itself, which apparently had something to do with our timing on the press. *Muddy* was the word Vida used most, along with *fool*, which I trust referred to the pressman. ". . . and then Carla forgot to run my wedding story on Shari Stuart and Ted Davis, but she did get in the birth announcement of their new baby. The Burl Creek Thimble Club piece got cut off after the line that read, quote, 'The business meeting ended when Darla Puckett removed her clothing,' unquote." Vida paused and I blanched.

"What?" I asked faintly.

"I told you, Carla dropped the last line," Vida said in an irritated voice. "It should have read that, quote, 'Darla Puckett removed her clothing drive suggestion from the agenda,' unquote. Naturally, Darla is *wild*."

"Oh." I kicked myself for letting Carla lay out the paper. Even Vida's hard-eyed supervision was no match for Carla's ineptitude. To be fair, it was Carla's maiden effort with layout, though I had hoped that the Pagemaker program would prevent any serious foulups. Computer technology has not yet found a way to overcome human error. I cringed at the thought of the typos that had gone unnoticed.

As usual, Vida seemed to read my mind. "Mayor Fuzzy Baugh is now *Wuzzy*. The county commissioners discussed construction of a new *bride* across the Skykomish River by the golf course. Elsewhere, it was a proposed steel *spam*. At least Carla didn't capitalize it. The 4-H Club speaker next week will be a well-known Everett dog *broomer*. Oh! Did I tell you how she spelled Darla Puckett's name in the Burl Creek lead?"

"No! Please!" I begged. The high standards I'd set

for the past three years had been washed away by a tide called Carla. "I should have asked Ginny Burmeister to help more."

Vida's snort was audible. "You can't expect Ginny to bail out your entire staff. She and I did our best. But I got stuck with all those summer vacation stories. How many ways can you write about Disneyland? My grandson's adventures there were more interesting than the rest of them put together."

That was all too true. Roger, the apple of Vida's eye, had jumped overboard on the jungle ride, thrown up on the Matterhorn, and pantsed Pluto. I had secretly hoped that Snow White and the Seven Dwarfs might give the little wretch the bum's rush down Main Street, but Disney employees are trained to be nice to terrorists. Maybe on their next trip Roger's parents will take him to Iraq.

The conversation with Vida ended abruptly when Cal Vickers came into the editorial office, asking why the ad for his Texaco station was upside down. Holding my head, I hung up so that Vida could calm Cal and whoever else would be surging into *The Advocate* after they received this week's edition. If I was lucky, I might get back to Alpine before they torched the place.

Paul Melcher arrived home while I was still thinking about taking some Excedrin. He had contacted the prosecutor's office. Of course they'd heard about the skeleton and were intrigued. They were also up to their ears in pressing business. However, they'd get the paperwork started and send an officer to the Melcher house in the next twenty-four hours. Like Alpine, Port Angeles officialdom worked at its own small-town pace.

Paul seemed to have mixed emotions. I wondered if he hated to part with his skeleton. Instead of regaling my host with the events of the day, I sent him off to the den. Jackie could explain everything. I wished I'd taken Mike Randall up on his offer of a drink. I finally steeled myself and called Dusty's.

The car would be ready by late afternoon, Thursday. Tomorrow. The fuel pump had arrived, but it had been for the wrong year. The replacement was due on the first ferry from Victoria in the morning. Dusty, or whoever he was, expressed mild regret. I had mixed emotions.

By the time I'd downed the Excedrin I carried in my handbag, I found Jackie, Paul, and Mike poring over the floor plan I'd brought from the third-floor storage area.

"Did you see this?" Paul inquired. He was on his hands and knees. He jabbed at the architectural rendering with his index finger. "Where's the billiard room?"

I knelt beside him. "It's right there," I said, pointing to the basement. "It's off the hall from what's now the rec room . . . Oh!" I stared at the blueprint. "I see what you mean. It was supposed to go where the unfinished part of the basement is now. The billiard room was never completed."

Paul tipped his head to one side. "That's right. Do you suppose that's because a dead body was there?"

My gaze flickered from Paul to Jackie to Mike. "Maybe," I allowed. "It might be a coincidence."

Paul got to his feet. "Jackie tells me I should call my aunt in Seattle. Do you think it'll do any good?"

I asked Paul if he'd ever met Sara Melcher Beales. He had, though only on about three occasions. She'd missed his wedding because of a two-month trip to Europe. The Samuel Melcher and Vernon Beales families not only lived in different cities, they also traveled in separate circles.

"Aunt Sara and Uncle Verne sent silver," Jackie chimed in. "We've only got place settings for three and a meat fork."

I consulted the family tree. "Sara's not old enough to know what might have happened involving Carrie. Still, she may have heard some family gossip." I wasn't about to surrender any possible leads.

"Go ahead," Jackie urged. "Maybe she'll be so tickled to hear from you that she'll send another place setting. Sterling silver costs the world."

Paul debated with himself, finally deciding to phone his aunt after five when the rates were down. The delay turned out to be a good thing because Tessie Roo rang up almost immediately. She asked for me.

"Three out of six are still alive," she announced in a chipper voice. "Not bad, eh? Joseph Malone is retired in Arizona, Mary Ann Malone Strom lives in the Chicago area, and Claudia Malone Cameron's address is Victoria, British Columbia."

I pictured the family tree I'd just been studying. "Claudia is actually one of Carrie's children, right? The other two are Minnie's?"

"Yes, indeed. Julia and Walter are both deceased. They lived in the Seattle-Tacoma area at the time of their deaths, but their children were all spread out. Daniel, the eldest of the children by Minnie, never married and died last year at eighty-two in a retirement home on the Kitsap Peninsula, not far from Bremerton. I believe he was a navy man. But Claudia is just a hop, skip, and a jump away in Victoria. Oak Bay, to be exact. Are you game?"

The question flustered me. "Well . . . I could call, of course . . ."

"Good heavens," Tessie exclaimed, "you could be there in less than an hour! Take the Victoria Express tomorrow morning. It's passengers only and fairly zips across the strait! If I had the day off, I'd go with you."

Before I could argue with Tessie, let alone myself, I had Claudia Malone Cameron's address in Victoria as well as her phone number. Tessie cautioned me to call first, after I arrived in the city.

"She's well into her eighties, so she may be deaf," Tessie added. "Judging from the address, she still lives at home, so her mind is probably keen enough. Good luck. Call me when you get back to Port Angeles."

I broke the news to the others, expecting one or all of them to volunteer as well. But Paul had to work, Mike met three classes on Thursdays, and Jackie wasn't yet feeling up to par.

"I'd get seasick," she said, clutching her stomach as if she could already feel the waves beneath the boat.

"Are you sure you want to go to all this trouble?" Paul asked, his earnest face displaying mixed emotions.

I wasn't, actually. But if I hung around the Melcher house while I waited yet another day for the Jag, I'd feel as if I were imposing. Two days and two nights of hospitality were plenty to ask of anyone.

"It could be a story," I said, surprising myself as well as the others. "I know I'm not local, but if we figured this all out, it might make a feature for the wire service around the state. Then the IRS would let me write my trip off." Suddenly I felt very clever.

Paul was nodding thoughtfully. "I got a call from *The Daily News* this afternoon. I put them off by saying we didn't want to talk about it until we had some more information."

I voiced my approval. "That's the way to handle the press. But I'd be glad to let them write the story if I'm not around for the ending. If there *is* an ending," I added.

Jackie sprang to life. "Emma! You have to be! You're the one who's done all the real work. As long as you've got to stay until tomorrow afternoon, you might as well take another day off from work and spend the weekend."

Paul chimed in, also urging me to remain in Port Angeles. Mike said nothing, but his blue eyes seemed hopeful. I, however, was immovable.

"Things aren't going so well at the office," I admitted. "If the Jag is ready before five tomorrow, I'll head straight back to Alpine and skip the rest of the Olympic Loop."

A chorus of nays echoed in my ears. This time, Mike had joined Jackie and Paul. Instead of arguing, I challenged them to organize the known facts of our little mystery. If Paul intended to phone his Aunt Sara and I was actually going to call on Claudia Malone Cameron in Victoria, we needed to see where we stood. I asked Mike to take notes.

"We'll stick with the theory that the skeleton is Carrie Rowley Malone, but we could be wrong," I said, sipping from a can of Pepsi I'd bought at Safeway. "We've come to that conclusion because of the earring we found, which we also saw in Carrie's photograph. Tessie Roo has cautioned me about discrepancies, inconsequential human actions that can alter family history."

Jackie wrinkled her nose. "Like what?"

I gave a little shrug. "Oh, like Carrie lending her earrings to somebody else. Or the earrings finding their way into the unfinished basement in some other manner. Lost, thrown away, maybe even stolen."

Mike's expression was very solemn. "That's true. There was another woman in the family about the same age as Carrie. Her stepmother, Simone."

Jackie demurred. "Simone looks tall. She would have worn bigger shoes. I'm still voting for Carrie."

It wasn't up to me to argue. "It might be someone we know nothing about," I went on. "If we believe what we hear, both Carrie Rowley Malone and Simone Rowley left Port Angeles around the same time in 1908, after Cornelius Rowley died. We're told that Carrie and her husband and children moved to Seattle. We have no idea what happened to Simone."

"We need to consult a lawyer," Mike asserted, looking up from the spiral notebook in which he'd been writing. "Somebody with a firm that's been around forever. All we know is that Eddie and Lena Melcher inherited the house. Who got Cornelius's money?"

Jackie and Paul exchanged blank looks. "We haven't had a reason to see a lawyer," said Jackie. "What about you, Mike?"

Mike flushed slightly. "I still use the family firm in Tacoma. The divorce, you know."

Jackie bounced off the sofa, where she'd been sitting next to me. "I'll get the phone book. We'll call around until we find some old-timers. Meanwhile, we need a cast of characters. Suspects, you know? Who have we got?"

Mike was tapping the notebook with his ballpoint pen. He shook his head. "We can't be sure of the victim."

"For the sake of argument, let's stick with Carrie," Paul replied doggedly, as Jackie scurried away. "We don't know that it *wasn't* her. Anyway, I want to sort out these people. They're my family, after all. Or at least somehow connected."

"We've got Cornelius," I noted, but I sounded uncertain. "We can't eliminate him just because we think he died before the victim did. It might not have happened that way."

Paul agreed. "Right. Then we've got his wife, Simone. There's Eddie and Lena, the odd couple. Then comes my grandfather, Sanford, and my grandmother, Rose. The skeleton can't be Rose or I wouldn't be here."

I found Rose on the family tree. "Sanford didn't

marry Rose until 1909, but she was local, so she would have been around. Okay, we'll count her in. And let's not forget Carrie and Jimmy Malone. Who else?"

Neither of the men answered. Jackie returned with the phone book. Apparently, she'd caught my last question.

"Servants," she said firmly. "You said so yourself, Paul. There had to be servants in this house. There are servants' quarters, and I can't imagine Simone lifting so much as a tea towel. Or Lena, either. She was too busy being a suffragette."

Jackie's point was well taken, but we knew nothing of the Rowley-Melcher staff. The den was silent as Jackie ran a finger down the listings for lawyers in the Yellow Pages.

"Oh, poopy! I can't tell much from all these names. Why don't they say stuff like 'Blah-blah and Blah-blah, established 1902—over a billion clients exonerated'?"

I glanced at my watch. "It's not five yet. You could call one of them, and they'd probably know which firms go back to the early days."

With an aggrieved sigh Jackie lugged the phone book out of the den. Paul, Mike, and I studied the family names on our list.

"As mysteries go," mused Mike, "this isn't much of a cast. Let's say that Carrie is the victim. Let's also say she was killed after Cornelius died. Carrie was listed as a survivor in her father's funeral notice, right? That leaves her husband, Jimmy, her brother, Eddie, and his wife, Lena. Lena's son, Sanford, and the stepmother, Simone. Oh, and Sanford's bride-to-be, Rose Felder. Six suspects in all. Now why would anyone want to kill a young wife and mother? Did she get the money instead of Simone? We know she didn't get the house. Did she quarrel with her brother over the inheritance? Did Jimmy Malone want out of his marriage?"

I had turned back to the photo albums, flipping through the thick black pages with their sepia-toned pictures: Cornelius Rowley, with his bristling beard, high forehead, and sharp eyes; Simone Dupre Rowley's exotic sophistication and undeniable beauty; Eddie Rowley's weak chin, his engaging smile, the cane not a prop but a necessity; Lena Stillman Melcher Rowley's chiseled features and the determined set of her shoulders; Carrie Rowley's soft blonde curls and innocent air.

"If Jimmy Malone was a bigamist, he definitely might want to get rid of a spare wife," I said. For the first time I felt a real connection with the Rowleys and Melchers of over eighty years ago. They were coming to life in my mind, possessing personalities, physical qualities, human emotions. I felt a rush of excitement. Ambivalence fled. I wondered what time the ferry left in the morning for Victoria. I'd call for a schedule as soon as Jackie was off the phone.

"Where *is* Jimmy Malone?" I asked out loud, searching through the album. At last, toward the back, I found a wedding photo. Weighed down by the ten-foot veil and train, a demure Carrie Rowley Malone stood behind her seated groom. Jimmy Malone looked smug, his broad features and burly build not quite in harmony with the satin-faced lapels on his frock coat and the high, white dress-shirt collar. I felt that he'd have been more at home in rumpled linen, leaning on the bar of a Belfast pub.

On the adjacent page I found another couple I hadn't noticed earlier. The young man was dark, with feral features, a forest creature frightened by the crack of a gun. Or maybe the soulful eyes were startled by the photographer's flash. The woman's head leaned stiltedly toward the man. She was no more than twenty, with a gentle face that was not quite spoiled by an overly long chin. I offered the album to Paul.

"Your grandfather, Sanford? And Grandma Rose?"

Paul studied the photo. "Yes, I've seen this picture someplace else. My folks must have had a copy. Or else I saw it here when I was a kid. Do I look like them?"

I considered. "Your coloring, maybe. Like Rose. But no, I don't see any resemblance to Sanford."

Lightly, Paul touched the photograph. "I vaguely remember Grandma Rose. I was only about four when she died. She stood and sat very straight. We had to mind our manners when we were around her. Luckily, it wasn't often." He smiled shyly and offered Mike a second beer. Mike volunteered to get it himself. I wondered if he preferred not to be left alone with me. Maybe Mike thought I was going to play the part of a wisecracking female journalist again. Paul went with Mike. It occurred to me that, like women going in pairs to the ladies' room, men must seek beer together.

Jackie wore a victorious air when she returned to the den. "The Smiths," she trumpeted. "A bunch of them, going back to eighteen-something-or-other."

I congratulated her on tracking down the law firm. "Did you talk to one of them?"

"No." She flopped down next to me on the sofa. "They're all dead. But their files are stored in somebody's back room. Meriwether and Bell took over the firm about twenty years ago. Or maybe it was forty."

Paul had rejoined us, carrying a fresh can of beer and a bag of Cheetos. "Did you call Meriwether and Bell, Sweets?" he asked.

Jackie had, but they'd left for the day. She'd try again in the morning. "I may ask them about my parking ticket. There were extenuating circumstances. I'm pregnant, after all. In fact, maybe that's what made me sick. I could sue the city for a threatened miscarriage." She brightened at the thought, then reached for the Cheetos.

My warning glance to abstain was ignored. Paul

didn't encourage his wife's litigious mood, but he did let her grab a fistful of Cheetos. Checking the time, Paul noted that it was after five o'clock. "I'll call Aunt Sara now. Let's hope she's home."

Jackie scrambled to her feet and rushed after Paul. "Hey, Emma and I'll listen in. Come on, Emma," she urged. "I'll go upstairs. You can use the phone in the basement by the washer and dryer."

Feeling like an intruder, I started to protest, but Jackie was already headed for the stairs. I surrendered, since three sets of ears were better than one. Probably this would be our only chance to quiz Aunt Sara. I took the spiral notebook with me, wondering where Mike had gone. He wasn't in the kitchen. Paul was already there, dialing his aunt's number in Seattle.

By the time I reached the laundry room, Paul was still answering Sara Melcher Beales's questions about renovating the house. Hearing the clicks as Jackie and I came on the line, Paul explained that his wife had joined him. He didn't mention me, which was just as well. As silently as possible, I moved piles of dirty clothes, empty detergent boxes, and bleach bottles. The laundry room was clearly Jackie's domain.

Aunt Sara had a strong, slightly reedy voice. I pictured her as a well-preserved dowager with a trim figure and expertly coiffed hair. I was probably wrong, but the image suited her voice and social status.

At last, Paul worked his way around to the pertinent questions. He surprised me with his cunning, by asking his aunt where Cornelius Rowley had come up with the idea of a small lift to haul firewood from the basement to the entry hall.

"Paul, dear," Sara Melcher Beales responded with a rich laugh, "I may be old, but I'm not *that* old. Cornelius Rowley had been dead for over ten years when I was born. I never knew any of the Rowleys except my father's stepfather, Edmund. Even he is hazy. Edmund—Eddie, he was called—came up with the wood-basket idea. He fancied himself an inventor. Otherwise, he took a backseat to Lena, as I'm sure you can guess if you know any of your family history."

"I know about Lena," Paul said. "Do you remember her well?"

"Daunting," Sara replied promptly. "All of us children were terrified of her when we were small. Grandmama was so *grim*. Very autocratic, very religious, very self-righteous. My papa—your grandfather, Sanford—was intimidated, too, I think. But my mother, Rose, would stand up to her. I don't believe Mama liked living with her in-laws. Looking back, I have the impression that my mother was never a happy woman."

Jackie's voice came on the line for the first time. "Rose? Wasn't she happy with Sanford?"

Sara hesitated. I envisioned her fingering a long strand of perfect pearls. "That's difficult for me to say. Children want their parents to be happy. But again, in retrospect, we all left Port Angeles as soon as we could. Except for Arthur. Our generation was quite daring. My grandparents and parents had stayed in the family home, and so had Aunt Carrie and Uncle Jimmy until they moved to Seattle. Of course, it was a big house, with plenty of room, but still, it probably wasn't emotionally healthy. Did you know that I was the first to go away even though I was the only girl?"

Jackie and Paul hadn't known and chorused their surprise. I clamped my lips together to keep from making any giveaway noises.

"Yes," Sara went on, warming to the tale of her youth. "I suppose I was a bit of a rebel. I got into a lot of trouble—oh, nothing by today's standards, but in a small town, in the Thirties, I was a scamp. Grandmama Lena thought I should go to a boarding school in Seattle, not merely to tame me but to get a good education. Naturally, she was a great believer in educating women as well as men. She offered to pay my way. I was thrilled, though my parents were not. Lena, as usual, prevailed. Off I went to St. Nicholas School, by St. Mark's Episcopal Cathedral. It was very strict, very exclusive in those days. At first I hated it—the discipline, the uniforms, the lack of privacy. But after the first year I began to discover the city. And myself, as one does. I never went back to Port Angeles except for the occasional visit." Her voice had taken on a brittle note. "I think I broke my mother's heart."

To my dismay, Jackie was weeping into the phone. "Poor Rose! Unhappily married! Estranged from her only daughter! A prisoner in her own house! Under the thumb of old Hatchet Face!"

"Really, Jacqueline," Sara said in mild reproof, "it wasn't as bad as all that. As I mentioned, Mama could get her back up when Lena became too overbearing. I was there for all the holidays. In any event, what's done is done. I had my life to live. The real tragedy is that Mama never got the chance to live hers. Like all of us, she had only herself to blame."

Jackie's sobs subsided. Paul spoke again, but in my mind I heard the voice of Lena, speaking through her granddaughter, Sara. Out of the corner of my eye, I glimpsed Mike Randall coming down the hall from the unfinished basement. I gave a little start of surprise, then signaled for him to be quiet. Pointing to the phone, I mouthed Sara's name.

"... a very gentle man," Sara was saying in response to a question about Sanford Melcher that I'd only half heard. "Papa spent most of his time in the music parlor, writing. He played the piano, too, quite beautifully. It was his inspiration, he said. I never saw him angry, though he was often melancholy. He would watch my mother with such sad eyes. Haunted, it seems to me now. Perhaps he blamed himself for staying at home with his mother and stepfather. As well he should. I don't recall that he ever held a real job. Occasionally he would sell a poem. In later years my parents weren't at all well off. Mama gave bridge lessons. Papa wrote more poems."

Mike hovered at my elbow, trying to listen in. I held the phone out from my ear, sacrificing some of the conversation in order to let Mike hear, too.

Paul had brought up the subject of the ghost. I strained to catch Sara's response. She laughed, that rich, brittle sound. "I never saw it! Oh, I remember listening in bed at night during a storm and *thinking* I heard a woman howl outside. But no, she never walked for me. My older brothers, Henry and Arthur, swore they saw her, with long black hair and a flowing cape. They made it up, I'm sure, to frighten John and your father and me."

Jackie had now composed herself. "Who was she? I mean, did anybody ever say who they thought she was?"

"Certainly," Sara answered calmly. "It was Cornelius Rowley's second wife, Simone. There was some silly story that she was murdered. But it wasn't true. Imagine! A murder in the Rowley house! Knowing the family, how could anyone believe such nonsense?"

Chapter Eight

PAUL MELCHER HADN'T contradicted his aunt. No doubt she would have scoffed at him and insisted that he was being fanciful. What really surprised me was Jackie's reticence. I'd expected her to blurt out the truth about the skeleton. But she didn't. Even Jackie occasionally succumbed to an attack of discretion. Or else she really wanted another sterling silver place setting.

After I called to get the ferry schedule, we reassembled in the den. I began to realize that it was here that the Melchers lived, the other rooms being too large and too sparsely furnished. Someday, perhaps, the house would come alive with comfortable chairs and cheerful drapes and cherished possessions. Most of all, it would wrap its walls around a family again.

Briefly, I chided myself for romanticizing the Rowley-Melcher house. As far as I could tell, it hadn't always been a happy home. Now, after hearing Aunt Sara describe her youth, I could picture Eddie Rowley, possibly relegated to the garage, seeking solace with his inventions; Sanford Melcher, playing sad songs on the piano and writing what I assumed was gloomy poetry; and his wife, Rose, restlessly going from room to room, readying herself for the next confrontation with her indomitable mother-in-law, Lena.

"It *could* be Simone," Paul allowed, tapping his beer can. "She borrowed her stepdaughter's earrings, maybe.

Or the other way around——Carrie had borrowed them from Simone for the photo session."

Jackie's eyes grew round. "What if they were both murdered. Carrie *and* Simone? We could keep digging and find another skeleton!" She was flushed with excitement.

Paul was shaking his head. "I don't know ... that's pretty farfetched. But so is finding just one of them."

I tended to agree with Paul. "It *is* odd that Simone seems to have fallen off the face of the earth right after her husband died," I remarked. "We have birth and death dates for everyone in the family except Carrie and Simone."

"She must have gone away," Paul said. "Back to Paris, maybe. She probably had family there. I wonder why she came to this country in the first place. And how did she get to Port Angeles? It seems like an odd choice for a young woman from Paris." His gaze flickered from Jackie to me to Mike.

I realized that Mike had been very subdued since returning from the basement. Jackie and Paul seemed to notice the same thing at the same time.

"Hey," Paul said, grinning, "what's up? You've turned into a clam, Mike."

Mike, who was using a packing crate as a seat, rubbed his scalp in an agitated manner. "It's bizarre. Especially the speculation about two women being killed. And yet ..." His hand now chafed his chin. "I went back down into that unfinished section. I felt inept, not noticing the damaged skull. I wanted to make sure I hadn't missed anything else. I had. So had the doctor. There were more bones."

Next to me, Jackie jumped. Paul fumbled with his beer can. I stopped thinking about my gnawing hunger pangs.

"From the skeleton?" Paul asked in a strange, dry voice.

Mike shook his head. "No. It's remarkably well intact. And this may not mean anything. The bones are tiny and there are only three of them. It could be from a cat or a dog. There might be more, but I didn't take the time to dig farther. To really go over all that dirt would be a major task."

"Where are the bones?" Jackie asked breathlessly.

Mike had found an old fruit jar. He'd left them on a shelf near the door to the unfinished area. "Maybe we could have them analyzed up at the college. Shall I go get them?"

We agreed that he should. Jackie was still agog. "This is so thrilling! To think I was about to give up! But it sounded like so long ago. And then Aunt Sara talked about these people as if it were yesterday!"

"She only knew some of them," Paul reminded his wife. "Not Carrie, not Simone, not Cornelius. Not Jimmy Malone, either. And we forgot to ask her about the servants."

Jackie dismissed the servants with a sniff. "She wouldn't have known them. Not the ones who were with Cornelius and Simone Rowley. I can't imagine Lena keeping on the same people Simone had hired. Hatchet Face is the kind who'd want to choose her own staff."

Jackie's assessment rang true. The portrait of Lena was coming into sharper focus. Yes, she had probably been a rigid, stubborn, obsessed creature, self-righteous and devoid of sentiment. But her motives were admirable, and she had matched word to deed by paying for Sara Melcher's tuition to boarding school. Lena also seemed to have instilled a sense of independence and self-confidence in her granddaughter. Some good qualities were emerging to offset the chiseled bronze image in the park.

"Frivolous," I said, apropos of nothing, certainly not of Lena.

"What?" Jackie gave me a puzzled look.

I offered her a wry smile. "I was thinking of what Lena would least admire in another woman. The word *frivolous* came to mind. It might apply to Carrie. Or Simone." My smile turned self-deprecating for Paul. "Your grandmother Rose doesn't sound lighthearted enough to qualify. Was she living here when she died?" I asked as Mike reentered the den carrying a dusty fruit jar.

"Oh, yes," Paul replied. "She stayed on with Uncle Arthur and his wife."

"And Sanford?" I inquired, hearing my stomach growl.

Paul's earnest face sagged. "That's weird . . . I'd forgotten about him. I mean, what happened to him. He had to be put in a home or something. I think he had a breakdown after Uncle John was killed in the war. My dad always said John was Grandfather's favorite."

Jackie pounced on her husband, who was sitting on the soft footstool. "You never told me your grandfather was crazy! There's insanity in the family! Our baby could be a maniac!"

Paul tried to pry Jackie loose. "I didn't say he was *crazy*. That was fifty years ago. It was probably depression. After listening to Aunt Sara, I'd guess he was a pretty depressed guy all along."

Jackie relinquished her hold on Paul. "He sounds morbid. I don't want a morbid baby, brooding all over the playpen. Maybe we should ask Dr. Carlisle about it."

Paul ignored Jackie and turned to Mike. "Well? Let's see those bones."

As Mike had said, they were tiny. They could have belonged to a chicken. "I'll take them to the college lab tomorrow," Mike promised. "If that doesn't work out, we can ship them off to the University of Washington."

Paul nodded. "Might as well. We're in too deep now to give up." His grin took in all of us. "This is so strange. One minute I'm scared I'll find out something really horrible about my relatives, and the next I can't wait to see where all this leads us. The worst thing would be if we never come up with an answer."

I disagreed. "The worst thing would be if I starved to death. You, too, Paul. Jackie and Mike have had a big snack, but we haven't. Why don't I make some pasta and a salad? I bought prawns on sale at Safeway and they won't keep forever."

It didn't take long to fix dinner. Jackie pitched in, though her efforts with slicing tomatoes and cutting up green onions were haphazard.

"Cooking makes me sick," she asserted. "Are you sure it wouldn't be easier to order a pizza?"

I didn't dignify her question with a reply. Instead, I tried a diversion. "Jackie, if you were a rich widow, what would you do?"

Jackie stared at a bunch of radishes as if they'd just arrived in a spaceship from Mars. "You mean like Simone?"

"Right. She was your age, more or less, when Cornelius died." I retrieved the radishes and gave them a good scrubbing under the kitchen faucet. "So what's your move, assuming you don't like Port Angeles?"

"I'd go to Calcutta and help Mother Teresa with the lepers. Or is it Bombay?"

Speculation clearly wasn't Jackie's strong suit, at least not at the moment. "Mother Teresa wasn't around then. And somehow I don't think charity was Simone's style."

Jackie made a face as she tried to concentrate. "How do we know she was rich? Simone, I mean, not Mother Teresa. I wonder what she did with that money she got from the Nobel Prize?"

"She blew it at the craps table in Reno," I retorted a trifle testily. "I assume Simone was rich—Cornelius must have left her some of his money, if not all of it. That's something else Aunt Sara might know, if we can't find out from the lawyers."

"We know Eddie and Lena got the house," Jackie said, back on track. "Eddie never made any money; in fact, he lost it, right? And Sanford didn't work. Lena had no money of her own. Maybe Rose had a . . . what do you call it? A dowry?"

"Could be." I whacked up the radishes. "Whatever money there was in the family, it petered out eventually, according to Sara. Maybe Lena spent it all on her social causes. Or Cornelius could have left it to Carrie and her husband, Jimmy Malone. They had three kids by the time the old boy died."

Jackie's manner had turned heated. "I know one thing—Paul didn't get any. Neither did his dad. We were darned lucky to inherit this house. Nobody else in the family wanted it because of the condition it's in. Besides, Paul's an only child and his cousins are all over the place."

I hadn't considered Paul's contemporary relations. "Like Sara and Verne's offspring?"

Jackie wasn't sure. "All I know is that the ones who came to the wedding were from places like Spokane and Billings and L.A. and Denver and a ranch in Wyoming. They didn't give a rat's behind about an old broken-down house on the Olympic Peninsula."

"Lucky you," I remarked, thinking about a few internecine family fracases over the years involving property no more lavish than a birdcage. It was amazing how excitable some people could be when it came to greed. Apparently, Paul's relatives weren't of that ilk. Jackie was right—she and Paul were very lucky.

We ate in the kitchen, seated on the tall stools at the counter. Jackie's thoughts turned domestic. She pressed Paul about the return of the electricians. Her husband informed her that it might be wise to put them off until the mystery was solved.

"Why?" Jackie wore a pugnacious air. "What's to find now? Mike said we'd have to dig forever to make sure everything was uncovered down there. We've got to get on with the project. The floor man is coming next week."

Paul confessed that he and Mike planned to do some more digging after dinner. If nothing else, they might find some other personal items that would pinpoint the date of the victim's death. Or perhaps verify the victim's identity.

"This rumor about Simone's disappearance muddies the waters," Paul explained. "Wouldn't you think someone would know what happened to the wife of a prominent, wealthy man like Cornelius Rowley?"

Paul had a point. Indeed, there were probably quite a few people who knew or suspected where Simone Dupre Rowley had gone after her husband's death. But that had been over eighty years ago. They, too, were now dead.

Unless one of them was Claudia Malone Cameron.

Mike raved about my cooking. I pretended to be flattered. How anyone could ruin a green salad, sautéed prawns, and fettuccine eluded me—until I thought of Vida. As multifaceted as she is, Vida cannot cook. Her pasta tastes like sponge, the only time I ever ate her prawns she had forgotten to remove them from the shells, and even lettuce is not safe in my House &

Home editor's hands. Vida is an ardent and capable gardener. She often raises vegetables. But she cannot cook them properly. Not that lettuce needs to be cooked, but one must first remove the slugs that infest it. Vida didn't.

There was no dessert. Paul and Mike retreated to the unfinished basement. Jackie and I perused the photo albums once more. We found nothing new, but we were becoming well acquainted with our cast of characters.

Jackie seemed mesmerized by Rose Felder Melcher. She went back up to the third floor and brought down some of the later pictures. We saw Rose grow from an innocent, fair-haired maid to a sad-eyed woman of middle age. Finally we studied the old Rose, withered and bereft of bloom. This was the Rose that Paul remembered.

"Aunt Sara may be right." Jackie sighed. "Grandma Rose looks like a woman with a broken heart. I wouldn't do that to *my* mother."

"You bet you wouldn't," I replied, thinking of my pal, Mavis, and her unquenchable spirit. At forty-eight Mavis had developed cancer of the uterus. Downing four martinis, she had simultaneously set the date for surgery and made plans for a trip to Fiji with her husband. Six weeks later she had sent me a postcard from the South Pacific: "Who needs the female parts you can't see at my age? Glad you aren't here—you'd be embarrassed. We're on our second honeymoon and much better at it than we were on the first. Practice, practice, practice!"

The dishwasher was making agreeably efficient noises when the men returned from the basement. They had a plastic basin full of small items: two more little bones, half a dozen buttons of varying styles and sizes, eyelets that might have come from a shoe, two safety pins, an I LIKE IKE campaign button, six Olympia Beer caps, a Captain Midnight decoder, a decaying faux leather watchband, a plastic barrette featuring cooing yellow birds, a child's thermometer from a play doctor's kit, a Rita Hayworth paper doll dressed as Carmen, a gold locket with strands of dark hair in it, several shards of broken crockery, and the mate to the garnet earring.

"Eureka!" I cried. "You've struck ... something. At least you found the other earring."

Jackie pointed to the mildewed cardboard doll. "Who's that? She's pretty."

Trying not to feel old, I told her about Rita Hayworth and *The Loves of Carmen.* "It was before my time, actually, but I saw it on TV. The movie was based on the opera, but they didn't sing."

Jackie shrugged. "Good. I don't like opera anyway. Let's see that locket."

It was heart-shaped, with a tiny circle of glass in the middle. The dark hair was soft. There was no inscription. I guessed it to be old but couldn't date it positively. Jackie asked if the men had found it near the earring.

"Within a couple of yards," Paul said a bit vaguely. "We dug sort of frantically. Like pups, I guess."

I reflected on the contents of the plastic basin. "That part of the basement wasn't closed off for all those years. This stuff covers a wide time span, at least from the Forties. But I suppose nobody did any actual excavation until the electricians went down there."

Jackie nodded. "It would be a neat place for kids to play. Sort of like being outside when you were inside. You know, when it rained and you had to stay in."

I gave Jackie a smile of encouragement. Her enthusiasm seemed to veer up and down, like a yo-yo. Some of her mood swings could be attributed to pregnancy, but I was certain that Jackie was mercurial by nature.

Juggling the garnet earrings, Paul frowned. "I played

down there a few times. When we were really little, the grownups would lower us in that wood-basket rig. It comes out upstairs under the inglenook seat next to the fireplace. That was fun because it was so scary. All the kids in the family loved riding in it. You could go down on your own if you jiggled the thing right, but you had to be cranked back up. Later we outgrew it, but we still horsed around downstairs. Once we made a fort."

Mike leaned forward on the packing crate. "Did you ever dig?"

"No." Paul's features twisted in the effort to recall. "The dirt was higher. Or maybe it seemed that way because we were smaller."

"It could settle over time," I commented.

"Earthquakes," said Jackie, then held her nose. "What about the smell? Don't bodies smell terrible when they . . . decompose?"

The question was relevant. Mike had a possible explanation. "Back then, this was a real mill town. I imagine it smelled most of the time. I'm from Tacoma, and I can tell you, before the environmentalists stepped in, when the mills were going full tilt, there were days when you could hardly breathe. You got used to it, of course."

I knew all about the so-called Tacoma Aroma; Everett, too, and almost any other place in the Pacific Northwest where pulp and paper were made had one. Mike was right—the smell would have masked almost any other odor. And Port Angeles's early fish-packing plants would have done the rest.

Mike was smiling at the plastic basin's contents. "Fascinating. Think what an archaeologist could make of this a thousand years from now!" He transferred his smile to me.

I sensed that Mike wanted to be admired. "Nice work," I said lightly. "As a matter of fact, my son and

my brother are involved in a dig in Arizona right now."
We digressed long enough for me to tell the others
about Adam's and Ben's adventures with the Anasazi.
My audience expressed polite interest, but it was obvious that they'd rather concentrate on the contents of the
unfinished basement.

It was Paul who brought us back to the past. "What
we need to do is figure out how the body got to where
we found it. Or where the electricians found it, I should
say. Why there? Was she dead before or after?"

Paul's logical approach was admirable, too. I was
quick to praise him. "Why would a young lady be in
the basement in the first place?" I posed the question after Paul had accepted my compliment with a self-
effacing shrug. "We must assume this is Carrie, if only
so that we can fixate on one person. She might go down
to the rec room—or whatever it was called at the
time—but she wouldn't do laundry or canning or stoke
the furnace." I unfurled the house plan again. "The rec
room isn't that close to the unfinished part of the basement. Was she lured there? Or killed somewhere else
and carried there?"

Silence filled the little den. Darkness seemed to be
descending earlier this evening, casting shadows in the
corners. The clouds had never quite disappeared. A
muted sunset filtered in through the leaded-glass win-
dows.

"The fissures," Mike said suddenly, leaping off the
packing crate. "The broken bones. Carrie goes downstairs with someone else—the killer, to be precise. X,
let's say. X leads her down that hallway to the door. The
door is opened. X has armed himself—or herself—with
something heavy. He—she—is behind Carrie and hits
her on the back of the head. Carrie is stunned, maybe
even killed, and falls off the ledge. Her legs are broken.
Isn't that what Dr. Carlisle thought?" He paused just

long enough for nods from Jackie and me. "X closes the door, locks it, and goes away. Or maybe X gets a ladder and goes down into the unfinished area and actually buries Carrie. Nobody has any reason to go there, and if Carrie was missed, a cursory look would show she's not there. Who'd think of digging up the place?"

Jackie had gone pale. "That's horrid," she whispered. "Why would anyone do such an awful thing?"

Paul grimaced. "People do awful things all the time. Pick up the latest newspaper or turn on the TV. How different were people eighty years ago? Not much, I'd say. People are people."

We didn't contradict Paul. Contemporary society had no monopoly on violence. "If we knew the why, we might know the who," I commented. "We talked about motives earlier, and even off the cuff we came up with several. At least for murdering Carrie Rowley Malone. Greed, sex, the usual reasons people kill for. Just go down the list."

Paul wore an expression of chagrin. "My family, the homicidal maniacs. Gosh, I sure hope we find out that the killer was an outsider." He gave Jackie an apologetic look.

But Jackie was in one of her effervescent moods. "Why? Having a murderer on the family tree would give it some color. Who wants everybody to be law-abiding and virtuous? That's so dull!"

Paul didn't appear convinced, but he was willing to be a good sport. "Okay, so let's check motives. Simone—maybe she didn't inherit Cornelius's fortune. If it went to Carrie, Simone might have wanted to do in her stepdaughter."

I had to quibble. "Even if Carrie died, her children would have inherited. There was no point in getting rid of just Carrie. Simone would have had to wipe out all the little Malones, too."

Mike nodded, clicking his ballpoint pen. "And we know they weren't. Okay, what about Eddie, the brother? A sibling rivalry?"

"Same thing," I noted. "The only way the inheritance motive works is if the money went to Carrie only for her lifetime. A trust, maybe. But we won't know about that until Meriwether and Bell come up with Cornelius Rowley's will."

Jackie snapped her fingers. "Jimmy Malone. He married Carrie for her money but really loved Minnie. He'd gotten into the Rowley family and now he wanted out. Divorce wouldn't do because he couldn't get his hands on Carrie's money. So *voilà*! He belts Carrie with an Irish shillelagh, or whatever you call them, on St. Patrick's Day. What *is* a shillelagh, anyway?"

I was bemused. "I think it's a sort of club. But I'm not Irish."

Paul's forehead furrowed. "Jimmy is a good pick. But why wait so long? He and Carrie already had three kids. Where was Minnie all this time?"

The problem didn't faze Jackie. "Stashed in Seattle. It was only five years. If Jimmy was counting on a fortune, that's not long to wait."

Again I had to contradict. "It might be to Minnie. It sounds like the old story: 'Stick with me, honey, I'm getting a divorce. But these things take time. . . .' " I choked on my own flippancy. Fortunately, nobody noticed. But suddenly my own dilemma was forced upon me. Not that Tom Cavanaugh had ever promised to divorce his wife, Sandra. Far from it. Her mental instability seemed to bind him even closer. Tom was too honorable to abandon a woman who needed him. Except I wasn't sure she did—Sandra needed a keeper, not a husband. But of course that was the role Tom had assumed. "On the other hand," I added in an acid tone, "some women are notoriously patient." I hoped no one would realize that I meant myself.

No one did. "So far," said Mike, "Jimmy has the best motive. If he was a bigamist."

"Sanford," Jackie put in. "Maybe he was gloomy because he'd killed somebody. Hey, let's get wild with this one. Sanford was gay, and why not? People didn't talk about that stuff in those days, right? He was crazy about Jimmy, a big, rough, tough, macho guy. Sanford killed Carrie in a fit of jealous rage." Jackie crossed her arms over her abdomen and sat back on the sofa, looking well pleased with herself.

"That's plausible," Mike said, offering Jackie a smile of approval. "I understand that loggers often used to exhibit homosexual tendencies, if only because they lived in isolated camps where there weren't any women. You may be on to something, Jackie."

Her husband seemed dubious. "I know we can't rule out any possibilities, but if this one is right, murdering Carrie didn't bring Sanford and Jimmy Malone together. Jimmy went off to Seattle and Sanford settled down with Grandma Rose."

Jackie was undaunted. "Jimmy rebuffed Sanford's advances. Being in the olden days Sanford couldn't admit he was gay. He had to live a lie, so he married Rose. That's why he was glum and she was unhappy."

As theories went, it wasn't bad. A major sticking point for me was the five children that Sanford and Rose had produced over a period of fifteen years. I had a variation to offer. "What if the Widow Simone was in love with Jimmy Malone?"

Jackie was aghast. "Not her type. Even if she got a pile of money from Cornelius, I can't imagine her running off with an Irish logger."

I didn't entirely agree with Jackie. When it comes to love, men and women are unpredictable. The heart follows its own highway, and didn't I know it. But Jackie had opened up some new avenues of thought for me.

"Let's go back to what we know—or think we know," I said. "Jimmy Malone went to Seattle. From what we've heard, he took Carrie and the kids along. If that's really true, then we may not have found Carrie after all." Jackie and Paul both tried to interrupt, but I waved them into silence. "My point is, a woman went with Jimmy to Seattle. How do we know for certain that it was Carrie? It could have been Simone. Or Minnie."

"Oh, poopy!" In frustration, Jackie twisted her wedding ring on her finger. "We don't know. We *can't* know. But I see what you mean, Emma—if Carrie had been killed, another woman might have taken her place. With those big hats, the same clothes, and long capes, how could anybody who didn't see them up close tell the difference? How would they have traveled? By train?"

"No," said Mike. "The railroad didn't come through here until much later. World War I, I think. They would have had all their belongings with them, so I'd guess they went by boat."

Jackie gave the rest of us a knowing look. "You see? They leave the house in a carriage or a wagon, go down to the dock, and sail away. Nobody sees them off because Simone has already left, or if she's still in town, she wouldn't give a hoot. Lena probably doesn't, either. Good riddance is how she figures it. And her husband, Eddie, is too henpecked to make a fuss over his sister's departure. Sanford doesn't care because he's not actually related to Carrie." Jackie paused, then gave her ring another frantic twist. "Oh, blast! This isn't getting us anywhere! Now we're back to the uncertainty of whether or not we've got Carrie in the basement!"

I stared at Jackie's hands. "Your ring . . . Where's Carrie's? We found the earrings, the silver bracelet, the cross, and the gold locket. But no ring. Carrie must have had a wedding set, maybe an expensive diamond."

Paul's expression was sheepish. "The rings may still be there. As we said, it'd take a long time to dig through that whole section of dirt."

Mike had an idea of his own. "Maybe the killer took the rings. If the set really was expensive, he or she might have wanted to keep them to sell or pawn."

"Who needed money?" asked Jackie.

"Grandpa Sanford?" Paul suggested. "If Lena ran the household, I have a feeling she kept her son on a short leash."

"We need that will," Jackie said, pouting a bit. "Why couldn't Meriwether and Bell have been in the office this afternoon?"

"We need marriage licenses," I put in. "We have to find out when Jimmy Malone married Minnie." I thought of Vida and how she would relish our task. We knew about Carrie and Jimmy's wedding, but the only way to verify a ceremony between him and Minnie Burke was through the county offices, either in Port Angeles or Seattle. Vida would expedite matters by revealing that one of her numerous nephews, nieces, cousins, or godchildren worked for the county clerk. I had no such ties, either in Clallam or King Counties.

"We might coerce somebody in Seattle to check the marriage licenses for 1908 or 1909," I said, finishing my third Pepsi of the day. "It would take time, though, even if we found a willing accomplice." Due in part to the Alaska Gold Rush, Seattle had been a rapidly growing city in the early part of the century. Off the top of my head, I estimated its population at between a hundred and two hundred thousand. Going through a full year of marriage licenses would be a big job. Jackie volunteered to make the call in the morning.

"You'll be off to Victoria at eight-thirty," she said to me. "I'll handle telephone research. Maybe when I call King County I'll pretend I'm a private detective."

Mike decided to call it a night. He had an early class on Thursday and also needed to finish grading some papers. I considered phoning Vida to see if there were any more crises in Alpine. Then I remembered that this Wednesday was her Cat Club meeting. She and several of her contemporaries got together once a month to eat gooey desserts and rake the rest of Alpine over the coals. The following day was always marked by their vows to go on a diet—and to rake over each other, usually by phone.

It was half-past nine when Mike left with his jar of bones. Since Paul also had to get up early for work, he, too, said good night. Jackie lingered with me in the den. She was studying the gold locket and looking poignant.

"Dark hair, black, really. Whose?" she inquired in a wistful voice.

I turned back to the photo albums. "It's hard to tell what shade of hair the people have in these pictures, since they're not in color. We can rule out Carrie and Rose because they were both fair. Jimmy, too, because he seems to be redheaded. That may be a cliché, given that he's Irish, but his hair certainly doesn't look very dark. Lena's hair may have been brown, but she appears to be going gray in the photos from this period."

Jackie leaned closer to me on the sofa, frowning at the album pages. "I feel I know these people now. Carrie may have been murdered, but it's Rose I feel sorry for. Maybe that's because she's Paul's grandmother."

"Probably," I agreed. "He knew her. That brings Grandma Rose into better focus." I turned more pages. "Eddie and Sanford were both dark. So was Simone. But the hair might be from someone further back. Cornelius or his first wife. Lena's first husband."

Jackie sniffed. "Lena with a locket? She wasn't the sentimental type."

I allowed that Jackie was right, though something she had said pricked at my mind. For the moment it proved elusive. "The problem is, if we assume the locket belonged to Carrie, wouldn't she have her husband's hair in it? Then it would be red or light brown, not black."

Jackie waved her hand, then gave the album a slap. "There's no locket in any of these photos. The women are all wearing pearl chokers or those high collars with tons of lace."

Again some small fragment of an idea passed through my brain, then danced away. But Jackie was on target about the locket. I hadn't been able to spot it, either. Maybe it came from a later period than the skeleton. Or maybe it was never meant to be seen.

"A lover," I said, startled to discover that I'd spoken out loud.

"A lover?" Jackie perked up. "Who? Carrie? Simone? Not Lena!"

"Probably not Lena." But, as Vida would say, *you never know*. Nothing could be ruled out with people. "But if it was Carrie or Simone, they wouldn't flaunt the locket."

"Simone might," Jackie said. "She strikes me as . . . What do you call it? Brazen?"

"No," I disagreed. "Simone knew what she was doing when she married Cornelius Rowley. She wouldn't do anything to throw a spanner in the works. If she had a lover, he was a well-kept secret."

Jackie had settled back onto the sofa. She was smiling slyly. "A lover. I like it. Simone would have done something like that. She was French, after all. Don't Frenchwomen always have a husband and a lover? Sort of like owning a washer and a dryer. They're practically a domestic necessity in France."

I didn't try to dispel Jackie's illusion. She was the French major, after all. "We're going in circles," I noted, then suddenly captured the elusive idea that had been needling me. "The cross—Lena wore a cross in that first picture. Let's compare it to the one we found in the basement."

One simple gold cross looks very like another. But at least the cross from the basement and the one that adorned Lena's pristine shirtwaist appeared similar.

"She was a religious woman, according to Aunt Sara. Her statue in the park doesn't show her wearing a cross. I wonder . . ." My weary brain tried to deal with the matter and failed.

"It's sure not Lena down there. She lived forever," Jackie pointed out. "Maybe she lost the cross. It might have fallen off the chain."

That was certainly a possibility. But there was another, uglier scenario. "Fallen off in a struggle?" I stared meaningfully at Jackie. "I can't figure a motive for Lena killing her sister-in-law, though. All this speculation is fine, but we need more facts. Maybe we'll get them tomorrow."

"We need more pictures." Jackie had gotten off the sofa and was going through a bandbox filled with loose photos. We had glanced at them earlier, but they seemed to be from a later era. Women in felt cloches, men in belted polo coats, children in pinafores and overalls recalled the period between the two world wars. But near the bottom of the bandbox were some earlier pictures. One was a duplicate of the Rowley-Melcher house photograph we'd seen on exhibit at the museum.

Jackie waved the eight-by-ten at me. "This is much clearer, even if it is smaller. I'm going to get that magnifying glass." She rummaged in the drawer under the glass-fronted bookcase. "Here, let's see if we can make out who the fifth person is, the one partly behind the front-porch arch."

But enlarging the photo under the magnifying glass had virtually the same effect as the blow-up in the museum. The figure became fuzzier, though we were able to discern that it was a woman. "If we could get someone to digitalize this, we could see it much better," I said. "Does anybody do that kind of work in Port Angeles?"

Jackie had no idea. Indeed, she didn't seem to understand what I was talking about. I explained that, basically, digitalizing was a process wherein an image was made sharper.

"It's costly, and probably not worth it," I added. "For all we know, whoever this is might be a neighbor."

"A neighbor!" Jackie's hand flew to her face. "The Bullards! They live next door. They always have. He was a banker. He's retired now, but his father is still alive. He must be about a hundred. I think he's in a home."

"Check him out," I said, half staggering to my feet. I was tired, though I hadn't worked half as hard as I did every day on *The Advocate*. Researching the past was tougher than I thought.

Jackie promised to speak to Mr. and Mrs. Bullard in the morning. She still seemed to be in high gear. As I headed up to bed, I envied her youthful energy. I was sure I'd fall asleep as soon as my head touched the pillow.

And I did, though I dreamed of straw-hatted men and tiny-waisted women, riding on bicycles built for two. They went round and round, never reaching their destination. We were doing the same thing in trying to piece together an eighty-year-old mystery. When I woke up shortly after seven, I felt a sense of futility. It was a wild-goose chase, and even if we somehow figured out a solution, there was no point to it. In fact, we could easily bring shame to the Melcher family.

On the other hand, it was better than thinking about my love life. Or was it the lack thereof that really bothered me?

I went into the bathroom and took a hot shower. I didn't need a cold one. That bothered me, too.

Chapter Nine

THE CAPACITY OF *The Victoria Express* was one hundred and fifty passengers. On this cloudy morning in July I doubted that the ship held more than half that number. Of course, there would be several additional crossings during the day. Meanwhile, *The Coho,* which carried a thousand people and also took on cars, would make at least two trips across the strait.

I had waited for breakfast until after I boarded. The menu wasn't elaborate, so I fueled myself on powdered-sugar doughnuts and coffee. My desire for a second cup led me to an encounter with an obstinate vending machine, which supposedly accepted both American and Canadian coins. It didn't seem to want to take either one, and I ended up giving the thing a swift kick. I didn't get my coffee, but I did acquire a sore toe and eighty-five cents in mixed change.

Midway, we encountered some heavy seas, and I was glad I hadn't eaten much. I'd forgotten that the open waters of the strait can cause seasickness. Jackie had been wise to stay home; she would probably have spent most of her time leaning over the rail.

My stomach settled down and my spirits picked up as soon as we approached Victoria's harbor. The capital of British Columbia is self-consciously English, yet it never fails to charm. The copper-domed Parliament buildings, the rambling granite mass of the Empress

Hotel, and the more modern hostelries that face the water are invitingly picturesque. The Inner Harbor seems to welcome visitors with a hug: It's not British to behave in such a familiar fashion, but somehow the Canadians have transcended their more austere roots. I caught myself smiling at the horse-drawn carriages, the red double-decker tour buses, and the overflowing flower planters hanging from wrought-iron lamp standards. Victoria is only seventeen miles from Port Angeles, but the city seems a world away.

I headed straight for the Empress and a phone booth. The hotel had undergone a lavish renovation since I'd visited it last. The fading dowager I recalled from years ago was now truly fit for a queen. Maybe I should have come to Victoria in the first place. I could have sipped tea in the lobby and contemplated my life. Or, more likely, I could have lost myself in the maze of shops that cater to dopey tourists like me.

Alexander Cameron had an Oak Bay address. I assumed that though he was dead, his widow had kept the listing intact. I dialed the number and was about to give up when there was no answer after seven rings. But a sprightly, if elderly, voice responded on the eighth ring.

I had readied my spiel while crossing the strait. Explaining that I was a newspaper editor and a friend of the Melcher family, I had undertaken a research project that dealt with early families in Port Angeles. As Mrs. Cameron was the eldest surviving member of one of those clans, I hoped she would permit me to visit and chat.

Claudia Malone Cameron was delighted, if a bit flustered. "I can't tell you how often I've thought about going back to Port Angeles," she said with a trace of self-reproach. "It's so close and yet I never do. I had no idea that younger members of the family lived there."

I had to hedge a bit, since I was actually representing

the Melchers, not the Rowleys. I told her that the present descendants had moved to town very recently. She didn't press for details but was more than willing to let me come out to her house. I found a cab under the hotel's porte cochere and was heading for the Oak Bay district moments later.

Claudia Cameron didn't live on the bay itself, which is an enclave of wealthy Victorians. Rather, her neighborhood was more modest, and close to the shopping area a few blocks inland. The house was typical of older, middle-class residences in Victoria, built of stucco, with dark green trim.

I paid the Iranian cab driver, added a generous tip, and mounted the four cement stairs that led to the walk and the small front porch. Like most gardens in British Columbia, Mrs. Cameron's was well tended and blooming profusely. Day lilies, roses, phlox, sweet williams, and hollyhocks grew in an orderly manner behind borders of ageratum, lobelia, and Saint-John's-wort. The porch was flanked by great shrubs of heather. I wondered if Mrs. Cameron was still able to tend her flowers.

It appeared that she was not. Claudia Cameron met me at the door in a wheelchair. She had a round, wrinkled face and twinkling green eyes. A shawl was thrown over her legs. She wore a gray twin set and a single strand of pearls. I got the impression that she was glad to see me, not for myself but because I was a connection with the outside world.

"The teakettle's on," she announced, leading the way into her cluttered, comfortable living room. A spinet piano displayed framed photographs, but I refrained from blatant rubbernecking. Later, perhaps, after we'd had a chance to get acquainted. First, however, I clarified my connection.

"So you know the Melchers," Mrs. Cameron said

with a winning smile. "My, my, I'd forgotten all about them."

I swiftly sifted through the family tree. "Paul is Sanford and Rose's grandson. They inherited the house from Paul's uncle Arthur. He died a year or so ago."

Claudia Cameron nodded slowly. "So many are gone. People of my age group, that is. It's very sad, living on, when the rest have passed away." Only the twinkle of her green eyes revealed that she took pride in having outlasted her contemporaries. "I don't recall any of the Melchers, really. My parents must have lost touch."

"You were raised in Seattle," I remarked, getting set to jot down items in my notebook. "What did your father do for a living?"

"He was foreman at a mill along the Ship Canal. It's gone now, I hear. So many places are." This time, Mrs. Cameron looked genuinely sad. Perhaps it wasn't as satisfying to outlive places as much as people. "We lived close by, in the Fremont district. Do you know it?"

I confessed that I, too, had been raised in Seattle, in the neighboring Wallingford area. Mrs. Cameron was delighted. "Then you must have gone to Lincoln High School. My brothers and sisters and I went there, too."

I was forced to disillusion my hostess. "My brother and I attended a private Catholic high school, Blanchet. It was built in the 1950s, just north of Green Lake."

"Oh." Mrs. Cameron definitely seemed disappointed, either by my failure to attend Lincoln or my Catholicism. Fortunately, the teakettle let off a howl and I volunteered to head for the kitchen. Mrs. Cameron, however, insisted on doing it herself.

"I get around just fine in this contraption," she said. "Arthritic hips, you know. I had them replaced twice, but they don't last forever. And at my age it seems like a waste of time and money." She smiled at me again and whisked off to the kitchen.

I took the opportunity to study the photos on the spinet. I recognized none of them. Most were graduation and wedding pictures, no earlier than the Depression era. There was one five-by-seven, however, which could have been of Claudia's parents. The heavyset man had a full head of white hair; the woman was plump, with frizzy gray curls. They were gazing at each other over a wedding cake. Or perhaps it was for an anniversary. Judging from the woman's fussy jeweled evening sweater, the picture dated from the 1950s. The man could have been Jimmy Malone, but I couldn't tell whether his wife was Carrie or Minnie. Time, weight, hairstyle, and the possibility of dentures defeated me.

I was back in my overstuffed chair by the time Mrs. Cameron returned, balancing a tray on her lap. Two English bone-china cups and saucers, a Royal Doulton teapot with matching sugar and creamer, spoons, strainer, and several napkins resided on the tray. I marveled at how my hostess managed not to spill anything.

"I never did go back," Mrs. Cameron said suddenly after we'd gone through the ritual of pouring and stirring our tea. "To Port Angeles, I mean. But of course I was a baby when we left. I felt no real pull. Victoria has been my home since 1929."

Boldly, I asked if the people in the photograph were Claudia's parents. She nodded. "That was their golden wedding anniversary. Sandy and I celebrated ours in 1979. Such a privilege to live that long together! And such a trial!" Her small mouth turned down at the corners, but the twinkle remained in her eyes.

I attempted a delicate approach for my next question. "And your mother was named ... Minnie?"

"That's right. Minnie, for Mary. So many Marys in those days. She came from a big family. One of her brothers had given her the nickname, I think."

"Irish," I remarked with what I hoped was an ingenuous smile.

"Yes." Mrs. Cameron nodded, her fingers clutching the rose-patterned teacup. "I never knew her people. Oh, I must admit, we were quite alone while growing up. My father's family was mostly in Ireland except for a brother who went out to California. We lost track of him, though."

I made a sympathetic noise. So far, I was discovering absolutely nothing. And how could I? Claudia Malone Cameron had been a year old when she left Port Angeles. Had I expected her somehow to have stored away indelible memories of her first year among the Rowley-Melchers?

Frustrated, I tried a different tack. "I realize you don't remember Simone, Cornelius Rowley's second wife. Have you any idea what happened to her after Cornelius died?"

Resting her cheek on one hand, Mrs. Cameron's expression grew sly. "Simone! Now there's a name that wasn't allowed to be uttered under our roof! My mother wouldn't hear of her, not a word. Naturally, that made one wonder."

Naturally, I agreed. It made me wonder, too. "Why was that?"

"Well." Claudia Cameron sat up straighter in the wheelchair. She looked rather excited, her cheeks taking on a delicate pink hue. "The fact that Mother wouldn't mention Simone's name made my sister, Julia, and me ever so curious. Finally we waited one evening until Poppa got a bit . . . ah . . . tipsy, which happened rather often." The wrinkled flesh along Mrs. Cameron's jawline hardened. "The Irish enjoy their dram, you know. So when Poppa's tongue became loose, we asked him about Simone. Alas, he wasn't drunk enough to be completely indiscreet, but he hinted certain things, his brogue thicker than ever. Winks and rolling of eyes, you take my meaning?"

I did, but was still in the dark. All I could see was Jimmy Malone, rollicking in his favorite chair and leading his daughters on with a lilting, if slurred, Irish voice.

"We gathered that Simone was no better than she should be, as we used to say. An adventuress who'd married Cornelius Rowley for his money. There was another man in the background, a Frenchman as you might assume. His name was Antoine or Armand or something like that, and he worked as a fisherman in Port Angeles. Mother had once overheard a quarrel between Cornelius and Simone. It seemed he had caught her with this Frenchman. She cried and carried on, promising to be a good wife. Cornelius vowed to run the man out of town. From that point on, Simone must have behaved herself."

Jackie's fantasy about a lover had turned into reality. "Do you think Simone left Port Angeles to join her lover? After Cornelius died, I mean."

Mrs. Cameron gave a slight shrug. "It's possible. She had the means." There was a bitter note in her voice.

I tipped my head to one side. "Simone inherited the family fortune?"

My hostess grew tight-lipped. "I couldn't say. But isn't that what she was after?"

My page of notes wasn't yet half full. I certainly hadn't gotten my money's worth out of the combined cab and ferry fares. I decided to confront the issue head-on. "I'm confused, Mrs. Cameron. Your mother's name was Minnie, for Mary. But my understanding is that her name was really Carrie, for Caroline. Caroline Rowley Malone. Why am I mixed up?"

The green eyes grew very wide. "I have no idea. My mother was a Burke, from Londonderry. Her family, all seven of them, came to America when she was a child. Her parents were taken early on, in Boston. One of her brothers had married and moved West. She came out to join him and took a post as a governess. That's how she met my father."

My brain was tripping over itself. "And that was . . . where?"

"Why, in Port Angeles, of course. They had a most romantic courtship. They eloped to Seattle. And then they moved there when I was not quite a year old. My two younger brothers and one sister were born in Seattle. Six, in all, though there are only three of us left."

"But . . ." I had begun to wonder if Mrs. Cameron's mind wasn't as clear as I'd thought. Or maybe it was my own that was fogged. "On the phone I mentioned that you were a member of the Rowley-Melcher family. You implied that it was so. Yet now you say you aren't?" I knew my face showed bafflement.

Mrs. Cameron smiled, a bit condescendingly. "You said *clan*, I believe. My husband was a Scot. To me, *clan* includes people outside of the immediate family. Which we were. You see, my mother was governess to the Rowley children."

There is no point in arguing with an eighty-six-year-old woman. In fact, there's not much point in arguing with anybody. It's always hard to change people's minds. It's damned near impossible when they are elderly and set in their ways.

Still, I was tempted. I wanted very much to say that I knew—had proof, though not with me—that Jimmy Malone had been married to Carrie Rowley and that she was Claudia Cameron's mother. But what if Carrie had left Jimmy and their children? What if she'd run away? Worse yet, what if she'd been murdered? Why suggest such awful things to a lonely, crippled old lady? She remembered Minnie Burke Malone as her mother. No doubt Minnie had been loving, selfless, understanding, and kind. If she had married James Malone somewhere along the line and borne him three children while taking on the trio from his previous marriage, so what? She had been as much of a mother to them as had Carrie Rowley. It wasn't up to me to turn Claudia Cameron's world upside down.

I uttered a lame little laugh. "I misled you. I'm so sorry. The family tree is sort of confusing, with several of the members marrying more than once. Stepchildren and all that."

Mrs. Cameron nodded complacently. "Oh, yes. It's even worse nowadays. So many divorces, and all these hyphenated last names. More tea?" She hoisted the pot and smiled encouragingly.

I couldn't say no. Nor could I quite let go of Jimmy Malone and the tale of two wives. "I feel silly," I said lightly. "I wonder how I got it in my head that your father had been married to someone other than . . . your mother?"

Mrs. Cameron's face took on a critical expression as she sipped her tea. "This has grown cool and much too strong. Shall I brew more?" I insisted that she not go to the trouble. Briefly, my hostess seemed unconvinced but finally gave in. She had, however, lost the thread of our conversation.

"Nievalle," she said suddenly, and I, too, was lost. Mrs. Cameron leaned forward in the wheelchair. "Armand Nievalle. That was the name of Simone Rowley's lover. Isn't it peculiar that I should remember it after all these years?" She chuckled, a merry sound.

"I suppose he might have descendants in Port Angeles," I remarked in a doubtful voice.

"Not if he'd been run out of town by Mr. Rowley." Mrs. Cameron's tone became quite stern. "It's interesting, though. I haven't thought about it for years. Which is odd since my sister and I were once quite obsessed with the subject. But so much else has happened since. And once we found out why Simone was anathema in our house, she lost her air of mystery."

I nodded. "Yes, I can see that. It's rather like you enlightening me about your father and his marriages. Marriage, I mean." I felt like kicking myself; I wasn't about to give up the chase.

Mrs. Cameron didn't seem at all perturbed by my single-mindedness. "People get confused, especially about the past. Their memories become hazy. And young people in particular have no sense of what's gone on before they were born. It's all one great cluster of events with no specific order. They have no feel for history. It's a pity."

My agreement was given halfheartedly. I was distracted. The interview hadn't gone as I'd planned. There was nothing else to ask Mrs. Cameron. Not without disturbing her. The steeple clock on the mantel showed that I'd been inside her house for less than an hour. I was anxious to get away. But I knew that she enjoyed my company. For once I succumbed to my better nature and asked about her own family. A flood of information surged from Mrs. Cameron's lips. Her husband Sandy's career with the provincial parks. Their two children's marriages, one satisfactory, the other not. The grandchildren, scattered from Vancouver to Toronto. The great-grandchildren, who she had seen only in photographs. I sat back and made appropriate comments.

"It's a pity to lose track of people," she said, now sounding a bit weary. "I should have gone over to Port Angeles. But they wouldn't have known me really. The Melchers, I mean."

"Well," I answered slowly, "they would have known who you were." I tried to envision Lena giving a warm welcome to the daughter of an ex-governess. Or Rose, throwing Sanford out of the music parlor so that she could entertain company. I knew nothing of Uncle Arthur's wife, but if she had followed in the footsteps of the other Melcher women, there would have been no rolling out of the red carpet.

"It's so hard," Mrs. Cameron was saying, and I realized I'd missed something. "Arizona is so hot and Chicago is so cold. Even though Walter and Daniel were closer, we seldom got together. I do regret that. For so many reasons."

Desperately, I tried to piece the conversation back together. Walter and Daniel were Claudia's brothers, now deceased. Another brother—Joseph?—was retired in Arizona. A sister lived in Chicago. Was it Julia or Mary Ann? It must be Mary Ann. Julia was dead. But unless I'd missed it, Mrs. Cameron hadn't mentioned Julia. Maybe she wasn't dead after all. I tried to remember what Tessie Roo had told me about the Malone offspring.

"Julia lived too far?" I'd tried to make the comment into a statement, but it came out a question.

Mrs. Cameron's lips pursed. "Julia." She lifted the lid from the teapot. "It's empty. Shall I . . . ?"

If I drank any more tea, I could float back to Port Angeles. Mrs. Cameron didn't press me. Instead, she twisted her swollen fingers together and frowned.

"I was so fond of Julia when we were girls. We had such fun together. How I've missed her all these years!" A faint tremor vibrated in Mrs. Cameron's voice.

"She . . . died?" As soon as I asked, I finally recalled Tessie Roo's information: Walter and Julia Malone had passed away in recent years in the Seattle-Tacoma area.

Mrs. Cameron regarded me with a sad yet wry expression. "They all do eventually. But I'm talking about years ago, when we were young. Julia ran away."

"Oh!" I leaned forward in the chair, eager for my hostess's confidences.

"Julia and my mother never got along. Never." Mrs. Cameron shook her head. "Isn't it strange how children can have the same parents and yet react so differently to them? It was cat and dog with Mother and Julia. When I was twelve and Julia was fifteen, she ran away. Like that!" The old lady made a feeble attempt to snap her fingers.

Julia. Julia, Julia, Julia . . . I found her on the family tree now imprinted in my brain. She was the eldest of Jimmy Malone's children. Carrie's eldest, too, according to the Clallam County genealogy records. If she'd been fifteen when she ran away, the year was 1919. The influenza epidemic came to mind.

"Where did she go?" I asked.

"I don't know." Mrs. Cameron's face sagged. "We never heard from her again. Not until she died. Someone I knew in Seattle read about her funeral in the newspaper and sent me a note at Christmas. Her married name was Olofson. She had two children, but they were scattered about, like all the rest."

"Goodness." It was all I could think of to say. Where would a fifteen-year-old girl go in the post–World War I era? Had she merely lost herself in the growing metropolis of Seattle? Had she found some of her Irish relatives in another city? Had she run off with a boy? I posed this last question to Mrs. Cameron.

My hostess was slow to answer. "There was no special boy that we knew of. But Julia would go off on the streetcar every so often and be gone for several hours. She was much too young to be on her own, riding around town. Julia was a pretty thing, so we had to assume it was a boy. At that time in our lives the age difference was such that she no longer confided her secrets to me. To her, I was still a baby. If she ran off with someone, it wasn't so much because of him as it was because of our mother. They couldn't get along, plain and simple. Poppa doted on his girls, especially when he was in his cups. He called us his little princesses. Julia's defection was hard on Poppa and me, but Walter suffered the most from her absence. He was always a shy little boy, but after Julia went away, he seemed to withdraw even more. He was very dependent on her, you see, since she was the oldest."

"Neither of you ever tried to find her?" I asked gently. "That is, after you grew up?"

Claudia Cameron's gaze looked beyond me, to the farthest corner of the room, or perhaps into a dark place in her soul. "No. I married and moved to Victoria. I had my children and . . . well, you get so caught up in your own life." She plucked at the shawl that was thrown over her legs.

"And Walter?"

"No." The word was emphatic. Claudia's thin lips tightened. "Not Walter. He had his own . . . difficulties."

A veil seemed to have descended between us. There didn't seem to be much left to say. Mrs. Cameron was obviously tired out from my visit, though she made a polite plea for me to stay on. It was after noon when I finally called a cab to take me out of Oak Bay and back to downtown Victoria.

The next passenger ferry left at one. I was tempted to delay my departure until the later sailing at four, but I knew that Jackie would be wringing her hands over my absence. Besides, my car might be ready. Grabbing an order of fish and chips wrapped in genuine English newspaper, I headed for the ferry slip.

As we left the Inner Harbor, the sun was trying to come out at least three hours ahead of schedule. I strolled the deck, noting that this time the ferry seemed much more crowded. Armed with a cup of coffee, I sauntered over to the stern to watch Victoria grow smaller as we headed out into the strait.

A man in a rumpled cotton sports coat was leaning over the rail. He seemed to be leaning a trifle too far, and I wondered if he was ill. Or, I thought fleetingly, suicidal. I smiled at my own fancy and came up within a few yards of him. Out of the corner of my eye I sensed that there was something familiar about him. A sidelong glance registered the sharp profile with the broken nose.

It was the drunk from the library, and judging from his desolate air, it looked to me as if suicide wasn't a fantasy after all.

Chapter Ten

I SPILLED MY coffee on purpose, then let out a little yip. Slowly, reluctantly, the man turned. He didn't seem very interested in my dilemma. But before he could look away, I burst into laughter.

"I'm such a dunce! Don't walk over here. You might slip and fall. Have you got a napkin?"

"No." The word fell out of his mouth like a stone. Again he tried to ignore me.

"Could you get me some from the vending area?" I assumed my most helpless air. "Please? I feel like a dope!"

With a sigh of resignation Leo Fulton Walsh moved off. The name had come to me as I visualized his California driver's license. I drank what was left of my coffee and waited. The other passengers, who had stared at my little drama, now resumed chatting and watching the water. I caught sight of Mount Baker over on the mainland. The big, snow-covered peak always reminded me of an ice cream cone. It crowned the North Cascades, a link in the range that led to Alpine. The idea made me smile, and I wondered if I was homesick. In the past three and a half years I'd never consciously thought of Alpine as home. It was my base of operations, the place where I had my job. But *home* was my native Seattle or my adopted Portland. Had I assumed the guise of the small-towner? No, never that; I was a born and bred denizen of the Big City. But maybe Alpine had sneaked into my heart, if not my soul. I smiled at the idea.

"You look pretty happy for a gal who damned near scalded herself," said Leo Walsh, handing me a dozen paper napkins.

Startled, I accepted the napkins, then bent down to wipe up the spilled coffee. Most of it had already drained overboard. I spent more time than I needed to swab the deck. What could I say to a man I thought was about to commit suicide? How should I initiate a conversation with somebody who was dead drunk when I last saw him? Should I stick to meaningless clichés or actually try to discover what was eating Leo Fulton Walsh?

"Did you spend the day in Victoria?" I asked, settling for triteness.

Leo arched his eyebrows at me. As I'd suspected, his normal complexion was faintly florid. He did not, however, seem marked by signs of excessive drink. Indeed, his brown eyes were clear and in sharp focus.

"I went over for the morning," he answered after a faint pause. "There's not much to see unless you're nuts about English bone china and fuzzy Eskimo sweaters."

"Oh, no," I said quickly. "There's a wonderful museum and the Parliament buildings are fascinating, especially when they're in session, and they've got an undersea garden and a wax museum and . . ."

His smile was crooked. It went with the nose. "You did all that in four hours?"

I blinked at Leo. "You saw me on the early ferry?"

He gave an indifferent nod. "Right. You were attacking one of the vending machines. I liked the way you kicked it and the coins flew out."

"Oh!" I uttered an embarrassed laugh. "Well, I hate those contraptions. They never seem to work for me. They're hexed."

The light in Leo Walsh's eyes went out. He looked away, beyond me to the open sea. "You were at the library." His voice had resumed its dull, deadly tone.

I hesitated before answering. There was no point in dancing around the issue. "You feel better now?"

"Better than what?" He had returned to the rail, leaning on it as if his body had no other means of support.

Having spent the better part of two hours trying to tactfully elicit information from an old lady, I didn't feel like playing word games with a middle-aged man. "Better than unconscious," I retorted. "I'll say one thing, you might have been a smart-ass when you spoke to me yesterday, but you sure were better-natured."

Leo refused to look at me. "I don't remember what I said," he muttered.

His manner was so dejected that I immediately regretted my own smart-assed remarks. "Come on," I said with a sigh, "let's go inside. We're out in the middle of the strait and the wind's up. I could use a full cup of coffee."

To my surprise, Leo followed me to the food-service area. I didn't make the mistake of trying to get coffee from a machine but slipped into the cafeteria line. Leo also got coffee. We paid separately, which suited me fine.

After we sat down at a small table, I waited for him to speak first. It took a couple of minutes. "What are you?" he finally asked. "A Saint Bernard for tourists?"

I gave him a wry little smile. "If I were, I'd think twice about offering you brandy. Are you staying in Port Angeles?"

"It doesn't look like it." His expression was now noncommittal.

I wasn't sure what to make of his reply. "You're making the Olympic Loop trip?"

Leo felt inside his jacket, scanned our surroundings,

and noticed the No Smoking signs. His hand came out empty and he sighed with annoyance. "This part of the country is too damned healthy. Whatever happened to the Bill of Rights?"

As an ex-smoker I often count time in terms of not smoking rather than forgetting all about my unwholesome habit. Thus, I sympathized. But only briefly. I was about to add that it was a good way to kill yourself, but so was jumping off *The Victoria Express*. I decided to change the subject.

"What did you think of Victoria?" I asked in my most casual manner.

"I told you. It's a tourist trap." Leo drummed his fingers on the table. "At least the sun came out."

"Big deal." I was having a hell of a time being polite to Leo Walsh. "You Californians would rather have a riot than rain. And how about those brush fires and earthquakes and that smog, Mr. Walsh?"

"You've got earthquakes up here, too," he grumbled, then stared at me. It was the first eye contact since we'd been out on deck. "How do you know my name? Or where I'm from?"

"I lifted your wallet. In the library." I gave a little shrug. "I'm not a local, either. I didn't know who you were. It was a dirty job, but somebody had to do it." Now I was the one who lowered my gaze.

For the first time Leo Walsh laughed. It was actually a surly sound, but not entirely unpleasant. "Okay, so who are you?"

I told him my name, adding that I was a visitor from the other side of Puget Sound. Leo didn't need to hear my life story. "My car broke down. What about you?"

"Hunh. My car broke down, too." Leo looked bemused. "In fact, it just plain died. It's got over a hundred and thirty thousand miles on it. I've got a lot more on me."

"Don't we all," I remarked lightly. "So how are you going to get back home?"

Leo gave me a sour look. "What home?" He gripped the table with both hands. "Hey, are you trying to pick me up or save me from my evil self?"

I let my eyes roam about the galley. "Oh, I just go around finding people with sad stories to tell and let them slobber all over me." Abruptly, I leaned forward and zeroed in on Leo. "What's yours?"

He gave another dour laugh. "We're about twenty minutes away from the dock. There isn't time."

"Try me."

But Leo Walsh shook his head. "No go, Emma Lord. You seem like a nice gal. You don't need it. Consider that you've done your good deed for the day. Get your car fixed and find yourself a stray dog to rescue." He got up, gave me his crooked grin, and walked away.

I wasn't about to chase Leo Walsh around *The Victoria Express*. Finishing my coffee, I sat at the table until we began to slow down for the maneuver into the ferry slip. If Leo really had been thinking about suicide, he wouldn't attempt it this close to shore. I hoped that it had been a passing mood. Better yet, that I'd misjudged him.

Whatever the case, the interlude with Leo had saved me from thinking about myself. Now that I was almost back in Port Angeles, I could resume thinking about the Melchers and their mystery. Love and death, I mused, heading for the passenger debarkation area, were the themes of my aborted journey. They were also the themes of my life, and everybody else's.

I went ashore in the sunshine, but I felt a big black cloud hanging over me.

Jackie Melcher was blooming like an English garden. "I did it!" she cried as I came through the back door. "I got somebody in Seattle to check the marriage licenses! Hurry, hurry, I've got tons to tell you!"

As I entered the kitchen, I suffered a sudden pang of guilt. I should have brought a hostess gift or even a baby present back from Victoria. A Royal Albert plate, a Hudson Bay blanket, a wee tartan kilt—all had been in easy reach, if maybe out of my price range. But I hadn't. Shamefaced, I offered my apologies to Jackie.

She waved my regrets aside. "Paul and I can go over to Victoria anytime. Sit, Emma, have some pop. Let me tell you about Meriwether and Bell."

"Hold it—what about the marriage licenses?" I asked, accepting a cold can of pop from Jackie and clearing away a pile of paint samples from the nearest kitchen stool.

Jackie clambered onto one of its mates, not bothering to first remove a couple of mail-order catalogues. "Desmond will call back later from the King County courthouse, tomorrow probably. He's a sweetheart. I told him I was a movie producer."

I didn't ask Jackie to elaborate on her lie. Instead, I steered her back to Meriwether and Bell. She grew serious and got out her notes.

"They weren't too happy about it. Digging in the files, I mean. Mr. Bell sounded like he was about a zillion years old, but it turns out he's the same age as Paul. His father's the senior partner. I told him I was—"

I held up a hand. "I don't think I want to hear—"

"—a romance novelist and I was using Simone Dupre Rowley for a true-life book." Jackie displayed her dimples. "That's how I found out how old he was. Mr. Bell, I mean. Richie. I told him the hero of my book was in his early thirties, and he said so was he, and I asked what he looked like, and he described himself, and I said, 'Wow, that's wild! My hero looks just like you!' So then he agreed to get the files out and call me back, which he did about an hour ago." She relapsed into her serious mode. "Do you suppose he'll want a free copy when it's published?"

I sighed. "Jackie, just tell me what Mr. Bell— Richie—told you about Cornelius Rowley's will."

"Oh." Jackie scrutinized her notes. "Cornelius Rowley left the house to Eddie and Lena, plus twenty-five thousand dollars. He left fifty thousand dollars to Carrie and her kids. The rest went to Simone except for some charities and five thousand to a sister in Saginaw."

I considered the bequests. "It sounds fair. But it raises some questions, doesn't it?"

"It does?" Jackie looked blank.

"Right. For one thing, how much *was* the rest?"

Jackie consulted her notes again. "It didn't say in the will, but Richie checked some other records. He figured Simone got over a quarter of a million, including stock in the mill. That would have been a big fortune back then, huh?"

I nodded. "But why not the house? A widow usually gets the house. Did Cornelius know Simone wouldn't stick around? Did he also know Carrie and Jimmy were leaving town? And what about the mill? Did Simone sell the stock? If Eddie ran the business into the ground, eventually the stock's value would have been nil."

Jackie was concentrating very hard. "Yes, I see. . . . Gosh, Emma, you're good at this stuff. You take these bits and pieces of dry facts and give them meaning. It's like magic!"

"It's like journalism," I said dryly. "If you've ever read a government press release, you wouldn't be so amazed. Ask your mother."

Still gazing at me with admiration, Jackie finally removed the catalogues she'd been sitting on and placed them next to the coffeemaker. "Carrie and Jimmy might have been planning to move for some time. But did Carrie go with him?"

I related the interview with Claudia Malone Cameron. It took me awhile, trying to recapture all of the data and some of the nuances. Even as I told my tale, I sensed that something was amiss. It wasn't just the basic inconsistency of who was whose mother but a feeling that there were other aspects of Mrs. Cameron's account that didn't mesh. I didn't think she'd lied. More likely, she herself didn't know the truth. Yet in going over the morning's conversation, I couldn't quite put my finger on what was wrong.

When I finally finished, Jackie jumped on the portion that had struck her as the most odd. "The sister—Julia—maybe she never got along with Minnie because she was older than the other two kids and knew she wasn't their real mother. I mean, she was around four when the family moved to Seattle. She could tell the difference between Carrie and Minnie."

"Good point," I remarked, my mind racing in several directions. "But Walter, the brother, was only two and Claudia was a year or so old. It must have been confusing for such little tykes, having a mother and a governess. Today we call them primary caregivers and we speak of bonding. Maybe Minnie was closer to the kids than Carrie was. The two younger Malones might have been happier with Minnie than they were with Carrie. But Julia was old enough to understand."

Jackie had gone to the refrigerator to get a bottle of mineral water. "Wouldn't Julia tell the other kids?"

I pondered the question. "Maybe she did. Maybe Claudia and Walter were into denial. Or it was like when one sibling tells the other, 'You're not Mom and Dad's real kid. You're *adopted*.' They might never have taken it in, especially if Minnie and Jimmy reinforced the idea that Minnie was their real mother. Then the

question is, Why would they do that? And getting back
to Cornelius's will, why did he leave the house and
money to Eddie *and* Lena, but the other bequest was
specified for Carrie and her children? Jimmy was left
out. Or did I hear you wrong?"

I hadn't. Jackie assured me that Jimmy Malone
wasn't mentioned in Cornelius Rowley's will. "It was
made in 1904, so Carrie was already married to Jimmy
by then," she explained. "The kids aren't mentioned by
name. It was one of those legal deals where they talk
about lawful *issue* and *legal heirs* or whatever."

Pensive, I sipped my soda. "Cornelius wanted Carrie
to have control of the money. He passed over Jimmy.
So if that's Carrie in the basement, the three kids got
the fifty grand." I shot Jackie an enlightened look.
"That, and another woman, make a motive."

"Wow!" Jackie wiggled excitedly on the stool.
"Jimmy gets control of the money because the three
kids are minors, right? He's in love with Minnie, so he
bumps Carrie off! Emma, we did it! We've solved the
mystery!"

I wasn't quite ready to celebrate. "We've got an awfully good theory," I admitted. "I wish I knew where
the money went. Did your pal Richie say anything
about a trust for the children or the administration
thereof?"

"No." Jackie was still rocking on the stool. "In fact,
the only other legal papers he found—besides the stuff
on Cornelius's estate—had to do with Eddie and Lena.
The mill, too. It went out of business in 1913."

I winced. "Terrible timing. That's just before the
town got electricity and the railroad came in. If Eddie
had held on, he might have made a go of it."

Jackie stopped rocking. "Poor Eddie. He's like the
forgotten man. A domineering father, a bossy wife, no
children of his own—nothing worked out for him ex-

cept that wood-basket invention. What happens to people whose dreams never come true? Are they crushed by failure? Do they stop dreaming? Do they give up hope and spend their lives on park benches feeding the seagulls and despising themselves? I'd like to tell every single person in the world that nobody lives in vain as long as they've loved somebody or had someone love them. How can I do that?"

I didn't know. Jackie's ruminations would have driven me crazy if they didn't demonstrate her kind, if whimsical, heart. "Sometimes our dreams may be what we want but not what we need," I replied. It was a pat answer, and of no help to anyone, myself included. Jackie gave me a quizzical look; I shrugged, feeling inadequate.

I was shaken from our philosophical mood by the realization that it was time to call Dusty's. My watch told me that three o'clock was drawing nigh and the Jag was supposed to be ready by four. Using the cordless phone, I dialed the number for the auto repair shop.

A recording came on the line. "Hi, this is Dusty's Foreign Car Repair. Our normal hours are seven to five, Monday through Friday. This Thursday, July 29, we will be closed at one o'clock in honor of our owner's birthday. Dusty sends you his best wishes and accepts yours with his thanks. Happy motoring."

It's dangerous to slam down a cordless phone, but I almost did it. "Damn! It's Dusty's birthday! I hope he chokes on his cake! Why didn't they tell me that?"

Jackie seemed unaffected by my dilemma. "I'll bet it's a surprise party. Dusty probably didn't know about it. Don't worry, Emma, I wanted you to stay the extra day."

I had jumped off the stool and was pacing the kitchen. "But I can't! I've got a paper to get out for next week! It's a special edition!" I felt like tearing out my hair.

Jackie had confiscated the phone book from me. "I know what let's do," she said, thumbing through the Yellow Pages. "Let's call Mike and we'll all go out to dinner. Someplace really nice like Downriggers. They've got a great view of the water."

The only view I wanted to see was of my car with its engine running. I grabbed my handbag off the counter. "Come on, let's go over to Dusty's and see if the party is at the shop. Maybe my Jag's ready and I can get it out of there."

Jackie's arguments were futile. She finally gave in, and ten minutes later we had found Dusty's Foreign Car Repair. Unfortunately, we found it locked and shuttered. My Jag was nowhere to be seen.

I glared at the big black letters that read CLOSED. Unpredictable work hours were one of the hazards of small-town life. I knew that only too well from living in Alpine. Muttering curses, I allowed Jackie to drive me back to her house.

"You see," she said cheerfully as we tooled down Oak Street, "it's meant to be. I'll call and make a reservation at Downriggers. How does six-thirty sound?"

It sounded like the toll of doom, but I tried to act enthusiastic. As soon as Jackie had phoned the restaurant and left a message at the college for Mike, I dialed *The Advocate*.

Vida was out. Carla was still sick. Ginny Burmeister, who is a borderline stoic, sounded upset. I explained my predicament, then anxiously asked how things were going at the office.

"Carla says she'll be in tomorrow," Ginny said slowly. "She still doesn't feel good. She isn't sick to her stomach anymore, but her head's stuffed up. Peyts has put her on a decongestant and nose drops."

I was thankful that Dr. Peyton Flake and my reporter were a romantic duo. At least I could be sure that Carla was getting professional tender loving care.

"Where's Vida?" I asked.

"She's taking a picture of Crazy Eights Neffel," Ginny answered, still in a strangely nervous voice.

"What? We just ran something on that old nut. Why is Vida doing such a thing?" My House & Home editor was acting out of character. Something must be going on, and I wasn't sure I wanted to hear about it.

Ginny sighed. "Crazy Eights is up a tree in Old Mill Park. He says the bear is after him."

"The . . . bear?" I remembered the bizarre story about the board games. "How long has he been in the tree?"

"Since last night. He says the bear chased him because he won."

"He won the board game?"

"Yes, but the bear said Crazy Eights cheated. Crazy Eights says he didn't. He wants Milo Dodge to arrest the bear. But Sheriff Dodge can't find him, and Crazy Eights won't come down out of the tree. The tourists think it's funny." From the serious sound of Ginny's voice, she didn't agree.

"Okay." I was accustomed to small-town oddities. The picture of Crazy Eights up a tree would make for good filler. Page four, I figured off the top of my head. "Where's Ed?"

Ginny was slow to answer. When she finally did, her response wasn't very helpful. "I don't know," she said simply.

"Is he coming back this afternoon?" I glanced at my watch. It was after three-thirty. As lazy as Ed was in the past, he rarely left the office so early. "He must have a pile of work to do with the Fixer-Upper edition next week."

"Well . . . actually, Ed's gone. I'm working on the

special section. And the rest of the ads." Ginny's gulp plunked in my ear. "I kind of hate to mention it when you're on vacation, but I suppose I'd better. Ed's not coming back at all. He quit."

Chapter Eleven

I HADN'T WANTED a drink so much since my son Adam asked me how you could be absolutely sure a girl was a virgin. Now I felt like an idiot, but I had to ask Jackie if she had any serious liquor on hand. She didn't. I'm not particularly fond of wine—I have no palate for it—and all the reds upset my stomach. I only drink beer when I'm with Milo Dodge.

I settled for another Pepsi. It crossed my mind that I could replace Ed with Ginny on a full-time basis. But while Ginny was eager and hardworking, she was too young and inexperienced. The older, conservative business men and women of Skykomish County wouldn't be keen on a twenty-three-year-old advertising manager. Nor did I know if Ginny wanted the job. She seemed perfectly happy running the front office and occasionally pitching in with the ad side.

The other nagging question was why Ed had quit in the first place. His wife, Shirley, worked part-time at St. Mildred's Parochial School as a teacher's helper. I didn't know if she got paid for her efforts. The Bronskys had five children, three requiring monthly payments at St. Mildred's and one freeloading in the public high school. Maybe Shirley was reimbursed with tuition credits. Whatever the situation, Ed and Shirley still had to live. I was mystified by Ed's sudden resignation. Ginny had promised to have Vida call as soon as she returned from Old Mill Park.

Though Paul sympathized with my plight over the Jag, he seemed pleased that I was staying on. When he arrived home from work around four, Jackie couldn't wait to tell him about what we'd deduced from our newly acquired information. I listened with half an ear while she rattled on. Paul's reaction was not unlike my own—he found our theory plausible but not conclusive.

"What about Simone?" he asked, fondling a can of cold beer he'd managed to snatch out of the fridge before Jackie hauled him off to the den. "Even if we think that's Carrie down in the basement and that Jimmy Malone killed her, what happened to Cornelius's rich widow?"

That line of inquiry seemed as cold as Paul's beer. "We may never know," I said. "I still wish we'd found Carrie's rings down there."

Next to me, Jackie leaped off the sofa. "The Bullards! I forgot to call them back!"

I'd forgotten who the Bullards were altogether. I started to ask, then recalled that they were the Melchers' next-door neighbors. Jackie raced off to get the cordless phone.

Paul was stacking more magazines and old newspapers. "I really should put these in the recycling bin. Jackie always forgets." He gave me a sheepish smile.

For a few minutes we spoke of matters other than murder. I asked Paul if there was any truth to the rumor that ITT Rayonier might close its local plant. He admitted to being edgy about the company's future in the area but confided that his dream was to set up his own consulting engineer's business. If his job disappeared down the road, he and Jackie would stay in Port Angeles. A free house was too good to pass up.

"You could sell it," I pointed out. "Once you've got it fixed up, it'll be worth quite a bit of money."

Paul presented me with his most earnest face. "We like it here. We're out of the big-city rat race. It'll be a great place to raise a family. The house is wonderful, really. Even with the skeleton."

I admired Paul's practical approach. I was saying so when Jackie returned to the den carrying her purse. "Let's go. Flint Bullard's in the nursing home by the college. I called Mike again and he'll meet us there."

"Whoa!" Paul raised his hands. "I don't do nursing homes. They depress me. And who's Flint Bullard?"

Jackie stamped her foot. "Mr. Bullard's father. He's ninety-eight and he used to be the sheriff. Or something like that. Come on, Mike will be waiting."

But Paul was obstinate. He'd worked all day; he needed to unwind; he had to shower before we went to dinner; he couldn't stand the way nursing homes smelled. At last, Jackie and I started off by ourselves. We got as far as the door when Vida called.

"Ed!" she shrieked into the phone. "Ed's a ninny! I've always said so!"

"Yes," I agreed, trying to keep calm, "you're right, but why did he quit?"

Vida made some grumbling noises, then settled into her response. "I told you he had an appointment Monday afternoon. It turns out it was with an attorney in the Doukas firm, that new fellow, Sibley. They've expanded, you know. We did a small story last May. Two new attorneys, Sibley and a woman named Foxx. Two x'es."

"I remember," I interrupted, waiting for Vida to stop refreshing my memory and get to the point. "What about Ed? Remember Ed?"

"Of course I remember Ed! Though I'd like to forget." Vida was being testy again. "As I was saying before you broke in, Ed had a four o'clock appointment in the Clemans Building with this Sibley. He—Ed, not Sibley—was notified that his aunt Hilda—Ed's aunt, not Sibley's—had died in Cedar Falls, Iowa, and left him two million dollars! In hog stock! Imagine! It figures, the hog part! Ed looks like such a pig! So does Shirley! I'm *wild*!"

I leaned on the kitchen counter, as dismayed as Vida. Or almost. "Two million. My word!" I could hear Vida panting at the other end of the line. "So Ed took early retirement?"

Vida snorted. "If you can call it that. The man's not yet fifty. Besides, as far as I'm concerned, except for his brief flurry of activity these past few weeks, Ed retired years ago."

There was some truth to Vida's allegations. I looked up to see Jackie leaning against the back door, an impatient expression on her face. "So that's why Ed was humming?"

"It certainly was," Vida replied. "I don't know why he didn't tell me straight off. I don't know why I didn't hear about it sooner. Three days, and Ed has to tell me himself! My niece Stacey is seeing the young man who drives the Federal Express truck that makes deliveries at the law office. She's a dud!" Vida's scorn for her niece almost curdled my ear.

"Well," I said, trying to ignore Jackie's mounting impatience, "we need a new ad manager. I'll call the Washington Newspaper Association first thing tomorrow and see if they have anyone looking for a job."

Vida's tone turned conspiratorial. "Where are you, Emma? All Ginny gave me was this phone number with a Port Angeles prefix. Are you in a love nest?"

I laughed. "No, Vida, I'm staying with friends while my car gets fixed. I'll explain it all when I get back, which will probably be tomorrow. I know I was supposed to come home tonight, but there've been some complications, mainly due to the Jag. It broke."

"Oh." Vida turned vague. She knew little about cars and cared less. Her big white Buick owed its reliability to Cal Vickers's Texaco station. "I suppose you've wasted your money. I· hope you haven't wasted your time, too."

This wasn't the moment to contradict Vida. Jackie was collapsing in the doorway, her eyes rolled back and her figure limp. Either her patience was at the end of its tether or she was fainting. Knowing Jackie, I suspected the former.

"I've got to run, Vida," I said, making an encouraging motion to Jackie. I had a final question for my House & Home editor. "Did Crazy Eights come down from the tree?"

"No," Vida retorted. "He won't until Milo gets a warrant for the bear."

I laughed, somewhat feebly. "I'll see you tomorrow. I hope. Give Milo my love."

"I certainly will not. You don't mean it. And if you do," Vida went on with fire in her voice, "you haven't been thinking properly, if at all. You were supposed to go to the ocean and watch the waves roll in. It sounds as if you've been gallivanting around the peninsula. You'd better spend the evening in solitude and do some soul-searching. Otherwise, you've wasted your days off and I've wasted my breath."

My smile was rueful as I replaced the phone. *The Alpine Advocate* had suffered in my absence and would require a large dose of editorial medicine upon my return. But Vida sounded like herself. Maybe the world wasn't coming to an end after all.

The receptionist at the nursing home informed us that Mike Randall had left a message. He was sorry, but he'd gotten tied up in an emergency faculty meeting. If he finished before five, he'd show up in Flint Bullard's room; if not, he'd meet us at Downriggers.

The corridor of the nursing home was lined with frail residents leaning on walkers. Wrinkled faces with vacant expressions stared up at us from wheelchairs. A few of the oldsters offered vague, hopeful smiles. I smiled back. On the rare occasions when I visit nursing homes, I always vow I'll come back soon. But I never do. I go away and close the door, shutting out the old folks who are left behind, waiting to die. I forget about them, like everybody else, including their children. They remind me of my future, and they shove mortality in my face.

Flint Bullard was propped up in a narrow bed under an artificial light that mocked the summer sunshine. Unlike the others, he didn't seem to welcome company. His watery eyes were suspicious as Jackie breezed over to his bed. I envisioned her wringing his hand and sending him into paroxysms of arthritic pain. But for once she reined in her enthusiasm and merely introduced us.

"You see," she said, pulling up a chair and sitting down, "Ms. Lord and I are researching the house that my husband inherited. It's next door to where you used to live."

Relieved that Jackie was telling the truth for once, more or less, I borrowed the visitor's chair from the next bed. There was no occupant at present, though a name tag reading "Hansen, George" was pinned on the wall. There was also a schedule, showing that Mr. Hansen was due in occupational therapy from four-thirty to five-thirty.

"The Rowley house," growled Flint Bullard. His deep bass voice belied his thin frame. His feet reached almost to the end of the bed, and despite the sunken cheeks and cavernous chest, I felt that he had once been a hulk of a man. "Then the Melchers. You're one of 'em, huh?" He didn't seem to approve.

Jackie wasn't discouraged. "Do you remember any of them? The early-day Rowleys and Melchers, I mean."

Swiftly, I calculated Flint Bullard's age in terms of Cornelius Rowley and his family. If Flint was ninety-eight, he'd been born in 1897. He would have been ten or eleven when Cornelius died, when the Malones allegedly left Port Angeles, and when Simone disappeared.

"Cornelius was a big shot," Flint declared with disgust. "His wife was a looker, though. But snooty. I don't know why—she couldn't even speak English so good. Hey," he said, gesturing at a water carafe on the nightstand, "hand me that thing. Just stick a straw in it."

Jackie complied, and Flint Bullard slurped up what seemed like a large amount of water. "The livery stable was in back of the house, up above, on the bluff. Still there, I guess, falling down. Good view property, too. Don't know why somebody doesn't buy it up and build a couple of houses. Make a mint." Flint handed the carafe back to Jackie.

"They probably would," Jackie said agreeably. "Now when you lived next door . . ."

Flint was shaking his head. "It wasn't the same house. Our first one burned down back in Oh-eight. We rebuilt, bigger, better. I moved out in 1917 to get married. I was working for the sheriff then, but thought I'd join the army and go over to fight the Huns. Never did. Had enough excitement right here to keep me down on the farm, as they used to say. You hear of the big windstorm of Twenty-one?"

Jackie started to shake her head, but Flint ran right over her. "Blew down five billion board-feet of overripe timber in Clallam and Jefferson Counties. Hell of a mess. There were big fights between the loggers trying to haul that blow-down out of the woods." He gave me a hard-eyed look, and I wondered if that was how he'd gotten to be known as Flint. "You say you're from Alpine? We had some of those numskulls come all the way over to the peninsula trying to horn in on the deal. Sonsabitches. They ran like Billy-Be-Damned when I waved my forty-five at 'em."

"Actually," I began in a mild voice, "we were more interested in the years before the war. . . ."

Flint was chuckling. "Same year that the Zellerbachs came to town. Decent people, in their way. Tom Aldwell was trying to sell that parcel of land where Ediz Hook starts. Good man, Tom. Not a blowhard like Rowley and some of the rest. The Zellerbachs weren't sure there was enough good timber to make it worth their while to build a mill. Some jackasses from Snohomish barged in and almost queered the deal. But the mill got built, and it was here for a long time. Now we got the Japs there. What's it called? Dish Chow? Dog Show? To hell with them!" Again his tone conveyed disgust.

The impatience that Jackie had displayed before we left the house resurfaced. "Just a minute, Mr. Bullard. We didn't come here to listen to you spout off about local history. No offense, but we want to find out about the Rowleys and the Melchers."

Flint Bullard bristled. He wagged a gnarled finger at Jackie. "You're missing all the good stuff. Bank robbers. Rumrunners. Bodies in Lake Crescent. You know it's bottomless? Sooner or later everything, including the stiffs, rises to the top."

"Yes," Jackie replied briskly. "All that's fascinating. But it doesn't help Paul and me with the history of our house. Tell us about Jimmy Malone."

Flint Bullard frowned, then his murky eyes lit up. "Smooth-Bore Malone? Hell of a guy. Those old-time loggers were quite a crew. Weather never bothered 'em.

Didn't know pain. And how they could eat! And drink!
Bull Sling Bill, Box Car Pete, Seattle Red, Haywire
Tom Newton. Now those were *real* men." After taking
another drink, Flint fell back against the pillow, a hand
on his chest.

I had been quiet for quite a while. I decided it was
time to jump-start this seemingly unproductive interview. "Was Smooth-Bore Malone crazy about the
Rowley girl?" I inquired, trying to speak Flint's lan-
guage.

He tipped his head to one side. "Oh—I suppose so.
Crazy about her daddy's money, anyway. Jimmy'd
come a-courting in his Sunday best, which wasn't
much. I saw him one time show up in his logging boots
and tin pants. We—my pals and I—would call him
Paddy and serenade him when he'd show up to call on
Miss Carrie. We'd sing 'My Wild Irish Nose.' It was a
takeoff. You know, a joke. Some of the bigger kids
thought it up."

"Right." I forced a smile. "That's cute. How did
Cornelius feel about Jimmy wooing his daughter?"

"Hell if I know." Flint Bullard was looking up at the
big clock on the opposite wall. "It's almost five. They'll
be bringing supper around pretty quick. You two almost
finished?"

Jackie and I exchanged quick glances. "Minnie
Burke," Jackie said. "Do you remember her?"

Flint made a face. "The parlormaid? Cook? No . . .
she was a what-dya-call-it. Nurserymaid? She watched
the Malone kids. Or was she the hoity-toity missus's
lady's maid? I forget."

Jackie proffered more water. "Was Minnie pretty?"

Flint waved the carafe away. He was growing restless
and seemed to have his gaze fixed on the doorway.
"Pretty? Yeah, pretty enough. Saw her knickers once.
Red-gold curls and an itty-bitty waist." A dreamy ex-

pression crossed Flint's seamed face. "Or was her hair dark red? I think she got fat. Most women did, in those days. My wife was six axe-handles across before she was forty."

Jackie was beginning to twitch, too. "What happened to her?"

"My wife? Got cancer and died twenty years ago. I tried to teach myself to cook, but it wasn't any good. I ate out all the time till I came to this godforsaken place." Flint's gaunt features were etched with aggravation.

Jackie gritted her teeth before she spoke. "I meant Minnie Burke. You must have been around when she . . . went away."

The watery eyes glared at Jackie. "She went away? Probably did. I don't recall. After the fire we moved over to Ennis Creek while the new place was being built. When we got back, everything had changed."

I inched forward on my chair. "Everything? Like what?"

Flint gave an indifferent shrug. His face was masked with boredom. "What I said. Old Cornelius was dead, Smooth-Bore and his family had moved, the Frenchie was gone, too. I suppose Minnie Burke went with 'em. No real loss—she was another foreigner you couldn't understand half the time. The only ones left were Eddie Rowley and that old bat he married. And her namby-pamby son. Eddie was all right, but I steered clear of the rest of 'em. The old girl—Lena was her name, but you had to call her Mrs. Rowley. *Everybody* had to kowtow to that one. She was always ranting and raving about this cause or that. I'll say one thing for her, she pitched in when we put through the port bond issue back in Twenty-five. Old Lena helped close down all the businesses that day to man the polls and get out the vote. There was a few that didn't like it, but we gave notice that their opinion wasn't real popular." Jerkily, Flint sat up. His thin fingers clawed at the sheets. "Where's that grub? They're late."

Giving Jackie a discreet nod, I stood up. But I had one last question for Flint Bullard. "When was the fire that burned down your first house?"

The old man answered promptly. "September sixth, 1908. We moved back in the day before Christmas, same year. As fires go, it wasn't much, just enough to put us out of house and home. Now back in Oh-seven, there was one hell of a forest fire in the Sol Duc Valley. . . ."

We thanked Flint Bullard for his time and trouble. He didn't say that we were welcome. With a querulous gesture he muttered something about a "bunch of bullshit. Nobody wants to hear about the important stuff. . . ."

Eager to escape, I almost fell over the tiny figure leaning on a metal cane. In the process of righting the little old woman, Jackie ran into me. We staggered and struggled, gaining the attention of two elderly men and a nurse's aide.

I apologized, but the old lady didn't seem perturbed. "I was listening in. Why not?" she demanded in a wispy, lisping voice. "What else is there to do in this place except make scrapbooks and play bingo? I've never been one for worthless pastimes."

"It's fine," I said hastily. I couldn't say much else, being an eavesdropper by profession.

"He's such a windbag," the old lady declared. The wispiness of her voice didn't detract from the accusation. "I'm Clara Haines." She put out a birdlike hand.

The cart containing the supper trays was moving toward us. Jackie and I stepped aside. Clara didn't budge. "I've known Flint since he was knee-high to a grasshopper," she went on as the orderly rerouted his cart.

"He's a conceited bully. What did you want to know about Minnie Burke?"

Swiftly, I glanced at Jackie. She was looking startled but game. "Is there somewhere we can sit down?" I inquired of Clara Haines.

The visitors' lounge was just around the corner at the end of a short hall. At this time of day it was empty. We sat on turquoise Naugahyde chairs and noted the view of the strait. Clara reached into the pocket of her housecoat and pulled out her dentures.

"My lower plate," she announced, then inserted it in her mouth. "It rubs my gum. I've got a sore spot right here." She pointed to her wrinkled cheek.

It was well after five and I was growing anxious to leave the nursing home. The arrival of the food cart hadn't improved the smell that clung to the atmosphere like a noxious fog. In theory my heart went out to these old folks; in practice I was antsy to get back to a world that included dinner in a restaurant with a view.

But Clara Haines wasn't one to dwell on herself. Neither did she seem interested in who we were. Or maybe she had been lurking at the door long enough to know.

"I knew Minnie," she said. "I'm not going to tell you how old I am, but when I was a girl, I lived down the street from the Rowleys and the Bullards. The house is gone, but we had berry vines all over the backyard and my brother and I used to sell them to the neighbors. Five cents a box. Blackberries, mostly, but some raspberries and boysenberries, too. Mrs. Rowley—the French wife—loved raspberries. It was Minnie, though, who bought them for her. That was because Minnie was the one out in the yard watching the children." Clara Haines paused, adjusting her dentures.

"Minnie was a livewire, quick to laugh. She was a hard worker, too, especially for a little thing. You can imagine that with two Mrs. Rowleys and one Mrs.

Malone, it wasn't easy to satisfy the women of the house. Minnie had that Irish brogue, and sometimes my brother and I didn't always understand her jokes. Teasing was more like it. We were sorry to see her go."

A couple in their middle fifties escorted a large woman with sparse white hair into the lounge. They nodded, then sat in the farthest corner from us. I suspected that they had stopped by after work to call on Mother.

"Where did Minnie go?" Jackie asked, sounding a bit breathless.

"I don't know," Clara replied, frowning. "Flint Bullard was right about that part. After Mr. Rowley died, it seemed as if most of the family—including Minnie—went away. We hadn't called on the neighbors after the berry season in August, but that fall my folks were hard up and my mother decided to sell some of her jam to make ends meet. We took a wagon filled with jars around town, but Mrs. Rowley's maid slammed the door in our faces. That was Mrs. *Edmund* Rowley I'm speaking of. The other Mrs. Rowley was gone, so was Mrs. Malone, and Minnie, too. My brother and I didn't bother to go back the next summer."

The time frame was shrinking. Cornelius Rowley had died in May; Clara had peddled her berries in August; the Bullard house burned in September; the departing family members were gone by December when the Bullards returned.

"Do you remember exactly when you were selling the jam?" I asked.

"Not exactly." Clara wiggled her jaw. "It must have been in late October because the leaves were on the ground. My brother was younger and I recall having to speak to him about rolling around in the piles that had been raked up. We didn't have many spare clothes if he ruined what he was wearing."

I tried to guess Clara Haines's age. She was remarkably unlined, especially for such a thin woman. I doubted that she was five feet tall. Her shoulders were faintly stooped, and she had walked to the lounge with a pronounced limp. Still, her mind seemed as clear as her hazel eyes. If she had known Flint Bullard forever, she must be at least as old as he was. Even older since she'd implied as much. Clara had to be a hundred. I marveled at her well-being.

While I was marveling, Jackie was interrogating. "Was the second Mrs. Rowley a good wife? Were Carrie and Jimmy Malone a happy couple? What about Minnie? Did she have a boyfriend?"

"My, my!" Clara fanned herself with her hand. "One thing at a time, dear. I couldn't tell you about Mrs. Cornelius Rowley. I don't think my mother approved of her, though. But of course she was young, beautiful, and foreign. That made a difference in how she was accepted in those days. As for Carrie Rowley, I know she doted on that Irishman. Oh, yes, some people thought she married him out of desperation—afraid of being an old maid—but my impression is that she loved him quite madly." Clara Haines stopped abruptly. Her hazel eyes were keen as she eyed us both in turn. "You must find me a loquacious old woman. I hope this is the sort of thing you're interested in."

"It's perfect," enthused Jackie. "It's wonderful of you to remember so much! I suppose that happens when you've lived forever in a small town."

"Oh, but I haven't." Clara came close to a smile but didn't quite make it. Maybe she didn't trust her teeth. "I spent forty years teaching astronomy at USC. I didn't move back here until long after I retired. I won't say when. Los Angeles became so difficult. Port Angeles is a better place for the elderly. They're coming here in droves."

There was no need to steer Clara back to the subject at hand. "Now Jimmy Malone was another matter. I think he was looking for the main chance. Or so my parents felt. An opportunist. To be fair, he seemed to treat Carrie well. He had to, I suppose, since she was the one with the money. And Jimmy was living under the scrutiny—not to mention thumb—of his in-laws."

"I don't get it," Jackie said, wearing a very serious look on her face. "Why didn't they move into a place of their own, especially after they started having children? I'd hate that, living with my relatives."

Clara nodded with understanding. "How very true. There was talk that they were building a house, first on Pine Hill, then on the bluff overlooking the strait, and finally way out by Morse Creek. Nothing ever came of the plans and they left town. Perhaps it was just as well. I don't think Carrie got along with her sister-in-law, Lena."

"And Minnie?" Jackie urged. "Did she create any problems for Carrie and Jimmy?"

"Minnie?" Clara's hazel eyes widened. "Are you suggesting that Minnie and Jimmy were romantically linked?" Clara paused briefly. Jackie gave a nod; I remained silent. "I understand why you might think so. They were both from Ireland, but so were a great many others at the time. Indeed, I have a vague sense that they may have courted early on. But once Carrie took a fancy to Jimmy, he wouldn't have given Minnie the time of day. Besides, she had her sights set on someone else. Perhaps she was an opportunist, too. You can't blame those emigrants. They came to this country to better themselves. Marriage was one way to do it."

"Do you know who Minnie was after?" Jackie was so eager that she ran the words together.

"Oh, certainly," Clara Haines replied blithely. "Sanford Melcher. My mother always wondered why it didn't work out."

Chapter Twelve

MY TRAVEL WARDROBE was limited. I hadn't expected to eat anywhere fancier than a pancake house. For Downriggers I would have to make do with a cotton denim shirt and a pair of khaki cotton slacks. The only outerwear I'd brought along was a black gabardine battle jacket. Fortunately, I wasn't out to make a fashion statement.

Dressing quickly, I had time to make a phone call. An idea had been brewing at the back of my mind ever since I'd left Oak Bay. I went downstairs very quietly, not wanting to alert Jackie and Paul. They were still in the master bedroom getting dressed. I was particularly concerned that Paul not know what I was about to do.

I took the cordless phone into the music parlor, where I'd have greater privacy should my hosts come down before I finished my call. It was after six, and I knew that Sheriff Milo Dodge was on night duty this week. I also knew that he was usually bored stiff. Criminal activity in Alpine comes to a virtual halt during the dinner hour. Even the speeders slow down as dusk descends over the mountains.

I had not confided in Milo about why I was taking my little trip. I couldn't, since he was part of the reason for it. Maybe I expected him to be thrilled to hear my voice. He wasn't.

"Where the hell are you?" he asked in that laconic

169

drawl I knew so well. "I was just going over to the Venison Inn to grab a steak."

"I'm in Port Angeles researching a story," I half lied. "I need a favor. You aren't in the middle of a big drug bust or hauling in local Mafia dons, are you?"

"I'm in the middle of a crossword puzzle. What's a four-letter word for *sluggish*?"

"M-i-l-o," I responded. "Or it will be, if you don't shut up and listen. I don't have much time."

I heard the sound of a newspaper being folded. "Okay, what is it?"

"I want you to check on criminal records for the following people." I gave him the list of names I'd put together in my head. "All of these will be from a long time ago, maybe back seventy years or more. Can you do that from your database hookup?"

Milo groaned. "Sure, and then I can go find Crazy Eights Neffel's invisible bear and serve him with a warrant. Damn it, Emma, you're as crazy as he is. This'll take all night."

"So what else are you doing, Sheriff?" I actually lowered myself to uttering a throaty laugh.

It was lost on Milo. "Who knows? Maintaining law and order, I hope." He sounded truculent. "I'm not sure I can pull records on a statewide basis that go back this far."

"Try. Please?" I turned meek.

"I'll see," he grumbled. "Don't count on it. If I do, you owe me two steaks and a fifth of Scotch."

"Done. I promise. You want candlelight, too?"

"Is that how you plan to cook the steaks?"

"Never mind. I'll barbecue. Afterward, I'll help you with your crossword puzzle. 'Bye, Milo." I disconnected the sheriff. Milo should have asked me for a five-letter word for *evasion*. It would have been d-o-d-g-e, in more ways than one.

* * *

Downriggers was located in a mall by the city pier and the Chamber of Commerce. The view was predictably spectacular and the menu was pleasantly varied. The specialties included steaks and seafood. I chose salmon, which I hoped was fresh—and not left over from the run before the killer whales arrived.

Mike Randall was wearing a tie, which surprised me. I wondered if he thought we were on a double date. He apologized again for missing our session at the nursing home. Jackie and I spent the cocktail round relating our interviews with Flint Bullard and Clara Haines.

Paul was taken by his grandfather's alleged romance with Minnie Burke. "Just think, if he'd married her instead of Grandma Rose, I wouldn't be here. That's amazing when you think about the quirks of fate."

"Well, you *are* here," Jackie said, fondling her glass of mineral water, "and that's not the point. Why didn't Sanford marry Minnie? I think she left Port Angeles with a broken heart."

"She mended it if she married Jimmy Malone," I pointed out. "Remember, we're getting all of this via hearsay. Clara Haines is a very sharp old lady, but she's relying mostly on what her parents told her. And that was mainly neighborhood gossip."

Jackie was perusing the menu for the third time. "I still think we've solved the mystery. Jimmy Malone loved Minnie, but he wanted Carrie's money. Maybe Minnie flirted with Sanford to throw everybody off-guard. You know, a blind. I'm thinking about the halibut now."

I was thinking about the view, or, rather, enjoying it. *The Coho* was making its last run of the day, just pulling into the nearby slip. One of the freighters I'd seen yesterday was still moored in the harbor. The other was anchored at the marine terminal to our left. In the opposite direction a group of bicyclists were getting ready to pedal off down the waterfront trail. The Hook jutted out across from us, sheltering a handful of pleasurecraft heading for the marina.

Upon our arrival, *The Victoria Express* had been making its six-thirty sailing. I'd thought about Leo Walsh and wondered if he was sitting in a bar somewhere, drowning his sorrows. Or maybe he'd gone off to a high bluff to jump and was just plain drowning. It was an unsettling idea. It occurred to me that I hadn't mentioned Leo to Jackie. But why should I? We'd had plenty of other things to discuss.

"You're drifting, Emma." Jackie reached across the table and tugged at my denim sleeve. "What do you think about Lena and Minnie?"

I gave myself a good shake. "Lena and Minnie? As a couple? What?"

Jackie giggled. "No, as in Lena disapproving of Minnie. For Sanford. Hatchet Face wouldn't have liked her son marrying a servant, would she?"

Mike came to my rescue. "Lena may have been a believer in equality and women's rights, but given her era she would have been very class conscious in spite of herself. I have to agree with Jackie. Lena would have frowned on a relationship between Sanford and Minnie."

Paul stroked the stem of his wineglass. "Let's not gloss over anything. This Clara Haines said Jimmy and Minnie actually dated, right?"

"Courted," Jackie quoted. "That's what they called dating in the olden days, Lamb-love."

"I know that, Sweets," Paul replied patiently. "What I'm saying is that Minnie had a history with Jimmy. That's why it'll be interesting to find out what turns up in the King County marriage licenses."

"A New York steak," Jackie said. "That sounds good,

with mushrooms and a green salad and a baked potato with butter and sour cream and bacon bits and chives." She gave all three of us a defiant look but spoke again before we could object. "I'm thinking Jimmy wasn't a bigamist. That golden wedding anniversary story was a fraud. I mean, Minnie and Jimmy got married after they left Port Angeles. But because they passed the first three kids—by Carrie—off as their own, they had to pretend they were married in 1903. So they just added five or six years on to the time they were really married to cover those kids' birth dates. Besides, they got their presents sooner that way. In fact, they wouldn't have gotten them at all if they'd waited for the real anniversary because they were both dead by then." Jackie glanced back at the menu. "I could get the green salad that comes with shrimp. That sounds good, too."

The waitress came to take our order. Jackie asked to go last; she still hadn't made up her mind. Mike joined me in ordering salmon, and Paul requested the petit filet medium well. To my surprise, Jackie asked for the sautéed prawns. They hadn't even been in the running up until then.

Mike traded his vodka martini in for a glass of Riesling; Paul went with a red instead of the white wine he'd been drinking; I decided to get wild and have another CC, water back; Jackie asked for Sprite.

"We've narrowed this down quite a bit," I pointed out after the waitress had gone off with our requests. "The big change in the family status must have taken place between early September and late October of 1908. That's about a five- or six-week period. I think it's amazing that we've been able to zero in like that."

"Absolutely." Mike Randall smiled at me as if I'd won the Nobel Prize. "I realize there's a certain amount of luck involved, but basically it's a question of research and following leads. I'm astounded at how you can ask the right questions and get the necessary answers."

"It's what I get paid for," I retorted, then felt a twinge of remorse. I smiled weakly at Mike. "You're right about the luck. Finding all those old folks has been a real help. Of course people are living much longer these days."

Now it was Paul who seemed to be off in his own little corner of the world. There were chickenlike marks on his cocktail napkin. Replacing his ballpoint pen in his pocket, he acknowledged the arrival of his red wine with an absent nod. "The timing is interesting, I guess, but I don't see that it adds much to figuring things out. We still don't know what happened to Simone."

Mike sipped thoughtfully at his wine. "We don't have any data on those bones yet."

I'd forgotten about the spare parts. "Where are they?" I asked.

"I gave them to the zoology teacher," Mike said. "I assumed they were from a small animal. She'll get back to me tonight or in the morning."

Jackie was stuffing sourdough bread in her mouth. She swallowed hard and clapped her hands. "We need to go to the library again tomorrow. If we take that six weeks in 1908 and concentrate on the local newspapers, we might find more clues." She looked at me. "Well? What time do they open?"

"Jackie," I began, shaking my head, "if my Jag's ready, I'll be gone. I've got a big crisis facing me at work."

Next to me, Mike leaned closer. "Really? That's terrible news, Emma. Tell us about it. Maybe you can sort through your feelings by verbalizing them."

I glommed on to my fresh Canadian Club. "I can tell you my feelings without any problem. I'm up a stump. My ad manager quit and half the town is ticked off because we screwed up. There's a special edition due out next Wednesday and not enough to fill it, editorial or advertising. If anybody here has fourteen hundred column inches of ads or eight hundred inches of copy, I'll walk out with a big grin."

Mike gave me a confidential smile. "You see? Don't you feel better? You've laid it all out."

"No," I responded, trying not to sound tart. "I didn't. Carla did, and that's part of the problem." Noting Mike's puzzlement, I took pity on him. "Look, it's nothing I can talk out. I have to *do* it, and that's impossible unless I'm on the scene. That's why I have to head back to Alpine tomorrow."

The hurt expression on Mike's face made me feel like a world-class worm. He meant well, I knew that. But his buzzword comfort was driving me nuts. I had a terrible urge to rush to a pay phone and call my brother, Ben. Or Vida. I missed Vida, even when she was huffing and harrumphing at me. Vida at her worst was an improvement over most people at their best. But I'd never dare tell her so. She'd fix me with her gimlet eye and mutter something that would feature the word *fool*.

Mike Randall was nodding, a font of understanding. "You've prioritized. That's so important. It's a sign of real maturity."

I might have screamed if our salads hadn't arrived just then. Jackie attacked hers with the verve of a rabbit, but she wasn't about to give up on me.

"I'll make you a deal, Emma. If you stay until noon, I won't bother you ever again. We'll go to the library first thing, at ten. I'm pretty sure that's when they open. Or call that Tessie Whoozits and ask her to let us in early."

I shook my head. "She's a genealogist, not a librarian."

"Whatever." Jackie forked up more lettuce. "I'll bet

she'd be able to dig up something that would help us now that we know more. Why don't we call her tonight?"

I started to protest, then reconsidered. Tessie Roo had been intrigued by our little mystery. If she could add anything to it, we might be able to wrap things up before morning. Then I could flee Port Angeles with a clear conscience.

I agreed. "I'll call her after we finish dinner."

Jackie's dimples flashed at me. Paul smiled at Jackie. Mike nodded sagely. I drank my Canadian Club to the dregs.

The pay phones were located just off the restaurant's lounge. Tessie was the only Roo in the local phone book. She answered on the second ring. Her delight in hearing from me warmed my heart.

"I thought you'd forgotten all about me!" she declared in that husky, engaging voice. "I was dying to hear what happened with Claudia Malone Cameron. Can you come by and have a glass of sherry?"

After two stiff CC's, I didn't need to add sherry to the list. I also didn't want to inflict the others on Tessie. I wasn't exactly sure how to proceed.

"Is there any way I could meet you at your office later on?" I inquired. "Say in about a half hour?" Jackie and Paul had ordered dessert; Mike Randall was sipping cognac. Perhaps the Melchers could drop me off at the museum. I could walk back to their house. The fresh air would do me good.

Tessie, however, volunteered to pick me up. I informed her I wasn't at the Melcher house but finishing dinner at Downriggers. We agreed to rendezvous on the museum steps at nine o'clock.

I was hanging up the phone when I heard a gust of laughter erupt in the bar. I turned to see what had caused the hilarity. A group of young men in their late twenties were sitting at a big table, apparently indulging themselves in the joys of youth and beer. I would have gone off without another glance if I hadn't seen a familiar figure hunched over the bar. Even from this murky distance I recognized Leo Walsh. That same aspect had been presented to me earlier aboard *The Victoria Express.*

I'd like to think it was my innate compassion that propelled me into the lounge. More likely it was the two CC's that did it. To be fair, I'd devoured a considerable amount of food since having the drinks and I was feeling quite sober. Often I have trouble giving myself the benefit of the doubt.

Boldly, I sidled up to Leo. The bar stool next to him was empty. He was drinking something on the rocks. Judging from the pale color, it was Scotch.

"Hi," I said. "How come you're not headed back to Culver City?"

Leo wasn't really drunk yet, but he was working on it. "Emma Lord, as I live and drink." He raised his glass to me. "What'll it be? Hot coffee?"

"Sounds good." Briefly, I questioned my sanity. Jackie and the men would wonder where I'd gone. But they were engaged in dessert and cognac. If concerned, they'd figure I was still talking to Tessie Roo.

The prompt arrival of my coffee caused Leo to order another Scotch. "You don't give up easy, do you?" His gaze was sardonic.

"I left the brandy cask in the parking lot," I said lightly. "Have you been here since you got off the boat?"

Leo sighed. Somehow, it was a painful sound. "I had dinner." He tapped the bar. "Here. Oysters. Not bad. You find any stray dogs?"

I shook my head. "No. Just a dead body." I bit my

tongue. Why had I said such a thing? Why didn't I drink my coffee and go back to the dining area? Why was I such an idiot?

"Oh, yeah?" Leo smirked, then lit a cigarette. The ashtray was already overflowing. "Anybody we know?"

"I'm not sure." I wasn't sure of anything, especially why I was sitting at the bar with Leo Walsh. His fresh drink arrived; I sipped my coffee. "Leo, where are you staying?"

He stared at me, then puffed on his cigarette. Deliberately, he blew smoke in my face. "You want to join me for a night of passion?"

"Drop dead, Leo." My voice was sharp, then I shook my head. "You bother me. I don't know what to say."

He rubbed at his crooked nose. "I've got a room at a motel out on 101. It's clean. It's cheap. It's lonely." A brief, poignant silence grew between us. "Hey," he barked, "go away, honey. You're a doll, and I could get to like you. You might get to like me, and then we'd both be miserable. Drink your coffee and go feed that stray dog."

The perverse streak in my nature dictated that I stay put. "Who are you, Leo? Why are you here? What makes you such a jerk?"

He stood up, drank his Scotch down in one gulp, stubbed out his half-smoked cigarette, and threw a twenty-dollar bill on the bar. "Whatever it is, you're too nice to know. So long, Emma Lord. Enjoy your dead body. It's probably got more life in it than I have." Leo lurched out of the lounge.

Tessie Roo was waiting for me in the shadow of the old courthouse dome. Jackie had wanted to come with me, but Paul had insisted that she go home and rest. Mike also expressed a desire to meet with Tessie. I fibbed a bit, saying that the genealogist would be upset to find anyone other than me on hand.

Tessie was raring to go. She had come prepared with a thermos of hot tea. But when we got up to her office, I had to confess that I might have brought her out on a fool's errand.

"It's the early newspapers I need more than the genealogy records," I told Tessie after recapping the day's investigation. "I don't suppose you have access to the library's periodical room?"

Tessie tossed her head. "I don't need it. Not for that era." She scooted over to an oak filing cabinet and began hauling out faded binders. "I don't have all the papers from that period, but I've got the principal publications. That's how I do my research. I can't be running back and forth to the library all the time, eh?"

The binders contained yellowed copies of *The Olympic-Leader* and *The Tribune-Times*. I suggested that Tessie take the former and I go through the latter. We settled on August 1908 as our starting point.

I expected that our first item of interest would be the Bullard house fire. However, I was determined to go over every inch of local news copy. Both papers were weeklies, which minimized the task.

The first reference I found was in the August fifth edition. Mr. and Mrs. Edmund Rowley were going to San Francisco for a visit. Mrs. Rowley wished to see firsthand how the city had rebuilt since the earthquake of two years earlier. Briefly, I pictured Eddie, leaning on his cane, while Lena surveyed the recovering city from Nob Hill.

"Ah!" Tessie tapped a page of *The Olympic-Leader*. "Here's a burglary at the Rowley house, reported on August fourteenth. The house apparently was broken into after dark. Jewelry, cash, and liquor were stolen.

The actual robbery was thought to have taken place on August eleventh."

"Eddie and Lena were probably out of town then," I mused. "Who would have been home? Simone? Jimmy and Carrie? Sanford? Minnie Burke and the rest of the servants?"

"That's a lot of people on hand," Tessie noted. "The burglars must have been bold as brass." She bent over the binder again and we grew silent. "It seems there was a series of robberies about that time. On August twenty-first three more were reported, fairly close by."

I found a brief story about the Rowley mill in the August 26 issue of *The Tribune-Times*. It was of little interest, merely stating the number of board feet that had been shipped during the first six months of the year.

With a sense of satisfaction Tessie noted that the burglar had been caught on August twenty-seventh while attempting to enter a house on Pine Hill. He was a twenty-two-year-old unemployed logger from Pysht. The crime wave appeared to be over.

The Bullard fire made both papers. By publishing two days earlier in the week, *The Tribune-Times* scooped *The Olympic-Leader*. Both reports made much of the blaze, describing flames "one hundred feet into the night sky" and "sparks flying like comets in every direction."

I read part of my account to Tessie.

Neighboring houses, including the stone and stucco mansion built by the late Cornelius Rowley, were in constant danger. Residents huddled in the street, anguished over the Bullards' loss and fearful for their own homes. Horses were evacuated from the nearby livery stable, after the terrified animals had first been blindfolded.

According to *The Tribune-Times,* it had taken over three hours to extinguish the flames. The fire had been started by an overturned oil lamp. The loss was estimated at almost three thousand dollars.

Having been scooped by its rival, *The Olympic-Leader* relied on the human aspects of the tragedy. " 'Mr. and Mrs. Fred Bullard and their children were stunned by the disaster,' " Tessie read to me. " 'Their daughter, Marguerite, and their son, Cosmo, were seen clinging to their mother's skirts and weeping.' "

Grinning, I interrupted Tessie. "Flint's real name is *Cosmo*?"

Tessie nodded. "Flint is for Flintlock. Or so I remember." She continued with the article.

A great fear erupted at one point during the evening when members of the neighboring household realized that two-year-old Walter Malone was missing. The child's father, James Malone, went in frantic search of the youngster. Little Walter was found a few minutes later, safe and sound, in the basement of the Rowley house. The reunion with his parents brought great sighs of relief from bystanders.

Tessie raised her eyebrows. "Interesting, eh?"

"Interesting—or a coincidence?" I remarked. "Is there anything else in that piece about the Rowleys and the Melchers?"

Tessie read down the column. It was a lengthy story. "Yes, there's a quote here about Eddie."

Edmund Rowley was walking from his garage to his house when he first noticed the flames. He was going to report the blaze when he heard the clang of the first fire wagon in the distance. Rushing to the Bullard property, he discovered that the family was already out of the house. He then returned to his own dwelling, where he alerted the household.

I could see Eddie Rowley, limping through the garden, checking on the Bullards, and then going back home to inform Lena and the others of what was happening. It was early September, late summer, and the weather was probably mild. The Rowleys and the Melchers and their staff would have trooped outside. Or so I speculated with Tessie.

"But they didn't," Tessie said. "Not all of them. There's one more note: 'Mrs. Cornelius Rowley, whose late husband built the handsome home next to the Bullards', refused to leave her boudoir. She had been feeling unwell earlier in the day and expressed no alarm over her personal safety.' "

Now I saw the picture of Simone, attired in a flowing negligee, looking not unlike Mme. Recamier reclining on her Grecian-style sofa. The widow had no compassion for the Bullards; she had no fear for herself. "Ego," I noted. "I see her as self-centered, vain, and unable to acknowledge that she, too, was mortal."

"Well . . ." Tessie sounded dubious. "I give you all that, but she might really have been sick."

It was true that I hadn't given Simone credit for any human emotions other than greed, vanity, and possibly infidelity. Yet I was seeing her through the eyes of her contemporaries. As Clara Haines had pointed out, Simone Dupre Rowley would not have had an easy time of it in the Port Angeles of 1908. In any small town, in any era, a newcomer is regarded with suspicion. After almost four years the residents of Alpine still considered me an outsider. I felt a pang of sympathy for Simone.

We returned to our task. There was a follow-up in both papers on the Bullard fire, but the stories were

brief, mainly dealing with the family's vow to rebuild
and their temporary stay at Ennis Creek.

We didn't find anything of interest until I got to the
September twenty-third edition of *The Tribune-Times*. A
stop-press box on the front page was headlined LOCAL
MAN SHOOTS AT INTRUDER.

Edmund Rowley of 820 West Sixth frightened off
an intruder at his home early this morning. Mr.
Rowley, who is assistant superintendent of the
Rowley Lumber Mill, was awakened by strange
sounds around two A.M. He discovered a man lurking
about the garden. Since the Rowley home was bur-
glarized last month, Mr. Rowley's sense of danger
was alerted. Taking his gun outside, he asked the intruder to identify himself. A stream of unintelligible
curses ensued, and Mr. Rowley fired twice into the
air. The man rushed off in the direction of A Street,
presumably heading for sanctuary in the gully. Mr.
Rowley described the intruder as fairly young, above
average height, and weighing about a hundred and
seventy pounds. He was dressed in work clothes and
high boots.

Tessie chortled in her rich manner. "The Rowleys
certainly made the news! Of course, they were prominent, and with so many papers being published in those
days, every little thing probably got reported."

I agreed with Tessie's assessment. I also wondered
why these items hadn't turned up in the periodical file.

Tessie had an explanation. "Those files contain only
major stories on individuals and events. It would be too
hard to cross-reference everything and everybody. You
might have found the Bullard story under *Fires*. Or possibly under *Bullard*. The Rowleys' presence at the scene
wasn't important enough to catalogue. Neither," she

went on, pointing to my binder, "is that bulletin. It would be different if Eddie had shot the fellow."

I understood. Our own file system at *The Advocate* was hit-and-miss. The founder and previous owner, Marius Vandeventer, had kept everything in his head. Our bound volumes were sorted only by year, with an index to major events. Someday I hoped to organize the back issues by subject, but there was never enough time or manpower. Now I had come up short on staff. I couldn't worry about past publications; there were enough problems with the present edition.

The Tribune-Times that came out two days later had a small story about horse thieves. A chestnut mare and a bay gelding had been stolen from the Lincoln Hill livery stable on the night of September twenty-fourth.

"That's the old wreck in back of the Rowley house, isn't it?" I asked Tessie.

She nodded. "That's interesting, too. I wonder if it ties in with the intruder."

It seemed that we had no way of knowing. In subsequent editions there was no reference to the intruder's apprehension or the recovery of the horses. The Rowleys and the Melchers weren't mentioned again until October ninth, when the D.A.R. gratefully accepted a donation of "fashionable ladies' apparel and fripperies" from Lena Stillman Melcher Rowley.

The bells in the courthouse tower had just chimed eleven o'clock when we got to December. For almost two months the Rowley-Melcher family slipped out of the news. Then, in both papers, the engagement of Rose Felder to Sanford Melcher was announced. *The Tribune-Times* ran a picture of the bride-to-be. Rose Felder's fair hair was piled high atop her head in an attempt to compensate for the overly long chin. The effect was sabotaged by the big pearl dog collar around her neck, which served to emphasize the length of her face.

The pose was graceful, however, and the dress had a modest chiffon fichu decorated with more pearls. Rose looked nubile, almost coy. Recalling the later photos of her, I sympathized for what lay ahead.

Mr. and Mrs. Conrad Felder of this city have announced the engagement of their daughter, Rose Anne Felder, to Mr. Sanford Stillman Melcher, the son of Mrs. Edmund Rowley and the late Mr. Ferris Melcher. The couple will be honored at a private fete December nineteenth hosted by the groom's mother and his stepfather, Mr. Edmund Rowley. The wedding is planned for St. Valentine's Day.

The stories in both newspapers were virtually identical. I suspected that they had been submitted not by Mrs. Conrad Felder but Mrs. Edmund Rowley. It should have been up to the bride's family to issue the formal announcement, of course, but Lena would have dashed etiquette aside.

In the final issue of December 1908, we found the item about the Bullards' return to Sixth Street. There was no account of the engagement party. I surmised that Lena had meant what she said about keeping it *private*.

The hot tea had long since been consumed. Traffic out on Lincoln Street had dwindled to an occasional passing vehicle. There were circles under Tessie Roo's eyes and my back was killing me.

"We needn't go into 1909," I said. "Let's call it quits."

Tessie, however, wanted to see the wedding picture of Rose and Sanford Melcher. It appeared in both newspapers, though the poses were different. Sanford looked faintly terrified; Rose wore a smug expression. The wedding sounded appropriately lavish, with five bridesmaids, banks of flowers, and a harpist imported from

Port Townsend. As with Carrie and Jimmy Malone, the Melcher reception was held at the Rowley house. The bridal couple planned to honeymoon at the brand-new Empress Hotel in Victoria.

"That's it," I declared, leaning back and stretching. "Tessie, you've been wonderful. Thanks a million."

Tessie didn't look at all pleased. "I haven't been wonderful at all." She spread a hand across the still-open binder of *Olympic-Leader*s. "What did you learn? That there was crime in Port Angeles eighty-some years ago just as there is today? That carelessness starts house fires? That Lena Melcher was involved with the D.A.R.? Where does that get us?"

I stood up and grinned at Tessie. "It gets me off the hook." Seeing Tessie's expression of chagrin, I patted her shoulder. "Look, it may be one of those situations where what we didn't learn is as important as what we did. That is, there were no obvious incidents that could lead us to airtight conclusions. When I've had time to sift through this information, trivial as it may be, I might think of something. But first I have to sleep on it."

Tessie was astute. She knew that I was, in effect, palming her off. "It's trivial, but it's not unimportant. While all these things were happening"—she jabbed at one of the binders with a stubby finger—"someone was being murdered. If you could look beyond the printed words, you'd know who—and why. You'd also know the killer. Don't give up now, Emma. I have a sixth sense about these things. When I'm getting close to connecting a farmer from Missouri with a lumberjack from Idaho, I have a feeling for it. I can't see the link until I look way out on the family tree. It's there, Emma. You just have to climb a little higher."

Chapter Thirteen

JACKIE WAS WAITING up when I got back to the Melcher house. Tessie had given me a lift after she gave me the pep talk. It was just past eleven-thirty when Jackie let me in and insisted we adjourn to the den. I tried to argue but failed.

"Don't fuss over me, I had a nap. Honest," Jackie insisted, settling onto the little sofa. "I went right to sleep while Paul and I were watching a rerun of *Seinfeld*."

I couldn't admit to Jackie that I was more concerned about my own weary state than I was about hers. I buoyed myself with a Pepsi and told Jackie what I'd learned from the old newspapers. She listened in a distracted manner, shifting and twitching on the sofa until I began to get nervous, too.

"Well?" I finally said when I'd concluded my account. "What do you think? Or should I say, what's wrong?"

"The police, that's what's wrong." Jackie was noticeably upset. "They came just after we left for Downriggers. Somebody named Arkwell put a note on the door. He's probably the same jerk who gave me the ticket."

"Well?" I prompted. "What did the note say?"

Jackie heaved one of her monumental sighs. "They'll come back tomorrow to remove the body. I don't want them to, not until we know for sure who it is and why

187

she was killed." She leaned toward me, her gray eyes pleading for understanding. "Once she's gone, the chain is broken. It won't be the same. She won't be *our body* anymore."

Jackie's feeling of kinship was justified, by real estate if not by family ties. On the other hand, she had to be reasonable. I knew that was asking too much, but I tried anyway.

"There are laws and moral duties involved here," I began, but Jackie scoffed.

"Poopy on the law," she declared. "As for moral duty, it's ours, to make sense of this tragedy. We're on the right track, I'm sure of it. All we need is a little more time." Jackie reached into the pocket of her cotton bathrobe. "I went to get the magnifying glass again to have another look at that picture of the house. You know how those drawers in the bookcase are sort of ... crammed?"

I nodded. Jackie's drawers were as jammed and cluttered as the other surfaces of her house. Or at least those for which she was responsible. "And?" I encouraged her.

A letter reposed in her hand. It was obviously old, with a pale green stamp featuring George Washington's profile. "I got the drawer stuck. I had to go underneath and take out the one below it. I found this at the back." She waved the envelope at me. "It must have fallen in there years ago."

The postmark was clear: Seattle, May 8, 1908. It was addressed to Cornelius Rowley. I slipped out three sheets of ivory paper and looked first at the signature. The handwriting was bold but precise. It was signed "Your faithful daughter-in-law, Lena."

Dear Mr. Rowley:
The convention here is most enlightening, though

frustrating as well. Too few of the candidates support the platform that we women and our supporters have fashioned. I spoke this morning to the Grant County delegation and found them exceptionally narrow-minded.

If anyone has doubts about the contribution that women can make to this great country, let them quarrel with our present venture. An outbreak of bubonic plague is feared in Seattle, due to the increased number of foreign ships coming into port. I am helping organize several women's groups to clean up the city and capture the disease-carrying rats. With God on our side, we shall be successful. Then our trip here will not have been in vain.

However, my political and social concerns must be balanced with those of a personal nature. I intended to speak privately with you about a certain matter before Edmund and I left for Seattle, but you were feeling poorly and I hesitated to disturb you.

The bald truth—and it must be told, I fear—is that certain shocking behavior has been going on behind my back. And yours as well. A highly respectable source from Quilcene has confirmed this. S—— has been seen in that vicnity in the unchaperoned company of M——. I cannot approve of these clandestine meetings some sixty miles from home. Naturally, your son agrees with me. M—— is an unsuitable object for S——'s affections in every way. Furthermore, he has had an understanding with R—— for some time now. She is a most sensible and modest young woman from a good family. I would hate to see their romance broken off because of some silly indiscretion on the part of S——, who no doubt has been led on.

I shall deal with S—— when I return next week. Meanwhile, I must request that you remonstrate with

M——. When you've thought through this matter, I should think it quite likely that you will dismiss her at once. In the meantime, I trust this letter finds you in good health and excellent spirits.

I refolded the stationery. "I wonder what Cornelius thought of that?"

Jackie was giving me her wide-eyed gaze. "Nothing," she replied. "He never read it. I was the one who broke the seal."

It required only a quick glance at the family history to note that Cornelius Rowley had died before the letter from Lena was delivered. Someone had thrown the missive into the bookcase drawer. Over the years it had worked its way to the back and finally fallen out to where it had been stuck forever. I could picture Simone, either grief-stricken or indifferent, tossing the letter aside and forgetting about it. I voiced my thoughts aloud to Jackie.

"Maybe," she replied, after hesitating. "Or maybe somebody hid it on purpose."

I considered, then shook my head. "No. Whoever got hold of the letter couldn't know what was in it. If they did and were alarmed, they'd have destroyed it."

Jackie laid a hand on the gentle curve of her abdomen. " 'S' must be Sanford. 'M' is Minnie. Who else could they be?"

"No one we know of," I said. "It fits what we heard from Clara Haines about Minnie chasing Sanford. Lena defends her son, saying he was *led on*. That may be true. But Sanford might have been willing."

"Yet Minnie went off with Jimmy Malone and eventually married him." Jackie was staring at the albums and photographs strewn on the floor. "What if Sanford was crushed by what she did? We know he and

Grandma Rose weren't happy together. Aunt Sara said so. What if the marriage was forced on him by Lena? I think Sanford was manipulated. Maybe Rose was, too. Poor things! Paul is the fruit of an unhappy union! Oh, dear!" Jackie seemed on the verge of tears.

I gave her a wry smile. "Paul's a generation removed from Sanford and Rose. His parents are happy, aren't they?"

Briefly, Jackie reflected. "They must be. They're in Hong Kong."

Tessie Roo had photocopied the newspaper articles pertinent to the Rowley-Melcher families. I gave half of them to Jackie and kept the rest for myself. Jackie seemed most taken with Eddie Rowley's intruder.

"Think about this, Emma. There had been a burglar who was caught. The loot may not have been recovered. If it wasn't, because it was pawned or stashed or whatever burglars did in those days, would a second burglar try to steal from the Rowleys? I know they were rich, but wouldn't that be dumb? Besides, the family must have taken precautions against another robbery. I can't imagine Lena sitting still for being victimized a second time."

Jackie had a point. "Okay," I agreed, "but so what have you got in mind?" I was getting my second wind. It often happens to me when I stay up past midnight.

"I wonder," said Jackie, speaking slowly, "if the intruder was that Frenchman. Armand. I don't remember his last name, but he was Simone's lover."

"Armand Nievalle." I searched for the few scraps of information we had about the French fisherman. According to Claudia Malone Cameron, Cornelius Rowley had tried to run Armand out of town. Maybe he hadn't succeeded. Maybe Armand had simply gone to ground in Port Angeles. "Or," I said in a burst of inspiration, "if Cornelius really did send Armand packing, it would have to have been in early spring. The old boy died in May. Where would a fisherman go that time of year? Alaska, of course, with the fishing season just starting up there. But he would come back in September or October. Maybe he knew Cornelius was dead by then and it was safe. Maybe he and Simone had kept in touch by letter. Maybe," I went on in a rush of enthusiasm for my own brilliance, "he and Simone stole those two horses and fled Port Angeles."

Jackie gave me a blank stare. "What horses?"

Tessie hadn't bothered to copy the story about the theft at the livery stable. The incident hadn't seemed to have anything to do with the Rowleys or the Melchers. I recounted the item to Jackie.

"It happened the night after Eddie shot at the intruder," I explained. "If it was Armand, maybe he was coming to get Simone and got scared off. See the part in the newspaper story about *unintelligible curses*? If the intruder swore, the reporter might have written *unprintable curses* or some such euphemistic jargon. But a startled, frightened Armand wculd have sworn reflexively in his native tongue."

"And Eddie wouldn't have understood it," Jackie said in growing wonder. "Eddie's stepmother might have used French now and then, but she wouldn't have sworn like a sailor. Or a fisherman."

"Exactly. So after Armand was scared off, he and Simone had to set up a second rendezvous, perhaps at the livery stable. They stole the horses and skipped town. Oh!" Excitedly, I flipped through the remaining news articles. "The ladies' clothes! And fripperies! Lena donated them to the D.A.R. a short time later. I'll bet they belonged to Simone. If Simone and Armand rode off on horseback, she couldn't take much with her. Lena wouldn't want the Widow Rowley's fancy Paris wardrobe cluttering up the house. I can imagine what

THE ALPINE ESCAPE 193

she thought of Simone's expensive 'fripperies.' Am I making sense?"

Judging from Jackie's elated expression, I was. Still, she had a quibble. "But would Simone leave all those lovely things behind?"

"She had no choice," I pointed out. "Simone had to choose between her clothes and her lover. She was French. *Vive l'amour!* Besides, she had all that money. The French are also practical." I was amused at my own reliance on clichés. In this case they made sense.

"It's terribly romantic." Jackie had grown misty-eyed. "Where would they go?"

I could only guess. "They wouldn't go west. There wasn't much civilization between Port Angeles and the coast in those days." Logging camps and the Indian reservation made up most of what was locally known as the West End. The Pacific Ocean rolled onto rocky beaches between Cape Flattery and Grays Harbor. It was a wild and beautiful stretch of land, leading to the rain forest and the Olympic Mountains.

"Seattle then," Jackie murmured, still looking moonstruck.

"Probably. Maybe they stayed there, maybe they took off for somewhere else. San Francisco, Denver, back east, even Paris." I stopped, another idea dawning. "Is it a coincidence that Simone took a French lover? Was it really like attracting like? She could have had her pick of eligible men. A fisherman didn't qualify. Socially, Armand Nievalle was no more suitable for the Widow Rowley than Minnie Burke was for Sanford Melcher or Jimmy Malone was for Carrie Rowley."

"But Carrie did marry Jimmy," Jackie reminded me.

"Oh, sure, but that was because she was afraid of being an old maid. I wonder about that, too." I picked up one of the photo albums and turned to a picture of Carrie. "She was good-looking, really. She came from a well-to-do family. Was she really desperate to marry? Or was she just plain nuts about Jimmy?"

"So why shouldn't Simone be nuts about Armand?" Jackie wasn't letting go of her latest romantic fantasy.

"I think she was," I replied. "I guess what I'm saying is maybe she was nuts about him for a long time. Like in Paris. I wonder if she didn't follow him to this country. Or maybe they ran away together, then quarreled and parted. Simone met Cornelius Rowley and decided to be a rich wife instead of a poor mistress."

Still paging through the album, I found the photograph of Simone with her flawless bosom and pearl dog collar. The jewelry tugged at my memory. I picked up another album. There was the engagement picture of Rose Felder in which she was wearing the same choker.

"That clinches it," I said, shoving the two albums into Jackie's lap. "Rose got her hands on Simone's jewels. Lena wouldn't give anything valuable away to the D.A.R. I wonder if Aunt Sara has Simone's baubles stashed away in Seattle."

In the kitchen the phone rang. It was a dull, distant sound, but it made both of us jump. Jackie rushed off to answer it. Mike, I thought, calling with a brainstorm. Or Tessie Roo, who had climbed out on a limb of the Rowley-Melcher family tree.

It was neither. Jackie came panting into the den, carrying the cordless phone. "It's for you," she whispered in wonder. "It's a *man*. He sounds so sexy, like butter melting on toast."

Puzzled, I accepted the phone. It was Milo Dodge, whose laconic voice sounded more like cold mayo on day-old rye to me. "You're damned lucky that Crazy Eights Neffel finally came out of that tree. Durwood Parker lured him down with some of his wife's blueberry pie. Crazy Eights said he was going to share it with the bear," he grumbled. "I waited until I was going off duty to call you back. You wanted felony convictions only, right?"

"Right." My grip tightened on the phone. I had the feeling that Milo had found something.

"No Rowleys, one Melcher, wrong time frame. Eleven Malones—bunch of troublemakers. Whoa!" I heard something drop, probably knocked off of Milo's desk by his big feet. He paused, swore under his breath, and then turned back to the receiver. "I lost my wobbler. It's a new kind Harvey Adcock got in this week. He says it's great for summer-run steelhead. Red, green, and yellow."

I grimaced with impatience. "Sounds like it'd match a skirt I saw at Francine's Fine Apparel last week. Give, Milo. Did you find the right Malone?"

"I found two Walters. One was up for armed robbery in the Sixties, but he was from Texas, born 1939. The other was a local, born 1906. That's your guy, right?"

"Right," I repeated with a weary sigh. My second wind was blowing out to sea.

"Nutcase, maybe. He was picked up and charged on September fifteenth, 1935, and convicted December fourth, same year. Four charges of rape. Malone was sentenced to twenty years in Walla Walla but got out six years early for good behavior. Plus he didn't use physical violence on his victims, only threats. One really weird thing—he always attacked them in a basement. He was known as the Root Cellar Rapist. Does that suit you?"

It suited me fine. It hadn't done the same for the victims, of course. Or for Walter Malone.

I was pushing Jackie out into the hall. She resisted. I tried not to use force or to raise my voice. I didn't want to wake Paul. As usual, he had to get up early.

"Jackie, it's past midnight. You need your rest. I need

mine. We can talk this over in the morning before I leave. It's probably a harebrained notion, anyway."

Jackie and I were a match in weight, but she had youth on her side. She refused to budge. I didn't want to put a hammerlock on an expectant mother. "At least you've got to tell me what put you on to Claudia's brother being a convict," she demanded.

I hesitated, then relented. If I didn't tell her, she'd lie awake fussing and fuming. But I wasn't going to mention the part about Walter Malone and the basements. Jackie didn't need to suffer nightmares on behalf of our investigation. "It was part whim, part intuition," I said, leaning against the doorjamb. "I was curious if any of the Rowley-Melcher-Malone clan had any criminal tendencies. I don't necessarily believe that such traits are inherited, but if somebody in the family was a murderer, then it was possible that the same somebody had committed another crime."

Jackie's baffled expression made me pause. "Not Walter! He couldn't have murdered anybody! He was a baby back then!"

"I know. I'm talking about other members of the family. As it turns out, none of the ones we've been considering had ever been convicted. So our murderer apparently never struck again. Or didn't get caught. This gives us a better profile of the killer."

Jackie didn't see how.

I tried to explain. "The murder in this house went undetected and the murderer was never apprehended. I think it's safe to say that much. This tells us several things. For one, the killer was very clever. But why wasn't the victim missed? If it was Carrie, as we're assuming, then we may already know the answer— Minnie Burke impersonated her. But there's another woman involved who isn't accounted for and that's Simone. We've got our theory about her running off with Armand, but we don't know that for sure. All along I've been slow to identify the body as Carrie. I still think it might be Simone. After all, Aunt Sara claimed that the ghost was Simone, not Carrie or anybody else."

The old house creaked in the summer breeze. Or maybe it merely groaned with the burden of age. Hearing the sound, I easily envisioned that in winter the wind could howl through the eaves and a specter might seem to wail on the cold night air. Outside, the trees and shrubbery would move, causing strange shadows and firing the imagination.

Jackie frowned. "Simone was tall. It can't be her skeleton."

"We don't know how tall Simone was. She dressed so beautifully and seems to have had wonderful carriage. That would make her look taller, but we can't be certain."

Suddenly, Jackie seemed to lose both her energy and her enthusiasm. "It's too confusing. You say the killer was clever. I'm beginning to think he—or she—was too clever for us."

"He—or she—was single-minded," I said, accompanying Jackie to the kitchen. "We can only guess that the murder was an isolated killing. But if that's true, then whoever did it had a single purpose, which was accomplished by the victim's death."

"Really." Jackie's footsteps dragged and her voice was hollow. She replaced the phone and started for the stairs. "You're right, we'll discuss it over breakfast."

I remembered to switch off the lights in the den, then followed my hostess. Halfway up the stairs Jackie stopped and turned to me. "Why Walter?"

I shrugged. "I gave Sheriff Dodge all of the next generation. The men, anyway. The only married name I knew was Claudia's."

"No, no." Jackie was deteriorating into fretfulness. "Why was he a pervert?"

I rested a hand on the banister. "I don't know. I'm working on that. But what made me wonder was the way Claudia talked—or didn't talk—about her brother. I sensed something strange about Walter Malone. That was my whim."

"Hunh." Jackie continued up the stairs. At the door to the master bedroom she gave me a feeble wave. I had the feeling that she would be sound asleep in a matter of minutes.

Somewhat to my surprise, so was I.

To my horror, I didn't wake up until after eight o'clock. By the time I got downstairs, Paul had been at work for over an hour and Jackie had already breakfasted.

"Look," she said proudly, "I had real food. Cereal and toast and a banana."

Distractedly, I smiled my congratulations. I was already at the phone dialing Dusty's number. Dusty himself answered. He was in a jovial mood.

"Sorry about yesterday, Mrs. Lord," he apologized over the noise of what sounded like a demolition derby. "These characters had to go and surprise me for my birthday. Al tried to call the Melcher place, but the line was busy."

I recalled Jackie's telephone research. No doubt she had had the line tied up when Al had placed the call. "Is the car ready?" I asked in a gulp.

"Just about," Dusty answered, still genial. "We got a little behind. How's noon?"

I winced. Noon wasn't good, but I had no choice. I could still get back to Alpine before whatever was left of my staff went home. I told Dusty I'd be there a bit early, just in case.

Jackie commiserated, but her heart wasn't in it. She was only too glad to have me hang around for another few hours of sleuthing.

I insisted on making my own breakfast. As I fried bacon and stirred eggs, Jackie listened to the details I'd withheld the previous night. Instead of shock, she exhibited titillation.

"Root Cellar Rapist! That's too weird! It's got to mean something!" Jackie was practically dancing around her butcher-block island. "It's . . . psychological! Or is it pathological?" She stopped next to the sink, her eyes wide and questioning.

Pouring the scrambled eggs into the frying pan, I replied in an even voice, "It's suggestive, I'll say that. It could be a coincidence. But I've had an idea ever since I heard about the Bullard fire."

Jackie hopped back onto her stool. "What? Tell me, quick."

"Because of the danger to this house," I said, gesturing with a spatula, "everybody cleared out. Except Simone. And little Walter. He was a toddler, around two years old. I can't imagine why somebody didn't bring him along with his sisters, but there was probably a lot of confusion. Maybe Carrie thought Jimmy had Walter with him or Minnie was in charge or whatever. But somebody—Jimmy, I think—went back inside to find the kid. Walter was in the basement. What had he seen? Or heard? Was he a witness to the murder?"

Jackie's eyes grew even wider. "You mean the murder happened *that* night?"

I drained the bacon, then buttered my toast. "I think it's possible. The setup was perfect for the killer. The fire was a big distraction. I suppose it's even possible that the killer set it. We didn't ask Flint Bullard about that part. Maybe we should. But even if it wasn't planned and the killer was trying to find the right opportunity to get rid of his or her victim, then the fire provided it. Why Walter was in the basement, I don't know. If that's his mother down there, then he may have been with her."

Leaping off the stool, Jackie rushed from the kitchen. "You're wrong, Emma," she called over her shoulder. "Wait—I'm getting those photocopies."

After clearing off an empty cereal box, I perched on one of the other stools and started to eat my breakfast. Jackie reappeared, waving one of Tessie Roo's copies.

"Look! It says in the story that little Walter was reunited with his parents and everybody was relieved, blah-blah-blah. Carrie must have been outside with the rest of them."

My theory was coming apart at the seams. Jackie was right. I'd forgotten about the reunion between parents and child. With a rueful expression I handed the copied newspaper item back to Jackie. "Well, maybe Walter could only get aroused when he was around a lot of fruit jars. For all we know, he had a marmalade fetish."

Jackie's giggle was cut short by the ringing of the telephone. I froze, fearing that Dusty was calling back to say that the wheels had fallen off my Jag. Judging from Jackie's expression, the news was indeed horrific.

"You're kidding! No! Wow! That's unreal! Yes . . . yes, I'll tell her. . . . She's right here . . . okay, 'bye." Jackie was leaning on the counter, agog. "Emma!" she breathed, "that was Mike Randall. His zoology buddy at the college gave him a report on those bones. They're *human*. They're from a baby about four months old!"

I was also aghast. "A *baby*?" My fork clattered onto the floor.

Jackie seemed to be gasping for air. "I don't mean a *baby* baby!" she gasped, clutching at her abdomen. "I mean a *fetus*! The victim was pregnant! Like me!"

She burst into tears.

Chapter Fourteen

JACKIE HAD ACQUIRED quite a collection of books and material on expectant motherhood. She found a beautifully illustrated volume that showed the various stages of fetal growth. Her forefinger jabbed at a drawing that depicted the child in the womb at sixteen weeks.

"See?" she said, her voice still choked with emotion. "That's about where I am. The bones are formed. That's why I should be chewing those Tums and drinking more milk." To prove her point, she dashed to the refrigerator and poured herself a big glass.

Mindlessly, I filled my face with toast, bacon, and eggs. The shock of learning that an unborn child had died with its mother was hard to shake off. "Who?" I whispered, still staring at the illustration.

Jackie, whose composure seemed to be returning faster than mine, wore a milk mustache. "Carrie had babies bing-bing-bing. I suppose she was expecting a fourth. Wasn't Claudia about a year old by then?"

"I guess so." I closed the big book and slid it down the counter, where I wouldn't be able to mar it with remnants of my breakfast. "But it could have been Simone."

Jackie gave me a dark look. "Carrying Armand's baby?" She was transformed, rocking excitedly on her stool. "It adds up! Cornelius ran Armand out of town in May! Simone had already conceived the baby!" She counted on her fingers: "May, June, July, August—the house fire! Four months! Emma, we did it!" She jumped off the stool and ran around the counter to hug me. "It was Cornelius!"

I went limp in her overenthusiastic embrace. "Jackie, Cornelius was dead. He must have run Armand out earlier than May." But, some part of me argued, maybe not. According to Lena's letter from Seattle, Cornelius Rowley was feeling unwell in early May. Perhaps the discovery of his wife's infidelity had made him ill. A volatile encounter with the Frenchman might have caused a heart attack. Jackie could be right about Simone's pregnancy even if she was off-base about Cornelius.

"Oh, poopy!" Jackie had released me and was looking subdued. "Well, it was a thought. How about Eddie? You know, defending the family honor?"

Eddie. I considered his somewhat shadowy figure, relegated to creating impractical inventions in the garage. Eddie, with his militant martinet of a wife, his crippled leg, his spirit of adventure forever quenched. Was Eddie's mind twisted along with his body? He had failed to live up to the accomplishments of his father. He had failed in keeping the Rowley mill going. He had even failed at his inventions, creating a disastrous contraption that had killed him. But why would he murder his sister or his stepmother?

I shook my head, though not with a great deal of assurance. "Eddie wouldn't kill Carrie. Or Simone. Unless . . ." My thought trailed off.

Jackie pounced. "Unless he was in love with Simone? Think about it, Emma. Lena or Simone. Let's say Eddie married Lena because she wanted it. She had such a forceful personality, and poor old Eddie couldn't withstand her. Lena needed a base of operations, she needed money, she needed a home for herself and

Sanford. Eddie was her ticket. Lena didn't marry a man, she married a household. Otherwise, she was stuck going back to New England and living off her relatives. It's obvious that Lena didn't want that. I think she bulldozed Eddie into marriage."

Jackie's portrait of the pair made sense. Ten years Eddie's senior, Lena would have been a formidable presence. I sensed that Cornelius Rowley would have liked her. He was another strong personality, and Lena would have appealed to him. They were kindred spirits. If he hadn't already fallen for Simone, he might have taken on Lena himself.

"So," I said slowly, rinsing my plate before putting it in the dishwasher, "Eddie discovers that being married to Lena isn't exactly a continual romp in the hay. Dad has a gorgeous young wife who's about the same age as Eddie and he goes nuts." I nodded thoughtfully. "It makes sense. Cornelius dies. Eddie figures he might have a chance ... but he's stuck with Lena. So why isn't she the one in the basement?"

Jackie groaned. "You're right, he should have knocked Lena off. Who would have blamed him? How would you like to be married to Hatchet Face?"

I arched both eyebrows at Jackie, never having learned the art of raising only one. "I? Wrong sex. Besides, I've never been married, period."

Jackie blushed. "Oh, Emma! I'm sorry! I forgot! It's just that ... well, most of Mom's friends are ... and you've got a son ... and ..."

I reached across the counter and patted Jackie's shoulder. "Don't get yourself all worked up. I've been an unmarried mother for years. Adam and I are used to it."

Still wearing a chastened expression, Jackie regarded me with a newfound shyness. "Mom says Adam is a good kid."

I shrugged. "He is. Unmotivated, unambitious, unfocused. But good nonetheless. Currently he's considering archaeology. Or anthropology, whichever applies to . . ." I laughed, and Jackie looked startled. It was my turn for chagrin. "Old bones. Adam would no doubt love helping us out."

As ever, Jackie was mercurial. She grabbed the phone with one hand and the directory with the other. "Let's call the nursing home and ask for Flint Bullard. We have to find out if he knows exactly how the fire started at his house."

I didn't try to dissuade Jackie. But Flint had no phone in his room. Whoever answered promised to pass Jackie's query along. Her call would be returned in due time.

Jackie sighed. "Flint will come up with some long-winded story about how he broke up a vice ring in Twenty-two or whatever."

I had poured us each a fresh cup of coffee. "Where were we? Eddie?"

Jackie nodded in a desultory fashion. "Maybe he killed Simone because he got her pregnant and she was threatening to tell Lena." There wasn't much conviction in her tone.

Silence crept over the kitchen for a few moments. The sun was out this morning, promising a beautiful summer day. Unless, of course, it clouded over and rained by afternoon.

"Sanford?" I spoke his name almost in a whisper.

Jackie looked up from her coffee mug. "Sanford? I thought he was hot for Minnie."

I lifted my hands in a helpless gesture. "Simone was ravishing, remember? All the men might have been crazy about her. Why not Sanford? He was in Simone's peer group, too."

"Then you have to include Jimmy Malone." Jackie's eyes danced with mischief.

I smiled. "I suppose you do, actually. But it seems unlikely." Even as I spoke the words, I wondered why. The French widow and the Irish logger weren't an impossible pairing. He seemed brash, virile, and adventurous; she was bold, beautiful, and capricious. But there was Armand Nievalle and Minnie Burke. It didn't quite mesh.

We finished our coffee. Jackie had loaded the dishwasher and was sprinkling detergent into the plastic container when the phone rang again. Quickly, she closed the machine and turned it on before grabbing the receiver. I held my breath, wondering what new horror this call portended. Dusty, I figured, saying my engine had exploded.

"Desmond!" cried Jackie, beaming into the phone. "You're a sweetie! What did you find?"

A rush of water cascaded into the dishwasher. The morning sun penetrated the kitchen, making shadows dance. A metallic noise clicked outside, no doubt signaling the arrival of the mailman. I waited for Jackie to react to Desmond, the helpful man from the King County's courthouse.

"Really," Jackie said with a frown. "How very strange. Oh, Desmond, I'm so grateful! I'll be sure to dedicate my novel to you!" There was a pause as Jackie suddenly looked stricken. "Yes, yes, I mean *movie*! But there'll be a novelization of it, you see. There always is with a blockbuster hit. If it's not already a bestseller. Oh, show business is so confusing, I know! You're a doll, and I love you! Mmmmmm-muh!" She kissed the receiver before putting it back on its cradle.

"Well?" I inquired.

Jackie leaned back on the stool, running a hand

through her hair. "I got mixed up! I forgot I was a movie producer instead of a romance writer! Yikes!"

"So I gathered," I remarked dryly.

Jackie sat up straight. Her ebullience had vanished. "Well. Desmond—he's so sweet—says that there was no marriage license taken out between a James Malone and a Minnie or a Mary Burke during 1908 or 1909. Do you think that's possible?"

I gaped. "I don't know. Unless they were married outside of King County. Tacoma, maybe. Everett. It's hard to say."

Jackie and I stared at each other. We still had no answer to our puzzle. Desmond had done a lot of work for nothing. And he'd never be honored in a book's dedication. Minnie and Jimmy's union remained a mystery. Maybe it would stay that way.

I felt obligated to inform Vida that I would be home by late afternoon. While Jackie was putting in a load of laundry, I took the cordless phone upstairs. I packed my meager belongings even as I waited for Vida to answer the phone.

She was in a hurry. Yes, Carla was back at work, already out taking pictures of a couple of gardens that had recently been landscaped. No, she hadn't seen Ed and didn't expect to. Certainly, Ginny was doing her best with the ads but was overwhelmed with the Fixer-Upper issue.

"I'm off to interview Rip and Dixie Ridley about their new deck. They put in a hot tub." Vida sounded as if she didn't approve. "Coach Ridley says he's going to use it for motivation with the football team when the Alpine Buckers start practice at the high school. Honestly, it's a wonder they won't all drown. What's wrong with a regular bathtub?"

I could offer Vida no justification for Coach Ridley's

game plan. A bunch of beefy Buckers wedged into a hot tub might make an amusing photo later on. But I put the idea on hold. It was a good thing, because Vida didn't give me a chance to talk.

"Your son called this morning. He didn't realize you weren't here. Don't you keep Adam posted with your whereabouts?" Vida's voice held a note of reproach. Again.

I hadn't, and Vida knew why—my decision to leave Alpine had been made on short notice. Adam was with my brother. I wasn't worried about either of them, not any more than I ever was. And I doubted that Adam was worried about me. Ever.

"What did he want? Is he okay? Is Ben all right?" Now I *was* worried.

"Yes, yes. Their flight has been changed for next month." Suddenly, Vida's tone changed. "Emma, are *you* all right?"

"Sure, I'm fine. Why?" Vida's abrupt transformation made me wonder.

"Well, you called Milo last night. I found that odd."

I closed the lid of my suitcase. Vida's pipeline was working efficiently as usual. One of her nephews, Bill Blatt, was a deputy sheriff. "It's no big deal, just some information for the people I'm staying with. You know, Mavis's daughter and her husband. I'll tell you about it when I get back."

"Oh! Mavis's daughter! So that's where you are! Why didn't you say so?" Vida sounded faintly put out. Maybe she really had thought I was in a love nest.

We rung off with mutual assurances, for her to hold down the fort, for me to drive safely. I immediately called the rectory in Tuba City, where Adam was residing with my brother. A soft voice I recognized answered. It was Violet, a thirty-year-old Navajo who worked as secretary, housekeeper, and Eucharistic minister when she wasn't being a registered nurse, a wife, and a mother of two. Ben hadn't returned from saying Mass; Adam had just left for the dig. Should one of them return the call? I thanked Violet but told her no, I'd ring back in the evening. Violet's soothing voice had calmed me. My son and my brother were fine, they would be coming to Alpine in less than three weeks, and we would have a summer family reunion. I tripped lightly down the stairs. It was a lovely morning, and I was going home.

I was back in the kitchen when I reminded myself that so far, my trip was a failure. Yet for some reason I didn't seem to care.

Jackie knew she couldn't avoid the grocery store forever. She also knew she had to stock her cupboards with more than the basic items I'd picked up Wednesday afternoon at Safeway. I volunteered to accompany her on a shopping expedition.

"I'll run interference to keep you away from veteran mothers," I promised. "I will spare you gruesome stories concerning veil of pregnancy, toxemia, and conniption fits."

Jackie took me up on my offer. At precisely nine o'clock we headed for the supermarket. I was browsing in produce while Jackie studied meat and fish. It seemed to me that she knew nothing about vegetables except for celery and green beans. I decided to introduce her to eggplant and broccoli and cauliflower. Corn was in season, of course, so I chose a half-dozen ears, some white, some yellow. Pleased with myself, I was contemplating brussels sprouts when I heard a familiar voice at my elbow.

"Hey, don't tell me you can cook, too! Why don't we say to hell with it and run off and get married?"

With a grimace I turned to face Leo Walsh. "Gee,

Leo," I said with more sarcasm than I intended, "how come your body isn't being washed ashore off Agate Beach? I thought you would have jumped by now. Instead you're scouting wholesome vegetables."

Leo's expression was mocking as he fingered a turnip. "I'm getting tomatoes to make Bloody Marys from scratch. What's your excuse? I thought you didn't live here."

I uttered an impatient sigh. "I don't. I'm shopping with a friend. Why don't you grab a lime for your vodka martinis?"

Leo picked up a long, large turnip. "I kind of like this. What do you think?" He leered at me.

"Leo," I said coldly, "you're a mess."

He flicked at the end of the turnip. "I'll bet you're wondering how I always seem to . . . turn up?"

I whirled away. "Hit the road, Leo." I didn't want him to see my smile. I'm a sucker for bad puns.

"Lettuce," he was murmuring. "Let us . . . what?"

Over my shoulder I managed a faintly appalled look. "Stop it. I'm leaving town in less than three hours. Good luck, Leo. Goodbye."

"I'm taking the Greyhound at two," Leo replied, mercifully replacing the turnip. "Where are you headed?"

"Mars." I had turned back to the brussels sprouts. I had a feeling Jackie wouldn't go for them. I reached for some peas instead.

"You got your car back?" Leo's voice held a note of envy.

"Almost." I was forced to look at him again. I couldn't stay in produce forever. On this Friday in late July Leo Fulton Walsh wore a faded plaid summer-weight shirt, gray Dockers, and the same loafers he'd had on in the library. The hollows under his eyes were dark, and his gaze seemed haunted rather than bloodshot.

Haunted. I recalled what Paul's aunt Sara had said about Sanford Melcher. His eyes had seemed haunted as he wandered through the Rowley house, composing his poems and playing the piano. Sanford had ended up in an institution, apparently the result of losing a son in World War II. Or maybe it had been more than that; maybe he'd always been on the verge of madness; maybe he'd cried for help, but no one had heard him.

"I'm going home," I said finally in a quiet voice. "I live in Alpine, up on Stevens Pass." Noting that my words didn't seem to mean anything to Leo, I amplified: "It's in the mountains outside of Everett."

Leo's face fell. "You're not headed for Seattle then?" I shook my head. "No. Is that where you're going?"

"I was." Leo's gaze went beyond me, somewhere in the vicinity of the chives.

The Kingston ferry plied the waters of Puget Sound between the Kitsap Peninsula and Edmonds, a suburb north of Seattle. I planned to hit the I-5 freeway out of Edmonds, hook on to the 405 link that went east, get off by Monroe, and head up Highway 2, also known as Stevens Pass. But it was possible to drive to Winslow on Bainbridge Island and catch the ferry that went right into downtown Seattle. I could reach I-5 from there, take 520 across the Evergreen Point Floating Bridge, and get on 405 in the maze of eastside suburbs. It would take a little longer, but not much.

"I'll pick you up shortly after noon," I said. "Where's your motel?"

Leo showed no sign of amazement at my generous offer. He was staying out on Highway 101, just inside the city limits. "I don't have much luggage," he added. "I'll be waiting in front of the motel office."

Briefly, we strolled the aisle side by side. Leo bagged a couple of Rome Beauty apples; I sniffed a cantaloupe to test its ripeness. A sense of panic overcame me. Was

I crazy to offer a ride to a virtual stranger? Leo Walsh could be wanted in eleven western states for all I knew. He might be a serial killer. He could be the Root Cellar Rapist reincarnated. Distractedly, I dumped the cantaloupe into my grocery cart.

But we'd be traveling in broad daylight on a busy highway. The ferry would be jammed with summer traffic. Before Leo got in the car, I could always pat him down for weapons. The idea made me smile. He noted my droll expression and jiggled my cart.

"What's up, Emma Lord? Are you thinking about pulling off the road and trying to ravish me?" Before I could answer, he gave a sad shake of his head. "Don't bother. You'd be beating a dead horse."

"Leo . . ." I was exasperated. "Has it ever occurred to you—or any other man I know—that sometimes women aren't thinking about sex? Once in a while we look at a man and consider him as just another human being. I realize that's a pretty tough concept for men, but for women it actually works that way. Honest."

On the other side of potatoes, onions, and summer squash two older women were standing in front of the frozen-food case, staring. It seemed that Leo and I were making a habit of drawing an audience. At the far end of the aisle I spotted Jackie, pushing her cart past dairy and wearing a dazed expression. I didn't want her to see me with Leo; I certainly didn't want her to find out that I planned to give him a ride.

Leo had started his comeback, but I waved him into silence. "I've got to run. I'm meeting a friend." Seeing the disbelieving look in Leo's eyes, I jerked my head in Jackie's direction. "There. I'm meeting her in cheese."

Jackie had fewer than a dozen items in her cart. "It's all so confusing," she complained as I briskly led her to the fresh pasta section. "I never really shopped for groceries until I got married. My roommates always did it."

Her lack of experience showed, but it wasn't up to me to teach Jackie the rudiments of food buying. For the next twenty minutes we scooted up and down the aisles. When I figured she had enough supplies for balanced meals to last a week, we checked out. The total was a hundred and seventeen dollars and fifty-three cents. Jackie was dismayed.

"I never spent that much on groceries in my life," she moaned as we loaded the Honda's trunk.

"That's because you've been eating junk, which costs more in the long run," I said sternly. "Shop once a week unless you're having company. Pay attention to the specials. Use coupons. Buy things like hamburger and rice in bulk. Didn't your mother teach you anything?" I couldn't believe that the practical Mavis had sent her daughter out in the world so ill-equipped to run a household.

Once more Jackie appeared tearful. "Cans. We should have bought lots of canned food for the poor. I keep forgetting. The only things I've given them were some marinated artichoke hearts and chocolate-covered ants we got at one of the wedding showers. Was that so wrong?"

It didn't sound exactly right to me. But I couldn't handle Jackie's peculiar attitude toward charity and nutrition at the same time. I sighed and closed the trunk. "Jackie, excuse me. I feel like an aunt. I've never raised a girl. I should keep my . . ." I stopped, my eyes widening. "Olive," I whispered. "We never checked on Olive!"

Jackie's sorrowful gaze followed mine over to Lincoln Street. I was looking in the direction of the museum. Jackie wasn't. "Olive," she repeated after me, her voice dull. "Olives and double cheese and Canadian bacon and green pepper. Emma, I can't stand it. *Please.*" Her knees buckled; her fingers were entwined in a pleading gesture.

There wasn't time to argue with Jackie. The courthouse clock was going on ten. I took the wheel, driving us over to Lincoln Street.

"Who's Olive?" she finally asked as I braked in front of Gordy's.

"Olive Rowley, the forgotten woman. Cornelius's first wife, the mother of his children." We were again blocking traffic. "Go. I'll pick you up in fifteen minutes."

I found a parking place in the block below the museum. To my relief, Tessie Roo was on duty. Her smile was wide when she saw me. While she hunted for the appropriate file folder, I told her what we had learned or surmised since the previous night.

Tessie was impressed. "I'm going to write down as much of all this as I can without jeopardizing my genealogical integrity. Much of it can be verified. The part about Walter Malone is shocking."

"If we figure this whole thing out, there may be more shocks," I said wryly. "We might hang a killer on the Rowley-Melcher family tree. That won't do them any favors."

Tessie didn't agree. "There's never any harm in the truth. It's the deep dark secrets that cause problems. Part of growing up is facing the fact that nobody is perfect, including your ancestors. Ah, here's Olive Rowley."

The first Mrs. Rowley was there, all right, but only in an obituary. Born Olive Ross in 1847, in Bridgeport, Michigan, she had married Cornelius in 1866. She had joined her husband in Port Angeles in 1895 after he had jumped his first land claim.

Mrs. Rowley was active in creating a wholesome social environment for the naval men stationed in Port Angeles. Her untimely death at the age of forty-nine is mourned by all, including her husband, Cornelius, her children, Edmund and Caroline, and numerous relations in Michigan.

A handwritten note was scrawled in the margin of the newspaper clipping. I couldn't decipher it. I asked Tessie if she could read the uneven script.

"I should think so," she replied, squinting at the page. "This was done by some busybody before me who knew all the local scandal. I'm rather used to it by now." A sharp chortle erupted from Tessie's throat. "Well! That's to the point! It says 'Died of syphilis'! That makes you think, eh?"

Chapter Fifteen

It did make me think, of course. The terse note also made my jaw drop. Afterward, I questioned my sudden urge to find out more about Olive Rowley. I suppose it occurred to me that I couldn't understand her children unless I knew more about their mother. She had always been there in the background, but if I'd seen her as the downtrodden wife of a successful man, I'd also unconsciously assigned her the role of the hand that rocks the cradle. It was Olive, not Cornelius, who had formed Eddie and Carrie. Oh, he'd definitely had his influence, but a man who would leave his family for months, even years, at a time to go off as a timber cruiser and make a fortune wasn't the one who guided his offspring through their youth.

Maybe Tessie and I were judging Olive too hastily. Mrs. Rowley might have contracted the disease from her husband. How had he amused himself during those long separations? I posed the question to Tessie.

But she gave a shake of her head. "Whoever wrote in the margins knew some of the early residents' intimate secrets. I've come across this same handwriting on other obituaries from the 1890s to the post--World War I era. 'Drank himself to death.' 'Opium user.' 'Died in a Seattle brothel.' There's no such annotation on Mr. Rowley's funeral notice."

Tessie was probably right. Cornelius had lived for another eleven years after Olive's demise. Maybe his wife's disease had been one of the reasons he'd left home in the first place.

"The navy?" I remarked, rubbing at my chin. I was still a bit shocked, trying to picture Olive Ross Rowley kicking up her heels with a bunch of randy sailors.

"Oh, yes," Tessie replied, her chortle gone and a sad expression now hovering on her piquant face. "They held training exercises up here in those days, out on the strait. That's how the local Elks Club was formed—to provide a lodge for the young men while they were in town. Half of the original Elks were from the navy. It was first called the Naval Lodge, in fact, number 353. I'm sure that part was quite above board."

I nodded. "Meanwhile, Olive was providing her own sort of entertainment. My, my."

"People are very peculiar," Tessie mused. "Isn't it odd how we tend to pigeonhole them?" She gave me a rueful smile.

I leaned back in the chair. "Oh, yes. I've seen everybody in a different light. Cornelius, the swaggering empire builder but cuckolded by his second wife. Now by his first wife as well. Simone, an adventuress yet a misfit, fighting for the man she really loved. Carrie, supposedly driven by the fear of becoming an old maid or obsessed with a virile Irish logger, take your pick. Sedate Sanford, marrying a sweet local maiden but turning morose because he loved Minnie Burke. Eddie and Lena . . ." I shook my head. "It never pays to jump to conclusions. I know that."

Tessie nodded vigorously. "We all do. But it's so easy. Especially when you're dealing with old photographs and dry facts." Carefully, she replaced Olive Rowley's obituary in the file folder. "But what difference does this make about the first Mrs. Rowley? In terms of the dead person, that is."

I thought before I answered. "I don't know." I re-called the later photographs of Olive Rowley, hanging back behind Cornelius, wearing her hat over her face. The poor woman had probably been concealing chancres. How had her husband and children borne the shame? Her death had sent her widower off to seek solace in the arms of a beautiful young Frenchwoman who loved another. Her son had taken to wife an older woman whose virtue was unassailable but whose ambition left him in the dust. And her daughter had married beneath her, apparently swept up by love for an unsuitable Irish opportunist.

They had all made a wreck of love. But who didn't? I had. I had fallen for a married man and borne him a child. For twenty years I had clung to that love while trying to pretend that the object of it didn't exist. Foolish and perverse, I'd cut Tom Cavanaugh off from our son. Adam had been old enough to be a father when he had finally met his own. My obstinate refusal to let Tom shoulder some of the responsibility had been unfair to all of us. Now I had to figure out if Tom was to remain my sometime lover or only my part-time co-parent. If I wanted a future, I had to let go. But for more than twenty years the hold was as firm as it was familiar. I nurtured my ill-starred love like a treasured keepsake. Every so often I could take it from its little box and thrill anew. It was, as Vida so pointedly told me, a safeguard against trotting my heart out into the world and risking the unknown. Or another hurt.

"Damn," I said, apropos of many things.

Tessie, however, discerned only one. "You've got Olive taken care of, eh? I trust it helps. Poor woman, she must have been a social anomaly around here."

"I hope so," I responded dryly, getting up from the chair. I put out my hand. "Tessie, you've been wonderful. I'm heading home in the next couple of hours, but either Jackie or I will keep you informed. If we learn the truth."

Tessie's grip was firm. "*You* call—or write," she insisted. "The least we can do after all this is exchange Christmas cards, eh?"

It was. The very least. Reluctantly, I let go of Tessie's hand.

Despite having been gone longer than I'd planned, Jackie was nowhere to be seen outside of Gordy's. I circled the block, then pulled into a loading zone. A moment later Jackie popped out onto the sidewalk. She carried a white paper bag and fairly bounced up to the car.

"The pizza oven wasn't fired up this early, so I got doughnuts. Want one?" She waved the bag at me.

I can't resist doughnuts. At the arterial I grabbed a cinnamon-and-sugar offering. The first bite told me it was delicious. "I thought you were in there gobbling pizza by the pound," I remarked, heading along Eighth Street to the Melcher house.

"Oh, no," Jackie replied. "I was sleuthing. Did you see that little museum when you were at Gordy's? I went in and looked around. You'll never guess what I found!"

I wouldn't, of course. Jackie was still bouncing. "What was it?"

"A pair of women's satin opera slippers with rhinestone buckles. Size seven. They belonged to Simone Rowley!"

I forced myself to concentrate on my driving as we crossed the bridge over the Valley Street gully. "Are you sure? That they belonged to Simone, that is."

"Oh, yes." Jackie was very definite. "I spoke to a man who knows all about the stuff they've collected. There's a hat that belonged to her there, too."

I remembered the hat with its jaunty green feather. "So it's not Simone in the basement after all," I said in a thoughtful voice. "Mike Randall guessed the skeleton wore a smaller shoe."

"I told you Simone was taller." Jackie's exuberance was still in high gear. "So if not Simone, we're back to Carrie. I was having some doubts about Simone. You know, it's possible that if she was pregnant, the baby could have belonged to Cornelius. Maybe she didn't want to leave the house the night of the fire because she was having morning sickness in the evening."

Jackie's reasoning confounded me. We were crossing a second bridge, above the truck route. I finished my doughnut, signaled for a right turn, and sifted through Jackie's logic all at the same time. I managed the first two tasks just fine but gave up on the third.

"If it's not Simone in the basement, then those aren't the bones of the baby she was carrying," I pointed out. "Simone left town. Lena gave her things away except for some of the jewelry, which Rose may have gotten. That means Simone had the baby somewhere else. Hmmmm."

We pulled into the Melcher driveway. Getting out of the car, I glanced up at the ramshackle livery stable on the bluff. The bright sunlight caused me to squint.

"I think we should deep-six the idea about Simone being pregnant," I said as we started to unload the trunk. "Madly in love or not, we have no evidence that she was going to have a baby. If she were, I doubt she would have undertaken a horseback journey from Port Angeles to Seattle. You're right, we seem to be stuck with Carrie. So to speak."

It required three trips to bring the groceries into the house. We were putting them away when Jackie finally responded to my latest remarks.

"It's terrible," she declared, unceremoniously dumping

vegetables every which way into the refrigerator. "If Jimmy Malone murdered his first wife, he also murdered his unborn child. What a brute he must have been!" She shuddered as I reopened the fridge and pulled out the crisper drawer.

"Vegetables in here, Jackie," I said firmly. "Any meat you're not going to freeze goes in the other drawer, underneath. Yes, it makes a difference."

"It sure does," Jackie agreed with fervor. "It's one thing to kill your wife, it's something else to kill a helpless baby."

"No, I meant the drawers in the—"

"How did Claudia Cameron talk about her father? Did she mention abuse? I'll bet he beat them. Minnie, too."

Jackie's haphazard approach to food storage had momentarily distracted me. Carefully placing corn, onions, and carrots in the crisper, I tried to address her assessment of Jimmy Malone. But it wasn't Jackie's heated statement that had tugged at some vague thread in my brain. It was someone else, speaking of the past . . .

I shook myself. "Damn, I just caught a snatch of an odd remark, but I don't remember who said it. Or what it was."

Jackie was on her hands and knees, putting canned goods in a cupboard. "About Jimmy the Jerk?" Her voice was a trifle muffled.

"Yes. Well, maybe." I placed a loaf of whole wheat in the wooden breadbox. "As I said, I don't remember. But Claudia didn't mention that her father was violent. He drank, though."

Jackie stood up. "You see? That's the usual scenario. The husband drinks, then beats up his wife. The kids, too. But in those days nobody talked about it. Claudia Cameron is an old lady, she wouldn't dream of bringing her abused childhood out into the open."

Jackie had a valid point. "You might be right," I allowed, dividing a five-pound hamburger chub into portions for two. "Yet Claudia spoke of her father only with fondness. On the other hand, there were serious problems with Walter. He grew up to become the Root Cellar Rapist." The allusion to sex—if one could term it so, as opposed to violence—made me think of Olive Rowley. I recounted my discovery with Tessie Roo. Jackie burst out laughing.

"Olive was a slut! Wow! Wait until Paul hears this one!"

"It's pretty tragic," I said mildly, wrapping hunks of hamburger in plastic. "It killed her. You know," I continued, putting the parcels into the freezer section of the refrigerator, "Olive must have had a history of promiscuity. She wasn't in Port Angeles long enough to have contracted syphilis and die of it. I'd guess that she was misbehaving back in Michigan, probably while Cornelius was out here establishing his claim to fame."

Jackie was still laughing. "Olive had one of her own, if you ask me. Oh, my!" Jackie wiped at her eyes.

My sense of humor is usually fairly acute. Yet I was having a problem matching my reaction to Jackie's. Nymphomania knows no time or place. How wretched it must have been for a nineteenth-century Victorian married woman to find herself deprived of her husband and yet trapped by her own rampant sexual desires. Clinically, I knew next to nothing about the social problem. I considered my own desires relatively normal, though I had lived a celibate life for stretches as long as five years at a time. My brother, Ben, claimed that celibacy was never as difficult a problem for him as obedience. As a priest he found it far easier to resist the temptations of seductive female parishioners than to knuckle under to a lamebrained superior. "Asshole priests," Ben had once told me, "are a hell of a lot harder to cope with than unhappily married women who want to be counseled by going to bed." Thus, I found myself inadequate when it came to judging Olive Rowley.

At last Jackie had her mirth under control. "I don't see where Olive's case of the clap helps us solve the mystery, though. I'm still voting for Jimmy killing Carrie, baby and all."

My nod was unenthusiastic. "You're probably right. It's all there: motive, opportunity, the whole bit. The reason I was curious about Olive was because I thought her character might provide a clue to her children's personalities. Now we discover that Olive suffered from some sort of aberration. I don't know how, but maybe it explains her grandson, Walter." I heard the doubtful note in my voice.

As ever, Jackie's mood swing was swift. She dashed across the kitchen and embraced me. "Oh, Emma, I hate to see you leave! This has been such fun! I can't wait to tell Mom about it!"

I hugged Jackie in return. "I'll write her a long letter as soon as I get home." Or, I thought to myself, as soon as I get my personal and professional lives straightened out.

Jackie squeezed me tight, then jumped back. "A souvenir! You've got to have something to remind you of your stay here!" She raced out of the kitchen and headed for the stairs.

I glanced at my watch; it was almost eleven. Dutifully, I followed her to the second floor. But she didn't stop there. She was headed for the finished attic.

I was huffing a bit when we reached the storage area. By now I knew it well. Jackie delved into the big trunk where we'd already found some of our treasures. She brought out a small velvet-covered jewel case I hadn't seen before.

"This was Lena's, I think," she said, prying the case open. "No flashy stuff, though I found a nice little gold circle pin I wear sometimes. Paul said it was made out of nuggets somebody brought back from the Yukon."

Jackie sorted through some modest brooches, a few gold and silver chains, and several pairs of men's cuff links. "Drat!" she exclaimed, wrinkling her nose. "There isn't much here that you'd really like. I guess the pin was it. You don't have pierced ears, do you?"

"No, I don't. I never saw the need to put any extra holes in my head."

Jackie held up a pair of small pearl earrings with gold posts. "You could convert them, I suppose," she said dubiously.

I pointed to what looked like a silver watch on a slim chain. "That's kind of nice even if it probably doesn't work."

Jackie picked up the round silver object and clicked it open. It wasn't a watch; it was a locket. The black hair lay soft and limp inside. We both stared.

"It's engraved," Jackie said, her voice rising with excitement.

She was right. The beautifully etched script read: SANFORD MELCHER, ON THE OCCASION OF HIS TWENTY-FIFTH BIRTHDAY, JUNE 17, 1904.

Jackie raced to the stairs. I followed, knowing that her brain was running on the same current as mine. In the den she scrambled among the debris of our previous research. The other locket was found in the plastic basin Paul and Mike had used for their most recent finds in the basement dirt.

Carefully, we studied the two locks of hair. The color and texture were identical even under the magnifying glass. There was little doubt that they had come from the same head. My gaze locked with Jackie's.

"Sanford?" she said in a breathless voice. "*Sanford?*"

I sat down on the small sofa. This latest discovery required some revised thinking. "It must be. The one we just found probably belonged to his mother. Didn't you say that most of the items in that jewel case belonged to Lena?"

Jackie had sunk onto the big hassock. "To Lena and Eddie. The cuff links were his. There was a watch, too. Paul is putting it on a chain so I can wear it as a a pendant. It's for my birthday, but he doesn't know I know it." She smiled like a pixie.

Absently, I smiled back. "If his mother had one of the lockets, you'd think his wife would have the other. But we know Rose isn't the body." A sudden, jarring thought struck my mind. I hated to give it voice. After all, Rose was Paul's grandmother.

Jackie, however, was still working on my wavelength. "Rose! Oh, Emma, what if the locket in the basement belonged not to the victim but to the killer? It could have fallen off in a tussle or something!"

The theory was credible. In 1908 Rose Felder was engaged to Sanford Melcher. The formal announcement had come late in the year, but according to the letter from Lena to Cornelius, there had been an understanding between the couple for some time. My knowledge of early twentieth-century courtship etiquette was sketchy, but I assumed that a lock of hair would not be a risqué gift for two people who were planning on marriage.

"But why?" I murmured, having been silent for at least a full minute. "What motive would Rose have for killing Carrie?"

"Money?" Jackie offered.

"We've been through that one," I replied, still fingering the silver locket. "The only person who benefited from Carrie's death in terms of money was Jimmy Malone and the children."

"Sex," Jackie said promptly. "We talked about the men being gay but not the women. What if Rose and Carrie were lesbians? Or if one of them was but the other wasn't?"

Again I was forced to contemplate an era of repression. How had homosexual women expressed themselves in a society that wouldn't admit any deviation from the so-called norm? A new scenario began to unfold in my brain.

"Rose wasn't happy in her marriage," I mused aloud. "Before that Sanford was carrying on with Minnie Burke. The match may have been proposed by Rose's parents in collusion with Cornelius and Lena. Rose really didn't want to marry Sanford, but she had no choice. Let's suppose that the object of her affections was Carrie. Carrie doesn't reciprocate and plans to leave town with her husband and children. That decision drives Rose over the edge—"

"And she does just that to Carrie!" Jackie exclaimed, rocking back and forth on the footstool. "By pushing her down into the unfinished basement! Emma, I think we've finally found the solution!"

Since this was approximately the fourth time Jackie had made such a pronouncement, I couldn't help but look askance. "Let's call it a hypothesis." Seeing Jackie's face fall, I hurried to add a note of reassurance. "It's a good one, though. The real problem is that we don't have any proof. We probably never will. All we can do is come up with every conceivable possibility and try to make one of them fit the crime."

Jackie was pouting a bit. "I like this one the best so far. How else do you explain the lock of Sanford's hair?"

I shrugged. "Rose might have lost it much later. Don't forget the other items that Paul and Mike found in the dirt. Some of them were left there fifty years after the murder."

Now it was Jackie who grew silent. "Lena," she said in a whisper. "Why couldn't Lena have two lockets with her son's hair?"

"Lena? What's her motive for killing her sister-in-law? We couldn't come up with one earlier when we speculated about the cross."

Jackie bounded up from the footstool. "The same as for Rose. Let's face it, Emma, Lena *looks* more like a lesbian. She was into all that women's stuff."

My expression was wry. "I don't think you can judge by looks alone. Or politics."

But Jackie wasn't giving in. "Don't be so broad-minded. Lena wore very masculine clothes. She didn't do anything to make herself attractive. She smashed up saloons and emptied beer kegs into the harbor. She only married Eddie to have a home for herself and Sanford." Swooping down on the pile of Tessie Roo's photo-copies, Jackie riffled through the pages until she found the one with Lena's speech. "Look! She says as much herself. Here, she's talking about meeting Eddie in Se-attle. 'His need of me was far greater than mine for him, which is as it should be when it comes to the mar-ried state.' Lena used Eddie. No wonder he invented a chair-lift that spun him off into oblivion! He was prob-ably trying to commit suicide in a really tricky way!"

Rising from the sofa, I had to laugh. "It was tricky, all right. Frankly, I'm still wondering about that cross. Why didn't Lena wear it in her later years? Why wasn't it on a chain? There are a couple of gold chains in that jewel case with nothing on them. That and the missing wedding ring—both bedevil me."

Neither seemed to perturb Jackie. "The cross fell off, the wedding ring is there somewhere. We just haven't found it. Think of all the stuff we didn't come across, like Lena's Bible."

Over the years the majority of family belongings had no doubt been thrown or given away. That was the way of a transient world. Most of what I had left from my parents were Christmas decorations and a few pieces of furniture. The rest was scattered, from cousins in Kansas to the St. Vincent de Paul.

"We're banging our heads against a brick wall," I said suddenly. "Jackie, it's almost eleven-thirty. I'll put my bag in your car, and we'll head for Dusty's."

The crestfallen expression on Jackie's face was alleviated by the ringing of the front doorbell. We both went out into the entry hall. While Jackie greeted her visitor, I paused by the fireplace. The recessed seats on both sides were covered with worn leather. I lifted the one on the right and discovered that this was where the firewood had been hauled up to the main floor. The crank turned with great difficulty. It was obviously rusty from disuse. I didn't have the strength or the inclination to bring the wood basket up from the basement. Still, Eddie Rowley's contraption gave me the seed of an idea.

Mike Randall was in the entry hall looking dejected. He hurried toward me with an outstre· ·ed hand.

"You're really leaving? I was sure y ·'d stay for the weekend."

Firmly, I shook his hand. "Duty calls," I said solemnly. "Jackie and I were just about to head for Dusty's."

"I'll take you," Mike volunteered. He hadn't yet let go of my hand. "My last class on Friday is at ten. Why don't we grab a quick lunch? The ferries shuttle back and forth during the summer. If you miss one, you won't have to wait long for the next."

I could hardly tell Mike—or Jackie—that I was picking up Leo Walsh. "Thanks, Mike, but I promised my staff I'd be in before the workday is over." I gave him my kindest smile and hoped he'd release me.

He didn't. He stood there, clinging to my fingers and staring into my face. "I can't believe you're going off without an answer to our little mystery. I thought you were considering a story about it." His blue eyes were dark with disappointment.

I felt a twinge of guilt, though I had no idea why. "Maybe the story is that there is no answer," I said. "Sometimes people like to read about things they can speculate on and create their own solutions. Provocative journalism, you might call it."

The phone was calling Jackie, who dashed off to answer it in the kitchen. Mike was nodding, his sad expression replaced by one of understanding.

"I admire your dedication," Mike said. "You have to forgive me—and Jackie and Paul—if we haven't been entirely supportive of your involvement with the newspaper. I'd be awfully pleased if you'd send me a copy of your paper. I've been over Stevens Pass dozens of times, but I've never stopped in Alpine."

"It's off the road a bit." I realized that my smile was becoming fixed. "You have to go out of your way." Frozen was more like it. "Most people are going somewhere else. They whiz right by." Stuck in place. Plastered on. I felt like a cartoon character.

Mike finally let go so that he could write down his address for me. I was slipping it into my handbag when Jackie brought me the phone.

"It's another man," she hissed, her hand over the receiver. "This one sounds like he's on something."

Startled, I took the cordless phone from Jackie. The voice that assaulted my ear was at once strange and yet familiar. It was Ed Bronsky and he was bubbling with excitement. Overwhelmed, I sat down on the padded seat next to the fireplace.

Ed wasn't merely humming; Ed was *singing*. I could hardly believe my ears. It was no wonder that the seedlings I'd been nurturing in my brain suddenly suffered from blight. I knew it would take a conjurer to resurrect them.

I should have realized that the conjurer was already preparing to wave the magic wand.

Chapter Sixteen

" 'CALIFORNIA, HERE WE come, right back where we ...' "

I didn't interrupt. Ed's off-key serenade ran its course, climaxing with a hearty chuckle. "I got your phone number in Port Angeles from Vida, who got it from Sheriff Dodge," he explained. "I know you're coming back today, but Shirley and the kids and I are heading for the airport in an hour. I thought I should at least say something before we took off."

"For where?" I asked, a trifle dully.

"Disneyland, Acapulco, wherever our fancy leads us. We've got over a month before we have to get the kids back in school. We decided to make the most of it."

The exuberance in Ed's voice was so unusual that I had to rub my forehead to make sure I wasn't hallucinating. "That's great, Ed. Congratulations on your inheritance."

"Hey, you could have knocked me over with a feather! I had no idea Aunt Hilda had so much money. We haven't seen her in ten years, since the family reunion in Fargo, North Dakota!" Ed's voice was bubbling over into the phone. I rubbed my head some more. "She never married, fought with all of her brothers and sisters except my dad, couldn't stand any of his kids except me! Do you know why?"

"Why—what?" I tried to come out of my daze.

"Why she liked *me*." Though still jovial, Ed's tone held a note of reproach. "It was because of my attitude. I was always the family optimist. Aunt Hilda called me her Sunshine Boy!"

I'd never met any of Ed's relatives, but I could only imagine what the rest of them must be like. No, I actually couldn't. For one thing, it would be impossible to see them through the heavy pall of gloom. I suspected that they had chosen Fargo as their reunion site because tornadoes had been predicted. Or maybe a cloud of locusts.

"I'm so pleased for you, Ed," I said hastily. "Give my best to Shirley and have a wonderful trip."

"We sure will," Ed replied with zest. "I just wanted to thank you for being so swell to me the last few years. We've had some good times, huh?"

"Oh, yes, sure we have, Ed." Like alienating our advertisers, cutting into revenue, being an eternal pessimist, loafing on the job, and, on one memorable occasion, going to sleep while standing up. But this was not the time to mention such things. It probably never would be.

"When we get back," Ed continued in his buoyant voice, "we'll have you and Vida and Carla and Ginny over for dinner. Thick steaks, champagne, the works. Hey, I'm at the office. I stopped to pick up the rest of my stuff. You want to talk to Vida?"

Nervously, I glanced at my watch. It was twenty minutes to twelve. Before I could demur, Vida came on the line.

"We're in a mess," she announced. "Ginny's doing beautifully with the ads, but Carla's still *ailing*." Derision dripped from the last word.

"I thought she was coming back today," I said, relieved that Jackie and Mike, who had been staring at me, were now engaged in earnest conversation.

"She did. But she's puny. Malingering gets my goat. We'll have to hustle over the weekend to fill up the news space. We need at least a half-dozen decent features with photographs. You're going to have to pitch in, Emma." Vida's tone gave no indication that I was the employer, she the employee.

"Okay," I responded. "Get Carla to do a piece on new housing starts in the last six months. Have her choose one house for a separate story about a family that's moving in. I'll cull some material out of the files on the influence of the railroad in shaping Alpine's growth. Let's do a big picture spread on some of the older houses, then write a historical feature on one of the founding families, somebody whose descendants are still around."

"Oooooh!" Vida was no doubt punishing her eyes with her fists. "Who? That's too tricky. If we play favorites, we'll never hear the end of it!"

Naturally, Vida was right. Of the two dozen or so families who still remained in Alpine from eighty years ago, any claim to preeminence could set off a full-blown feud. Still, it was a good idea.

I had a brainstorm. "You, Vida. The Runkels and the Blatts. Your father-in-law, Rufus, was here almost from the beginning. He co-founded the ski lodge. Nobody would argue with your right to do the story. Use the first person. It's a natural. No research, just your own account of the two families."

Vida protested, "That's self-serving. I wouldn't dream of it."

It was time to assert myself as the boss. "Now listen, Vida, who is related to more people in Alpine than you? Who knows every snippet of local lore? Who has more old photographs of the town's residents and events? If you write that story, I'll bet it'll be the best-read article in the whole edition."

"Well ..." Clearly, Vida was weakening.

I went for the jugular. "You can run some of those old photos and new ones, too." I gritted my teeth as I shot my wad: "Think how much Roger will like having his picture in the paper!"

"Well!" Warmth was flooding into Vida's voice. "Roger would get a kick out of it, certainly. I could have him pose with his pet spider."

I shuddered but retained my encouraging tone. "There you go. Use as much space as you want. Four pages if necessary. We'll key it into the middle of the special section."

By now Vida was almost purring. "I must call Roger and tell him. Maybe I should run over to the mall and buy him that black leather jacket he's been wanting. It's been such a cool summer, his little arms might get chilled."

A picture of Roger in a straitjacket flashed through my mind. Roger in leather was almost as frightening an apparition. Silver studs. A skull and crossbones stitched on the back. Tattoos all over his little arms. But to give the little devil his due, he was unwittingly helping me out of a hole. I told Vida I'd see her in a few hours and clicked off the phone.

"Mike's going to ride to Dusty's with us," Jackie said. "I told him about the lesbians."

"Oh." I was somewhat jarred. My conversations with Ed and Vida had drawn me away from the Melcher mystery. Indeed, I felt as if I were already gone from Port Angeles and immersed once again in Alpine and *The Advocate*. "What do you think?" I inquired of Mike.

"Fascinating." He picked up my suitcase, which Jackie had brought into the entry hall. Then he paused, watching me in a questioning manner.

"That's it," I said, realizing that he thought I had

more luggage. I wondered if he would have let me carry the suitcase had he not thought there was more. Mike Randall wouldn't want to deprive me of my right to bear equal burdens.

We were in the Honda before Mike elaborated on his remark about the lesbians. "I think you have to define the term *crime of passion*," he said from his place in the backseat. "Does it refer to the act or the cause? If it's the act, then we must rule it out. It strikes me that this was a well-planned crime, nothing spontaneous or impulsive." He tapped my shoulder lightly. "Do you agree?"

"I think so. But it's like everything else about the case. We can't really know for sure."

"Yes, that's true." He leaned back. "Now if we're talking about the cause, or motive, crime of passion means a crime *caused* by passion. Agreed?"

"Definitely," Jackie responded.

"That's right," I allowed.

"Repression." Mike spoke the word under his breath. "If Rose—or Lena—was a lesbian, one of them might resort to violence when spurned by the object of their desire. Somehow this theory makes more sense to me than the one about the men being homosexual. I don't know why, but . . ." He leaned forward again, this time tapping Jackie. "Do you mind swinging by that statue of Lena? I looked up the Latin inscription."

It was almost noon and I was getting antsy. My greatest fear was that Dusty's would close down for lunch and I would have to wait another hour to retrieve my Jag. But Jackie dutifully turned toward the little park. I consoled myself with the reminder that it wasn't much out of our way.

Mike got out of the car. Reluctantly, I joined him. The sun was almost directly overhead. Lena Stillman Melcher Rowley's image wasn't improved by daylight.

" *'Finis coronat opus,'* " Mike recited in a low voice.

"According to Bartlett's *Familiar Quotations* at the college library, it means 'The ending crowns the work.' " He glanced at me, his blue eyes ironic. "It can be used in a good or a bad sense."

Momentarily, I was puzzled. "You mean . . . Oh, I see. Not the end justifying the means, but instead life's closure being appropriate to whatever the person did along the way." Despite the press of time, I grew thoughtful. A soft breeze was rustling the trees in the small park. In the past two days a bed of dwarf dahlias had burst into riotous bloom. A gray squirrel darted across the grass, glancing first at us, then up at Lena's statue. It raced off into the shrubbery. I didn't blame the little guy; Lena didn't look like she wanted company. "Do you suppose Lena chose the inscription herself?" I asked after a long pause.

Mike gave a faint shake of his head. "I've no idea. How did she die?"

For the first time I realized that Tessie Roo and I had never looked up Lena's obituary. She had lived into the Forties, as I recalled. Our natural assumption was that Lena's death was quite ordinary, undoubtedly from old age.

"It probably isn't pertinent," Mike said, a hand at my elbow as he guided me back to the car.

Jackie was behind the wheel, looking bored. She didn't show much interest when Mike translated the Latin inscription for her. "We stopped here for that? It would make a better epitaph for Olive Rowley than for Lena."

There was truth as well as bite in Jackie's opinion. Dying of syphilis was, alas, too fitting for a lifetime of promiscuity. But the Rowleys, the Melchers, and all the rest were erased from my mind when I saw my beloved green Jag parked at the curb in front of Dusty's. I was so overjoyed that I could have kissed the hood. Or bonnet, as the manual called it.

The bill, however, brought me back down to earth. The price of a new fuel pump was two hundred and eighty-five dollars; labor came to a hundred and ninety. There were some other small items listed on the invoice that I felt no compunction to understand. Car mechanics are like doctors—if their tinkering keeps either me or my car alive, I don't need to know the gruesome details. With tax the total was over six hundred dollars. I held my breath as Dusty waited for approval on my bank card.

Miraculously, the charge was given the green light. Accepting my car keys and thanking Dusty for impoverishing me, I looked around for Jackie. Mike motioned toward the small office. Jackie was inside talking on the phone.

"What's she doing now?" I asked anxiously. It was a few minutes after noon. I pictured Leo Walsh, sitting despondently in the motel, waiting for the ride that never came.

Mike cleared his throat. "Jackie changed her mind about that inscription. She decided it was intriguing after all. She's calling your friend Ms. Roo at the genealogy room of the museum."

I rolled my eyes. But Jackie came out almost immediately. She was wearing a smug expression.

"So *that's* what it means," she declared. "Lena Rowley didn't die of old age even if she was eighty-four. Lena got run over by a drunk driver."

It was possible that someone had a black sense of humor. On the other hand, the words were appropriate for a woman of Lena's accomplishments. *Finis coronat opus.* Either way it worked.

I had to pry Jackie loose. She clung to me as if I were her mother, though I couldn't quite imagine Mavis putting up with such sentimentality, even from her own daughter.

"The house will be so empty! What will I do? How will I grocery-shop? Where do I put the grapefruit?"

I hugged her, I patted her, I soothed her with words. "Thank Paul for me," I said, finally managing to free myself. "I'm sorry I missed him this morning." Giving Jackie a final kiss on the cheek, I reached for Mike's hand. "I'll send you the Fixer-Upper edition," I promised. "Feel free to write back with any editorial comments."

Mike gave me a broad smile. Obviously, he interpreted my offhand remark as an entrée to future intimacies. "A letter to the editor? I'd enjoy sending you one." He was still holding my hand.

Before I could respond, Paul Melcher pulled up in his Wrangler. "I thought I might catch you here," he said with his diffident grin. "It's my lunch hour. I decided to come and see if you got your car. What all did they do?"

I handed Paul the invoice, which he read with great care. "They adjusted the fuel gauge," he said. "Tightened nuts on the underside of the dash. Checked the electrical system. Hmmmm."

"Well?" I turned toward Paul, hoping that the move would force Mike to let go of my hand again. He held fast, however. "Did I get screwed?"

Handing the invoice back to me, Paul shook his head. "Oh, no. Dusty has a good reputation. But it always pays to check things out. That way, when you go in for your regular tune-up, you can let the mechanics know what's been done recently."

The only thing I ever say to Cal Vickers when I pull into his Texaco station is "How's Charlene?" Charlene is Mrs. Vickers and a member of the bridge club in which I often serve as a substitute. Asking about Charlene is much cheaper than complaining about peculiar noises emanating from my car. Still, I expressed my appreciation to Paul for his concern. Mike finally surrendered my hand so that I could bid my host farewell.

But Paul wasn't finished with his automotive advice. "Keep all your records in chronological order in the glove compartment. You might want to code them with colored index stickers so that you know what kind of work was done when. You'd be surprised how keeping track of the smallest details can save you money in the long run. You think you'll remember everything that's been done, but you don't. It's natural to forget things. Not all car mechanics are as honest as Dusty or the guys we go to at the Chevron station."

I felt my eyes glaze over. But two phrases stuck: *keeping track of the smallest details* and *it's natural to forget*. The seedling in my brain was trying to germinate once more.

Jackie, however, was definitely wilting. "I suppose we'll have to let the police in and call the funeral home and have the remains hauled away. I think I'm going to miss her. But not as much as I'll miss you, Emma."

I finally made it to the door of my Jag. My thankyous were effusive. Jackie begged me to come back soon, certainly after the baby arrived. Paul assured me of a warm welcome. Mike's face was suffused with sensitive regard.

"If we discover the solution to the mystery before you write the story, we'll let you know right away," Mike promised. "But don't feel pressured. You've got a lot of stress in your life already."

Mike didn't know the half of it. I got behind the wheel, took a deep breath, and switched on the ignition. The engine started immediately. My shoulders slumped in relief. The six-hundred-dollar outlay hadn't been a trick after all.

"We learned some fascinating things," I said, leaning

out the window. "It was a wonderful exercise in family research. I think we exhausted just about all the possibilities, as far-fetched as some of them might be. Maybe it's a good thing we didn't find a solution." I offered my trio of well-wishers a wan smile. "We might not have liked it."

Jackie burst into tears. I blew her a kiss and pulled away from the curb.

There was one more stop before I could put Port Angeles and the Melcher mystery behind me. I had to get on with my life. Maybe I could think about it over the weekend. Except I'd be too busy getting the paper out. Odd, I thought, how events crowded in, how people caused distractions, how time seemed to drain away like water in a funnel. Of course, it wasn't my fault that the Jag had broken down or that Carla had gotten sick or that Ed had quit his job. I'd had every intention of going to the ocean; I'd been committed to making some big decisions.

My plans hadn't worked out. The ocean was still there, but now it was at my back. My problems were still in front of me.

Leo Walsh was waiting outside the motel, smoking and holding his sports coat over one arm. His luggage consisted of a large suitcase and a small briefcase. Like his clothes and his wallet, they were of good quality but worn.

Leo put out his cigarette in a concrete container next to the motel office. "You're late," he remarked, more amused than annoyed.

I opened the trunk so that he could load his belongings. "It's a long story. Do you want to eat lunch on the way or wait until we get on the ferry?"

Leo professed indifference. Not wanting to lose any

more time, I opted to eat while we made the crossing. Moments later, we were on the highway heading east toward Sequim.

I searched for an opening conversational gambit. "I hear that Sequim is full of Californians, especially retirees. What drew you up this way?"

Leo emitted a chuckle that was more of a grunt. "I wasn't exactly drawn. Port Angeles is as far north as you can go on Highway 101 without falling into the strait."

"Oh," I remarked casually. "You took the coastal route."

"More or less." Leo was shifting around in his seat, apparently trying to get comfortable. He wore a faded denim shirt and jeans with cowboy boots. The boots looked real, not like a pair from a Beverly Hills designer boutique. Leo didn't seem to be in a talkative mood this afternoon.

"But you were heading for Seattle?" I prompted.

"No," he answered.

I waited. Leo didn't elaborate. "Shall I shut up?" I asked, irritation rising in my voice.

"No," he repeated. I waited again. Leo turned to look at me, but I kept my eyes on the road. "The story of my life is sad and boring, as most people's stories are," he said in a flat tone. "Maybe yours is better, but I don't want to hear it. I came up from California looking for a job. There were three or four openings along the way, including Port Angeles, but every damned one of them was filled by the time I hit town. Or so I was told. Now I'll see what Edmonds has to offer."

"Edmonds?" Briefly, I stared at Leo. His face was tired, not just from lack of sleep, but, I suspected, from lack of hope. "But we're going to Seattle. I thought that's where you were heading."

"Seattle? You said you were going to Edmonds." Leo was frowning, not at me but at the passing landscape.

I hadn't realized that I'd neglected to mention my revised itinerary to Leo. "I changed my mind. It isn't that much farther to get to Alpine from downtown Seattle than it is from Edmonds. It'll be easier for you to get to wherever you're going next. Edmonds is a suburb. You'd have to take the bus into Seattle."

Leo didn't respond. He sat with one knee propped against the dashboard, fingering his lower lip. As we drove past the tiny town of Gardiner, I decided that he really didn't want to talk after all. But I was wrong. We were skirting Discovery Bay when he suddenly laughed. It was another strange, truncated sound.

"You really are a good kid, aren't you, Emma Lord? For Chrissakes, it's not an act."

The note of surprise exasperated me. "No, it's not an act. I'm trying to be helpful, that's all. It isn't going to kill me to take the Winslow-Seattle ferry."

Leo shook his head, as if in awe. "It's been awhile since anybody did anything nice for my benefit." He put out a hand but didn't touch me. "Thanks."

"Sure. When we get into town, I'll drop you off at the Four Seasons Olympic Hotel because it's right by the freeway ramp. They can give you directions to anyplace you want to go."

Reaching around, he pulled his sports coat off the back of the seat. "I've got today's *Post-Intelligencer* here with the classifieds. I didn't find much, but I'll pick up some other local papers when we get to Seattle."

Discovery Bay cuts deep into the land, with clusters of old and new beach houses just off the highway. A century earlier, the town had had its own railroad and sawmill. Both were gone now, but several construction sites indicated fresh growth. I could smell the low tide this afternoon, a mixture of wet sand and salt water. Wrapped in silence, we followed the curving road. Then, perhaps to repay my generosity, Leo began to talk.

"The funny thing about women is, they never shut up, but they don't say anything." He hesitated; I made no reply. "Liza never bitched about me," Leo went on. "She'd yak her head off about her relatives or the neighbors or the other teachers at the high school. I could never keep track of all of them and their problems. And our kids—she'd rattle on until my ears would damned near fall off. Katie's boyfriend's doing coke, Brian's wife can't cook, Rosemary's husband quitting graduate school. Yakkety-yak-yak. But Liza never—*never*—tells *me* what's bothering *her*. So what does she do? She packs up and moves in with the guidance counselor from the high school! Some guidance! Some counselor!" Leo snorted in disgust. "Twenty-seven years of marriage down the toilet! And our kids blame *me*!"

The indictment seemed to demand my response. "Why?" It was the best I could do while negotiating the turn from Highway 101 to 104.

"I ignored my wife. I worked too much, I was too self-absorbed, I didn't show enough interest in *her* career. Hell, who told her it was okay to go back to college? Who gave her the go-ahead to get a teaching job? Who listened to all that bullshit about Aunt Lorena's broken toe and Principal Mendoza's new rockery? What more did she want, and why the hell didn't she say so?"

I didn't know if Leo expected me to provide an answer. He seemed like a runaway train. Maybe my best bet was to stick to driving and let him get the bitterness out of his system. I suspected he hadn't vented his frustrations until now. Or that he hadn't done so while sober.

"It was New Year's Day, not this year but the year before. I was sitting there watching the Rose Bowl, and I look up to see Liza in the hallway with a bunch of suitcases. She says, 'Goodbye, Leo. I'm going away. You think you're going to miss me, but you won't.' And she left." He snapped his fingers. "Like that!"

We passed the turnoff for Port Ludlow. Leo was shaking his head, apparently still marveling at his wife's defection. "You didn't try to stop her? Or were the Huskies about to score?"

Leo gave me a shamefaced grin. "It was the Wolverines. They trounced the Huskies that year. Hey, you like sports?"

"Sure. Baseball especially."

Leo seemed amused. "Liza hated sports. When we were going together, she pretended she didn't. I used to take her to all the Bruin basketball games. That's where we met, UCLA. Back then, in the early Sixties, Walt Hazzard and Gail Goodrich were the big guns. Remember them or are you too young?"

I nodded. "Goodrich went with the Lakers. Hazzard played for the Sonics' expansion team. They traded him to the St. Louis Hawks for Lenny Wilkens. It seemed like a bad idea at the time, but it wasn't. Leo, let's skip the sports stuff. That's probably part of what got you into trouble in the first place."

He stretched out his legs and chuckled. This time the laugh was almost authentic, if wry. "Liza and I had quite a bit in common, though. Music. Movies. The kids."

We were coming onto the Hood Canal Floating Bridge. Its two predecessors had sunk, but I never had any qualms about making the long crossing. The steel-blue water was too calm and the forested shoreline too green for alarm. We, too, seemed to float across the natural canal. Neither of us spoke until we were on the other side.

"Pretty country," Leo remarked. "I haven't been up this way in twenty years."

"Did you go on vacations with Liza?" I asked, taking the turn for Winslow.

"Sure." Leo sounded defensive. "We went to Banff and Lake Louise one year. Mount Rainier. The Oregon coast."

"That's it?"

"I'm not counting places in California." His tone was growing hostile. I didn't say a word. "Okay, so we hadn't been anywhere together in the last few years. So what? I was busy, she was taking summer courses, we couldn't get away. It happens."

Another silence filled the car as we headed south on the Kitsap Peninsula. This time I was the one who broke it.

"So you quit your job and decided to make a fresh start."

"I got fired. I was drinking too much. I was feeling sorry for myself. I just hung around for about six months, like a sabbatical. We'd already sold the house. The divorce was final this past April. Good Friday. What's good about it?" Leo's laugh had disintegrated again.

"You're still feeling sorry for yourself," I said firmly. "You're still drinking too much. When are you going to change all that?"

"Yesterday," Leo replied swiftly. "I didn't drink last night. I went for a long walk."

We were passing Poulsbo, a town like Alpine with a proud Scandinavian heritage. "And didn't feel sorry for yourself?" I sounded a trifle arch.

Leo gave me a sour look. "I can't change everything

at once. What about you? You've been letting me do all the talking."

"So? Weren't you griping about Liza never shutting up?"

Leo rested his arm on the edge of my seat. His ill humor was receding. "Hey, you're doing me a favor and I bleat all over you. Your turn, Emma Lord. What brought you to Port Angeles?"

"Just a getaway," I responded casually. "I haven't taken much vacation lately, either." Before Leo could start prying, I went on: "I'm a single mom, with a son in college. I was born in Seattle, attended the University of Washington, graduated from the University of Oregon, and I've supported Adam and me ever since. I've got a brother in Arizona and various relatives scattered around the West and Midwest. One of these days I'll take a real vacation and go see the ones I like."

"Who dumped who?" Leo asked.

"What? Oh—you mean Adam's father? No dumping on either side." I refused to explain. I'd share my car with Leo but not my life.

Leo got the message, which surprised me a little. He settled back in his seat as we crossed Agate Pass to Bainbridge Island. Pointedly, he changed the subject.

"So what did you do in Port Angeles? Did you really find a body or was that a joke?"

I told Leo about the Melchers' mystery. It seemed harmless and it was certainly a safer topic than our personal histories. Leo absorbed the details like a sponge. By the time we had boarded the ferry and were in the galley on the upper deck, I expected Leo to come up with some theories.

He didn't. While I ate a hamburger and Leo tried the peach pie, he shook his head. "See what I mean? You women—getting caught up in everybody else's business. Hell, you don't know any of these people, most of

them are dead anyway, and the connection with your
buddies is pretty remote. So who cares?"

I started to bridle, but Leo had a point: the most that
could be accomplished by solving the mystery was the
satisfaction of our curiosity. It appeared that Leo, however, wasn't as curious as the rest of us.

"You aren't one for seeking truth?" I remarked
lightly as the ferry slowed to maneuver into the slip.

"Truth, schmuth," Leo retorted, throwing half of his
pie into a nearby receptacle. "A lot of good truth did
me. On the last day at work my boss asked if I'd been
drinking on my lunch hour. I said, 'Yes.' He said,
'You're out of here.' So much for truth."

We were one of the last cars to get off the ferry at
Coleman Dock in the heart of downtown. For much of
the year Seattle is various shades of gray. Clouds and
rain suit the city, which is like a beautiful woman who
doesn't need cosmetics. But when the sun comes out, as
it did on this July afternoon, Seattle shines like the belle
of the ball. Elliott Bay dances with diamond waves;
Mount Rainier sits comfortably in the distance, keeping
watch. The tall buildings catch the sun and take on a
warm, amber hue. Steep hills rise up from the waterfront and cut through the commercial district. There is
bustle but not much hustle. For all of its imported residents from California and New York and the Midwest
and Asia, Seattle remains almost perverse in its reluctance to change. It's true that smaller towns, like Alpine, are slower of pace. But it's all relative. Boasts of
being a cosmopolitan city are only obligatory civic promotion. In reality, Seattle is just another mill town that
got too big for its tin pants. Maybe that's why I love it
so much.

The driveway curving into the Four Seasons was
flanked with brilliant summer flowers on one side and
officious uniformed hotel staff on the other. I wedged

the Jag in between a white rental car and a Yellow Cab. Leo and I got out to open the trunk. He grabbed his two cases and slung the sports coat over his shoulder. The brown eyes were keen; the smile was crooked.

"Thanks for the lift," Leo said quietly. "In more ways than one." He shook my hand, briefly but somehow with feeling.

"Good luck, Leo." I realized my smile was a little tremulous.

"You, too, Emma Lord." He waved off the bellhop's attempt to take the luggage. "This is a great hotel," Leo said over his shoulder. "I wish I could afford it." With a spring in his step he disappeared behind the gleaming brass-edged revolving door. I had the feeling that the hotel's grandeur had swallowed him up. I had the fear that despite his bursts of bravado, the world was doing the same thing to Leo Fulton Walsh.

Chapter Seventeen

IT WAS FRIDAY on the freeway. I didn't travel it often enough to remember that traffic could be bumper to bumper on I-5 from three P.M. until early evening. On a brief trip to the ladies' room aboard the ferry, I had soothed my soul by promising to do some heavy thinking between Seattle and Alpine. But for the first half hour I had to concentrate on my driving. It was only after I had crossed Lake Washington on yet another floating bridge and exited at the Monroe turnoff that I was able to relax a bit.

Love is intangible. I think. It strikes without warning and there's no defense for it. Two decades ago, I had never intended to fall in love with Tom Cavanaugh. My goal was a degree in communications at the University of Washington. It was a time of student dissent, of enormous social upheaval, of noisy rebellion. I chose to abstain. I was going to be a journalist, and I had to keep my perspective. Even then I'd questioned my refusal to join the many protests and causes. Was it a cowardly way to avoid committing myself? An excuse for not jumping into life with both feet? Was this what my desire to go into reporting was all about? Did I want to write about the doings of other people while I stood on the sidelines and merely observed?

Twenty-odd years later I still didn't know the answer. There were only two things I knew for certain: I loved my work and I loved Tom Cavanaugh. I had progressed in my profession, but my personal life was stagnant. Was it possible to move on and find a man who could replace Tom as the object of my thwarted affections? Tom would always be in my life. Tom was Adam's father, and in the last two years he had asserted his paternal rights. That was okay with me, now that I'd gotten used to the idea. Making mad, passionate love with Tom at Lake Chelan was also okay with both of us. But as a couple we had no future.

There had been other men, four in all. Number three had seemed the most promising. He was an attorney for the city of Portland I'd met while doing an in-depth series on rapid transit. Jack was in the middle of a divorce at the time, and we would rendezvous at the Red Lion Motor Inn. One of us always brought food, since we were too discreet to order from room service. After almost a year of sexual delight, I arrived early one afternoon without having had breakfast. We were engaged in amorous conduct when Jack asked if I wanted to proceed swiftly or slowly. I knew he was in the mood for a leisurely pace. Wanting to accommodate him, I said, "Slow is fine." Then I added, "But can you reach that ham sandwich from here?" Given our physical involvement, he couldn't. It had been the last time we saw each other.

Except for the reunion with Tom, there had been no romantic attachments for me since I'd moved to Alpine. Milo and I had shared a lot of things, including an impulsive kiss, but otherwise we were very careful about avoiding intimacy. He had his potter, Honoria Whitman; I had my old love, Tom Cavanaugh. Milo and I didn't seem to make magic together. But then we'd never really tried.

And yet I'd been aware that while I was in Port Angeles, I missed Milo. With a dawning sense of wonder

I realized that Milo's laconic, unimaginative common sense was a source of solace in my life. Milo might not be the most exciting man in the world, but he sure was dependable.

As for other men, they didn't seem to exist. Mike Randall probably was a decent sort, but his contemporary man act drove me nuts. Mike Randall didn't exist. He was a walking textbook, full of platitudes.

Driving through Sultan, I thought about Leo Walsh. Leo was the flip side of Mike's coin. Leo was living in a time warp, where women were only allowed to do things of which their men approved. Phooey on Leo.

The bald fact was that any man in my peer group was going to be burdened with the problems of having lived for five decades. He would, most commonly, have at least one ex-wife, various children, and as many neuroses as I had. In addition to my personality defects, I was also Catholic. A divorced man would present spiritual problems. The church had grown more lenient about granting annulments, but I hadn't. A dozen canon lawyers couldn't convince me that after twenty years of marriage and four kids, the sacrament was invalid because the couple had wed in a state of delirious confusion.

I was passing the turnoff to Index. Traffic was still heavy but moving at the speed limit. Shafts of sunlight filtered through the tall stands of Douglas fir and hemlock. Involuntarily, my lips curved in a smile. I was climbing steadily, going up the pass, almost home.

There were no eligible men in Alpine. Not for me with my college education and my city rearing. Except for Milo, small-town native that he was. If I wanted to meet a man who could fill in all the blanks on my imaginary future-husband application, I'd have to find him in Seattle. That would take a concentrated effort.

I passed Deception Falls. Did I want a husband? I'd

never had one. I didn't know what marriage was like. A shared life, juggling schedules, allergies to my favorite foods, dirty socks, all sorts of compromises. I was accustomed to living alone. And liking it. Usually.

Why was I beating myself up? I had a fine son, a rewarding job, a nice little home. If someone came along and we fell in love, that would be wonderful. But what was the point in putting pressure on my life? Who really cared but me?

I turned off the highway and crossed the Skykomish River. Vida had urged me to reflect, to think, to make decisions. Why? She had been widowed in her forties, left with three girls. Had Vida tried to find a second husband? She had not, as far as I knew. Instead, she had gone to work for *The Advocate* and seemed to love what she was doing. What gave her the right to meddle in my life?

Friendship, concern, affection—these were the reasons for Vida's attempt to give me guidance. I could argue that I didn't need it, but I couldn't fault her for trying. In her brusque, unsentimental manner Vida was like a second mother. My parents had been killed in a car crash while I was in college. I missed them dreadfully. It was an unexpected comfort to meet Vida twenty years later.

Alpine's version of rush hour was different from Seattle's. Both lanes of Front Street were busy with cars, trucks, and RVs. In the three blocks between Alpine Way and *The Advocate* office I spotted four out-of-state license plates, from Oregon, California, British Columbia, and Texas.

There were a few wispy clouds hanging above Mount Baldy, but otherwise the town looked summer fresh in the late afternoon sun. Most of the shops along Front Street were still open, and quite a few people roamed the sidewalks. The Chamber of Commerce's flower planters were flourishing. A banner proclaiming Fixer-Upper Week was stretched across the street by the Venison Inn on one corner and the Whistling Marmot Movie Theatre on the other. After four days in Port Angeles, Alpine seemed to have shrunk. There was no wide vista of open sea, no sculpted harbor, no major highway cutting through the heart of town. The Cascade foothills closed in around Alpine, as if holding the inhabitants in a cradle. But I felt no sense of claustrophobia: The rocky ground and thick forest in which Alpine had been built, log by log and shingle by shingle, provided sanctuary. I was home, and happy for it.

It was close to five-thirty when I walked into the news office. Only Vida was still at work. She was sitting at her desk going over what appeared to be a large diagram. At first I thought she was laying out the paper. Vida refused to use a computer program or a word processor.

"Well, you made it." Vida spoke without looking up. "Whatever have you been up to these past four days?"

"It's a long story," I said, sinking down into the chair by her desk. "What's that?"

At last Vida looked at me. Her paisley blouse was more rumpled than usual and her gray curls needed taming. "My family tree. It's difficult, but it's all there, going back to my grandfather and my husband's grandfather. Pre-Alpine. Well? If this isn't a job, I'll put in with you!"

Vida's version was even more crude—and extensive—than the Rowley-Melcher family tree we'd put together in Port Angeles. I couldn't make head or tails of it. "Are we going to run this?" I asked.

"Yes. But not in this form." Vida removed her tortoiseshell glasses and rubbed her eyes, though not with her usual vigor. "Carla knows someone who has a family tree computer program. They can adapt my version and print it out. It'll fill a half-page. We can use the copy."

"Okay." I wasn't entirely convinced. "Why do you need the grandfathers if they weren't in Alpine? Couldn't you save space by starting with the next generation?"

Vida bristled. "I didn't say they were never in Alpine. They weren't born here, that's all. My Grandpa Blatt worked for the Great Northern Railroad. He used to stop on his way through Alpine for pie and coffee with some of the local ladies. Grandpa Eldon Runkel knew Carl Clemans in Snohomish. He got jobs for his sons, Rufus, my father-in-law, and Rupert in the woods." Vida tapped the page with her pencil. "That was back in 1919. Rufus and Rupert were mere teenagers. Neither finished high school."

I was able to make out the Runkel brothers' names on the family tree. Rufus had married Ingeborg Stensrud; they were the parents of Vida's late husband, Ernest, and thus her in-laws. I didn't recall Rupert.

I pointed to the younger brother's name. "What happened to Rupert?" I inquired.

"He was killed in the woods. Twenty-three years old." Vida clucked her tongue. "Not an uncommon tragedy, but it ruined Rufus's logging career. He couldn't bear to go back after Rupert died. That's why Rufus was so intent on starting up the ski lodge when the original mill was closed a few years later."

I nodded. Logging was still a dangerous business. Like other timber towns, Alpine had its share of amputees and people with missing digits. Casually, I checked to see if young Rupert had left a family.

He'd had a wife. Her maiden name was Julia Malone.

It was a coincidence, a similarity of names that had nothing to do with Port Angeles. I refused to believe that Vida could be connected, however tenuously, to the Rowley-Melchers. Julia Malone Runkel's year of birth was noted by Vida as 1904, but even that could be co-incidental.

Yet I knew the ties between the logging towns of western Washington were strong and intertwined. Part of it was the nature of logging, the nomadic existence that so many woodsmen lived, going where their work or their whim led them.

"Tell me about Julia Malone Runkel," I said, feeling faintly light-headed.

Vida put her glasses back on and frowned. "Aunt Julia?" She traced her finger across the page to the Blatt branch. "After Rupert died, she married my uncle Elmer. They moved to Sultan while I was in high school. When Elmer passed away in the Sixties, she married an Olofson, from Seattle. She buried him, too, and died about twelve years ago. She was Marje Blatt's grandmother. Why do you ask?"

I heaved a deep sigh. "Vida, are you hungry?"

"Well . . ." Vida glanced into her wastebasket, where I suspected the remnants of her latest diet lunch reposed. "I've been working like a dog all day. I could use a little sustenance."

The Venison Eat Inn and Take Out was crowded. We managed to snag the last booth, stepping nimbly in front of a couple who had *tourist* marked all over their deeply tanned faces.

I spent the salad course relating the events of my stay in Port Angeles as well as the background. I tried to keep to the basic facts, stressing only Julia Malone's relationship to the mystery. Vida listened attentively, occasionally cocking her head to one side like an owl. By the time I finished, I was hardly surprised to see her nod.

"Oh, that's Aunt Julia, all right. She was from Port

Angeles originally, though I honestly don't know much about her family. Except that it wasn't a happy situation for her or she wouldn't have run away."

"Why Alpine?" I asked. "She was only fifteen. It seems like an odd choice."

"Oh, no." Vida allowed her empty salad plate to be removed. "She had a stepmother here. Well, not really a stepmother, a stepgrandmother, but she was too young to be called that." Abruptly, Vida's mouth turned down. "Her husband was a cook at Camp Two. They left town after the mill closed." Vida was showing some signs of distress.

My hot turkey sandwich and Vida's pot roast arrived. I was somewhat confused as well as alarmed. "What's wrong, Vida?"

Regaining her composure, Vida assaulted her dinner. "I'm not telling this at all well. Let me back up. It might help you with your little mystery. This cook was an out-of-work fisherman from Alaska. It was a year or so after the Great War and he'd met someone in Ketchikan who knew Carl Clemans and was heading for a job in Alpine after the fishing season was over. It was suggested that he come along, since the cook at Camp Two had recently quit, and this fellow was French, which doesn't mean he was a *chef*. But you know how people think in such clichés. And as it turned out, the Frenchman *did* have a knack for cooking. Armand Nievalle brought his wife, Simone, to Alpine in the fall of 1919. Julia joined them soon after they set up housekeeping."

"Armand! Simone!" The names shot out of my mouth. "That was the second Mrs. Rowley and her lover!"

Vida gave a little shrug. "Was it now? I don't think I knew who Simone had been married to before. You must remember that this was before my time. I was only aware that she had been close to Aunt Julia."

"But how? Julia was very small when she and her family left Port Angeles."

"Aunt Julia knew Simone and Armand in Seattle. Simone was left by herself for months at a time while Armand fished in Alaska." Vida paused to administer great sprinklings of salt and pepper on her mashed potatoes and green beans. "Aunt Julia used to take the streetcar and sneak across town to visit Simone in West Seattle. Simone was very pretty, very gay. Julia was very fond of her, much more so than of her own mother. That's why it was quite natural for Aunt Julia to run away to Alpine."

I had always said that not only did Vida know everybody, she was related to most people, too. Given her numerous nieces and nephews and the rest of her extended Runkel-Blatt family, it wasn't much of an exaggeration. Now I discovered that she had a connection with the Rowley-Melcher family. I was surprised, but I should have guessed. When it came to knowing everything about everybody, Vida was an oracle. Or, in this case, a conjurer.

For a few moments I was silent, eating my hot turkey and sage stuffing and gravy-soaked white bread. It wasn't a summer meal, but the long drive had given me an appetite.

"I gather they'd had quite a bit of money somewhere along the line—no doubt from Simone's first husband, if you're saying Mr. Rowley was rich—but they'd frittered it away," Vida explained, employing both knife and fork in her attack on the pot roast. "Simone had expensive tastes, even in Alpine, and I heard Armand liked to gamble. Then there was a child," Vida said, her voice dropping a notch, her eyes not on me but on the aisle that separated us from the other diners. "He'd been born while Armand was in Alaska that summer. They named him Charles. He was very strange, never fitting in, going his own way."

"A different drummer?" I suggested.

"An entire marching band." Vida spoke without humor. "Charles was always a problem."

"Did Julia help care for him?" I inquired, wondering why Vida seemed so uneasy.

"Certainly. Aunt Julia never shirked a task." Vida acknowledged Durwood and Dot Parker's exit from a rear booth. "When Carl Clemans closed the mill in Twenty-nine, the Nievalles moved away, as so many of the earlier people did. They left Charles in Alpine with Julia and Elmer."

I was surprised. The boy couldn't have been more than ten. "Why? Where did they go?"

"They were headed for San Francisco. Simone wasn't well. She'd never been robust. I think they intended to send for Charles once they got settled. But they never did. Simone kept in touch, but she died a few years later, when I was about eight. Armand dropped out of the picture." Vida nodded at the Lutheran minister and his wife, who were being escorted to the booth vacated by the Parkers.

My portrait of Simone Dupre Rowley Nievalle was changing. Yes, she had been vain, self-indulgent, extravagant, and amorous. But she had also possessed a good heart or she would not have taken in Julia Malone. Yet something about this revised portrait jarred me, as if the colors clashed.

"I don't get it, Vida. Simone abandoned her own son, while on the other hand she took in a troubled runaway teenage girl. That's not consistent."

"I told you," Vida replied doggedly, "Simone was sick by the time she and Armand left Alpine. I'm not excusing her, mind you. But there was a big difference

between Aunt Julia and little Charles. Julia wasn't troubled in the sense that you're implying. She didn't get
along with her mother. There may be two sides to every
story, but in this case I'd take the daughter's side. Or so
my mother did. When Julia married Uncle Elmer, she
became my mother's sister-in-law. They were rather
close."

Somewhere in the back of my mind certain small
scraps of information were dancing about, demanding
my attention. "Details," Paul Melcher had said. *Details
were important.* Momentarily, I shut myself off from the
bustle of the restaurant. My greetings to Harvey and
Darlene Adcock were somewhat distracted.

"Harvey's taken it well," Vida whispered as the
Adcocks headed for the cashier.

I gave Vida a startled look. "What?"

"The ad for the hardware store." Vida's expression
reproached me. "You've forgotten Ed's debacle?"

I had. I'd forgotten Ed, too, at least temporarily. "I'm
sorry, Vida. I'm trying to remember something. I think
it's important." Taking a last bite of turkey, I slid out of
the booth. "I'm going to make a phone call. It shouldn't
take long."

Vida arched her eyebrows but said nothing. I hurried
to the pay phone in the hallway between the restaurant
and the bar. Digging in my purse, I found the number
for Claudia Malone Cameron in Victoria. I had only
two questions for her, but if she had the right answers,
the Melcher mystery was solved.

"Boysenberry pie," Vida said upon my return five
minutes later. "It's fresh this time of year. It wouldn't
be right to pass it up, do you think?"

"Go ahead," I replied, wearing a big grin. "I'll settle
for coffee."

Vida seemed absorbed in the dessert menu. "I haven't

had a hot fudge sundae in years. Roger's so fond of them. The last time I took him to Baskin-Robbins in Monroe, he ate two."

My grin was fading, but I was on the edge of my seat. "Vida . . ."

"They've got poppyseed cake, but that's awfully heavy, especially this late in the day." Vida leaned forward, her manner conspiratorial. "They don't bake it here, you know. They get it from the Upper Crust Bakery."

"Vida." My tone was severe. "Don't you want to hear what I found out?"

Vida was wide-eyed, then blinked several times behind her big glasses. "Certainly. Though I can't think why you didn't tell me any of this over the phone. We spoke several times. I thought you wanted to keep this your little secret."

"I never had a chance to tell you about the body," I protested. "You were always in such a tizzy about the problems with the paper."

Vida uttered a faint snort, then smiled warmly at our waitress and ordered the boysenberry pie à la mode. "You seemed to be a world away from Alpine," Vida said after our order had been taken.

"It was your idea for me to go." Now I was on the defensive. "Damn it, Vida, you're just irked because you weren't there to help figure all this out!"

"Well, now!" Vida looked affronted. "I daresay I could have made a contribution. At least I knew some of the people involved. You didn't."

"I do now. Or I feel as if I do, even though most of them are dead." I was turning sullen. Vida had stolen the ball and slam-dunked right over my head. Now that I was trying to go for the winning basket, she was committing a flagrant foul.

Her pie and my coffee arrived. Vida seemed appeased

by the generous slice with puddles of berry juice and the mound of vanilla ice cream. "Very well. So tell me what you learned from your mysterious phone call."

I relaxed against the back of the booth. "I called Julia's sister, Claudia, in Victoria. Now don't tell me you know Claudia Malone Cameron intimately."

Vida's attitude was vague. "I recall Aunt Julia speaking of her. But they weren't close. I didn't realize Julia's sister was still alive."

"Two of her sisters and a brother are still living, but Claudia was the only one I met." I explained how I had gone over to Victoria and spent most of a morning with Claudia Malone Cameron. Vida's resentment faded in the face of hearing about her late aunt's sister. When I got to the part about Walter, the Root Cellar Rapist, Vida choked on a mouthful of boysenberries.

"Oh, good grief!" she exclaimed after taking a drink of water. "No wonder Aunt Julia never mentioned her brother! How disgusting! Obviously, it wasn't only her mother who was evil!"

Vida's choice of words electrified me. "Evil," I repeated. "That's right. Julia's mother was evil."

"Malicious Minnie, that's what Aunt Julia called her. She spread scandal about Simone, too." Vida patted her mouth with her napkin. "I imagine she did that because she knew Julia was fond of Simone."

"No," I said. "She did it because she was afraid. Julia's mother couldn't risk meeting Simone in Seattle. Just now I asked Claudia Cameron if her mother wore a wedding set. She did, with a beautiful diamond that Claudia had remounted but can't wear because of her arthritis. I also asked if Mrs. Malone had a thick Irish brogue like her father's. Claudia said she did not."

I couldn't resist pausing for dramatic effect. But Vida's gaze was blank. "So?"

"That's because Claudia's mother wasn't Irish. She

wasn't Minnie Burke. She was Carrie Rowley, and yes, she was Julia and Claudia and Walter's real mother as well as the mother of the three children who were born after the family moved to Seattle. But she was never Mrs. James Malone. She murdered Jimmy's wife. The victim was Minnie Burke Malone, and she was going to have a baby."

Chapter Eighteen

THE MAIL HAD piled up during my four-day absence. The box at the edge of the street was crammed to overflowing. The separate delivery containers for *The Advocate* and the Seattle papers were also full. I needed two shopping bags to carry everything into the house. The reading material could wait. At a cursory glance, the mail looked mostly like bills and advertising circulars.

Vida was already in the kitchen, putting the teakettle on the stove. We had adjourned to my cozy log cabin for a couple of reasons: I was anxious to get home, and we were taking up much-needed space at the Venison Inn. Also Vida and I wanted to discuss the Melcher mystery in more comfortable circumstances. She had followed me up the hill in her big Buick, announcing upon arrival that we must have tea. Having just gulped down two cups of coffee, I wasn't in the mood, but I was willing to humor Vida.

A quick check of the answering machine revealed a total of eleven messages, which wasn't too daunting for a four-day absence. Of course the business calls would have piled up at work. I fast-forwarded through the answering-machine tape, pausing for Adam in Tuba City.

"Hey, Mom, where are you? I need some new jeans and a pair of khaki shorts and some Nikes and—" I cut

Adam off. He could whine at me later. Besides, he and Ben would be in Alpine soon.

I pressed the button again. Jackie Melcher squealed at me from Port Angeles: "Emma! You forgot to take the pearl earrings! I owe you for groceries! Did you want the elephant bracelet?" She stopped, probably gasping for breath. "I finally talked to Flint Bullard. What an old crank! He went on and on, blah-blah-blah! I don't know why people can't come to the point! Finally I said to him, 'Mr. Bullard, I don't think you remember zip about the day the fire started except that your house burned down.' And he said, he did so, his father had gone down to get a tub of beer and he'd made him— Flint, I mean—rub lard around the tub so they wouldn't cheat him—his father, I mean—and put a bunch of foam on top and when he and his dad got back just before supper, Carrie Malone was there with two of her kids, borrowing one of his mother's hats and talking too much! But she wasn't lighting any matches." Jackie's voice took a downward turn. "It's not much help, is it? Call me. I think I'll send you the elephants." I was about to shut the answering machine off when Jackie resumed speaking: "Oh, guess what? I'm going to volunteer up at the nursing home. I really liked Clara Haines, and if I can stand Flint Bullard, I can put up with any of those ornery old coots. Besides, when the baby comes, they'll enjoy that. It'll be like having a whole bunch of grandparents. Or great-grandparents. Or whatever. 'Bye."

Vida stood in the doorway to the kitchen, hanging on every word. "That's your hostess?" She sniffed in disdain. "From what you've said of Mavis, I thought her daughter would have more sense! She sounds like a jabberwocky!"

Vida and I settled in the kitchen. It was still daylight at seven-thirty. My house smelled faintly stuffy. The

sun was coming down over Western foothills, but I left
the front door open to clear the air.

"You must go over all these people again," Vida insisted. "I knew only Aunt Julia and the Nievalles."

I started with Cornelius Rowley and his first wife,
Olive. Vida affected shock at the cause of Olive's demise, but I knew better. Inwardly, Vida was probably
smirking her head off.

I moved on to the Rowley children, Eddie and Carrie.
I explained Lena's background, her first marriage, the
birth of her son, Sanford, and her subsequent remarriage
to Eddie Rowley. Counterpoising Eddie's business fail-
ures with his wife's political success, I awaited Vida's
reaction.

"Lena sounds overbearing but admirable." Vida got
up to remove the whistling teakettle from the burner.
Somehow, I could see Vida face-to-face with Lena.
They would have made a great match. "I suppose she
henpecked Eddie. No backbone on his part. Poor soul."

I was getting a couple of mugs from the cupboard.
"That's how we figured it. Then there was Carrie, the
daughter, who seemed to be the victim."

Vida allowed the tea to steep. "Slowly, Emma. What
about Lena's son, Sanford? Let's keep to one side of the
family at a time. That's how I managed with the
Runkels and the Blatts this afternoon."

I told Vida how Sanford had married Rose Felder.
"There was a pattern there," I noted as we sat back
down at the table. "Lena's first husband was a weak-
ling, so was her second. And her son didn't sound much
better. None of them had a will of his own, unless you
count Ferris Melcher's desire to roam the country as a
sign of determination."

Vida considered. "Ferris may have been weak physically but not emotionally. Certainly he got Lena to go
along with him on his travels to pursue whatever it was

he wanted from life. It's probably a good thing—otherwise, Paul Melcher might have been a washout. I take it the young man has some gumption."

I hadn't thought about Ferris Melcher's many moves as willful. Will-o'-the-wisp was more like it. But perhaps Vida was right. Paul Melcher wasn't exactly a ball of fire, but somewhere under that anal-retentive exterior I sensed that he had a spine. He'd have to, in order to survive his rollercoaster ride through life with Jackie.

"The point is," I impressed on Vida, "Grandpa Sanford rebelled, if briefly. He fell for Minnie Burke, the governess to the Malone children. I think he wanted to marry her. He gave her a locket with his hair in it, and she led him on."

"Maybe she loved him," Vida commented, stirring a great deal of milk and sugar into her tea.

"I wondered about that, even tonight, after I talked to Claudia Cameron. I came up with an alternate theory, that Minnie was pregnant with Sanford's child and Lena was so set against her son marrying an Irish immigrant that she killed her. But it didn't fit with the rest of what I knew, especially Carrie's impersonation of Minnie."

Vida gave a short nod, now obviously impatient to hear me out. "So Sanford caved in to his mother and married this Rose?"

"Yes, but that was later, the year following the tragedy. We—Jackie, Paul, Mike, and I—had some notion that Carrie was afraid of becoming an old maid, which is why she latched on to Jimmy Malone. His social standing wasn't any better than Minnie's, and certainly Cornelius Rowley must not have been keen on the match. Cornelius could have quashed it and sent Jimmy packing. That's what the old boy did with Armand Nievalle, his wife's lover. But Jimmy stayed. Then I began to realize that Carrie's will must have been powerful, too, and that maybe she was madly in love with

Jimmy. As for Jimmy, he had the chance of a lifetime—to marry well and to live a comfortable life. The only obstacle was Minnie Burke. Jimmy had married her already."

"Well, now!" Vida set her mug down so hard that tea spilled on my plastic tablecloth. "Jimmy was a bigamist?" Hastily, she mopped up the tea with a paper napkin.

"That's right. But Jimmy couldn't pass up his big opportunity. I'm guessing at so much of this, but I assume he met Minnie first, maybe in Seattle. Jackie and I foolishly asked King County to check marriage licenses for the years *after* the Malones left Port Angeles. We should have inquired about *before* Jimmy and Carrie were married. We even toyed with the idea of Jimmy being a bigamist because of the discrepancy in golden anniversary dates."

Vida's eyes sparkled behind her glasses. "Well, now. Jimmy and Minnie married in Seattle, then he found work in Port Angeles and met Carrie Rowley. She fell in love with him, they married—illegally—and Minnie followed her husband to his new home. Then Carrie started having babies and Minnie got herself installed as governess where she could keep an eye—and other things—on Jimmy."

I nodded with appreciation for Vida's quickness of grasp. "That's right. There would be no need for a governess until the children started coming. It must have been a horrible situation, though. Two wives under one roof, Jimmy caught in a cage he'd built for himself bar by bar, Simone and her lover making assignations, Cornelius playing master of the house, Lena manipulating everyone, Sanford mooning after Minnie and ignoring his fiancée. I marvel that there was only one murder. It's a wonder they didn't all kill each other!"

"People had better manners in those days," Vida declared. "Still, it must have been particularly difficult for Minnie. I can't think how she stood it, waiting so long and watching Jimmy be a husband and father to another woman."

I refused to spare too much sympathy for Minnie Burke Malone. I also refused to ask myself why I was so uncharitable. A first wife wasn't always the right woman for some men. "Jimmy must have convinced Minnie that he'd stay with Carrie only long enough to get his hands on her money," I said, my voice unduly harsh. "They were probably a pair of schemers. Minnie used Sanford as a cover. He was smitten, and provided not only a backup suitor but good camouflage. Then the situation got out of control. I'm guessing that after Cornelius Rowley died—that was in May—Minnie put pressure on Jimmy to leave Carrie. Minnie got pregnant about then and she may have figured that Carrie's inheritance would go to both her and her alleged husband. But Cornelius's will wasn't written that way. It went only to Carrie and the children. I think Cornelius may have had his suspicions about his son-in-law's devotion to Carrie."

Vida poured more tea. "Cornelius sounds shrewd. He was probably a good judge of character except where his wives were concerned. It's often that way with men. They're not like other people."

I acknowledged Vida's oft-repeated aphorism with a faint smile. "When Carrie found out—and I don't know how, maybe Jimmy told her, maybe she just *knew*—she pitched a jealous fit. I think she was aware that Minnie was pregnant. They lived under the same roof. The governess's condition would have been hard to conceal, especially from a woman who had already borne three children. Even Flint Bullard knew it in some undefined, childish way. He told Jackie and me that he recalled Minnie getting fat. At four months she wouldn't have shown much, but given the stylishly tiny waists of the period, a sudden change would seem to a young boy like putting on weight."

Vida looked askance. "Shocking, really. What women will do to themselves to be chic. I haven't worn a girdle in years." She shook herself and her buxom figure rippled under the paisley blouse. It was an awesome sight.

"Think of the scandal," I went on, ignoring Vida's imposing bust. "Legally, Carrie wasn't Jimmy's wife. Her three children were illegitimate, which was utterly unacceptable in 1908. Carrie was afraid that Jimmy would leave her. He may have made earlier threats, which is why they kept postponing their plans to build a house. Possibly he'd already connived with Minnie to move to Seattle. The house fire next door at the Bullards' gave Carrie her chance."

"Did she set it?" Vida asked.

"I don't know that, either. Jackie's conversation with Flint Bullard tells us that Carrie was in their house that day." I waved vaguely at the living room where my answering machine reposed. "I'd like to know if she was borrowing a hat with a heavy veil. She may have worn it when she and Jimmy left town to give the impression of secrecy. It's possible that Carrie did something to set the fire in motion, but the point is that the blaze provided a big diversion. Everybody cleared out of the Rowley house except for Carrie, Simone, little Walter, and maybe Minnie. Simone was lounging around upstairs, unafraid. That suits her character. But Carrie was putting her small son into the wood basket and lowering him into the basement. It was a game the children in the family played quite often, according to Paul Melcher. Carrie then summoned Minnie to look for Walter. Somehow she lured the governess to the other end of the basement, the unfinished section, where she bashed her in the head, pushed her off the ledge, and killed her.

All she had to do was shut the door and worry about burying her later. Then she raced out of the house and announced that Walter was missing. Jimmy went after his son. He knew where to find him, since the woodbasket game was such a favorite with the kids. The furnace and the woodpile are quite a distance from the unfinished part of the basement. Jimmy came running outside with Walter, and as the newspaper story said, he was reunited *'with his parents.'* I realized then that Carrie Rowley was still alive. But I didn't put it all together in terms of the timing."

Tipping her head to one side, Vida pursed her lips. "Well—you might be wrong about when the murder occurred."

"I might, but I don't think I am. There was another signal I missed when I interviewed Claudia Cameron. She told me how Simone's name was never allowed to be spoken in their home. The real Minnie Burke wouldn't have cared if Cornelius Rowley's wife was unfaithful. But Carrie did. Her own mother, Olive, had been a tramp. Her stepmother was accused of infidelity. And Minnie Burke was trying to take Jimmy Malone away."

The kitchen grew quiet. The wind picked up, blowing through the evergreens in my backyard. I could hear a crow caw in the distance. On the other side of town the Burlington Northern whistled as it slowed on its passage through Alpine.

"Why the impersonation?" Vida demanded. "Why couldn't Carrie simply pack up with her husband and children and go away?"

This was the question that had plagued me since I'd discovered that Carrie was the killer, not the victim. "Carrie never intended for Minnie to be found," I said slowly. "But she knew it could happen. If it did, she wanted to divert suspicion. I think she tossed her own earrings into the dirt along with Minnie. We never found a wedding ring in the basement. That's because Minnie didn't dare wear one. Claudia Cameron told me tonight that her mother had a big diamond that she'd had reset. Naturally, that was Carrie's ring, no doubt paid for by Cornelius Rowley. Jimmy Malone couldn't afford it.

"But the main reason was that Minnie was Mrs. James Malone. Carrie wasn't. In order for her to marry Jimmy in the eyes of the law, Minnie would have to be either dead or divorced. Consider the problems of Jimmy, trying to divorce a wife he couldn't find. Think of the scandal back home in Port Angeles. Jimmy and Carrie were moving to Seattle. No one knew them there. Not until Simone and Armand showed up a few years later."

Vida was looking thoughtful. "So Carrie avoided the Nievalles and would have had a fit if she'd known Aunt Julia was sneaking off to visit Simone. But, Emma, surely the Malones must have run into people who knew them in Port Angeles!"

"I doubt it. I have the feeling that Carrie stayed close to home. In later years she changed. She put on weight, went gray, switched hairstyles. Naturally, she aged. I saw her picture in Claudia Cameron's house and I didn't recognize her. The Malones' home life was probably a bit peculiar, to say the least. I never saw a photo of Minnie Burke, though I suspect she was the obscure figure on the front porch of the Rowley house."

Vida sipped her tea. "Do you think Jimmy knew?"

"He had to. Oh, Carrie could have talked him into the impersonation simply on the grounds that he'd lose out on any of her money if he didn't pretend she was Minnie, his lawful wife. She might even have given him some story about Minnie going away to have the baby and never coming back. But what could Jimmy do? Declare that his mistress had murdered his wife? Announce that he had committed bigamy to get his hands on the Rowley riches? Jimmy Malone was backed into a corner."

"And poor little Walter got stuck in the basement. My, my!" Vida refilled the teakettle. "Do you suppose he was so psychologically damaged that he became a rapist?"

I shook my head. "Who knows? He was very young. He may have sensed what was going on. He was probably fond of Minnie. But I'm not going to play psychologist and try to figure that one."

Vida plunked herself back down in the chair. "No wonder Aunt Julia couldn't stand her mother! Julia was a very sensitive woman. She insisted that Minnie—I mean, Carrie—was evil. I simply gathered that Mrs. Malone had a wretched disposition."

"We had so many wild theories," I said, thinking back to our brainstorming sessions in the Melcher den. Had ghosts been looking over our shoulders? Was Lena sneering at our modern mores? Were Sanford and Rose shaking their heads in dismay? Had Carrie mocked our efforts to bring her to justice? Did poor Minnie will us to find the truth?

But Minnie had been no innocent maid. She had been part of a conspiracy to better herself at the expense of others. Still, she and her unborn child hadn't deserved to die.

"Even when we thought Jimmy might be a bigamist, Carrie made the perfect victim," I continued. "Of course, that's what Carrie wanted everyone to think."

Passing a hand through her jumble of gray curls, Vida wrinkled her brow. "There's another point of view, it seems to me. What if Jimmy had fallen out of love with Minnie? What if the baby was Sanford's? Why couldn't Jimmy have killed Minnie? If he no longer loved her, wouldn't it be more likely that he was the murderer?"

Dutifully, I drank my tea. "I certainly put him at the top of the list, either as the killer of Minnie or Carrie. You may be right about his affections shifting from one woman to the other." It could happen, I thought to myself. It had happened to Tom Cavanaugh. Or so he had led me to believe.

"You might even be right about the baby belonging to Sanford," I went on doggedly. "But it was Carrie, not Jimmy, who Julia hated, and maybe even feared. It's not natural for a daughter to have such hostile feelings for her mother. There's nothing in what Claudia Cameron said that indicated anything but affection and compassion between Julia and her father. I'm making some of my deductions from studying their characters, and Carrie emerges as the strong, willful partner in the Malone marriage. I don't think Jimmy Malone had it in him to commit murder."

Vida was gazing around the kitchen. I knew from experience that she was contemplating cookies. I didn't have any. I offered her cinnamon toast.

"Heavens, no!" Vida professed horror. "I couldn't eat another thing!" Concealing her disappointment, she retrieved the teakettle once more. "Rose had a good motive for killing Minnie. I'm sure you considered her."

"Briefly. But I sensed that the murderer hadn't stayed in Port Angeles. Paul told us how the children had played in the unfinished basement over the years. Rose and Sanford lived there then. Neither would have permitted unsupervised children in the basement if they knew there was a body buried under the dirt."

"What about Eddie and Lena?" asked Vida, pouring more tea.

I felt I was about to float away. "I considered them both. Especially Lena." My smile was ironic. "Eddie had no reason to kill his sister or Minnie. Lena did, at least as far as Minnie was concerned. But Lena was innocent. Still, I think she knew Minnie's body was there. Her feelings were ambivalent about it being found."

Vida's eyes widened. "Lena *knew*? How?"

I shook my head. "I'm not sure how. But she wasn't the sort to miss a trick. Of everyone involved, she would have kept track of all the players. When the Malone family left town, either Carrie or Minnie wasn't with them. Lena would have figured it was Minnie who was absent. Since the governess was involved with Sanford, she would have wondered where the young woman had gone. It's possible that she discovered Minnie's body. She would have realized that Minnie was pregnant and thought that the child was Sanford's. Maybe it was. Had Sanford murdered his mistress? Lena couldn't deal with that. She couldn't risk a scandal, she was too involved with her social and political concerns. Being a God-fearing woman, I think she took her cross from the chain and put it with Minnie, then closed off the basement, canceled the plans for the billiard room, and never revealed her darkest secret. Maybe Lena recorded Minnie's death in her Bible. We never found it. She literally may have taken it to her grave. *Finis coronat opus. The ending crowns the work.* Maybe that was meant for Minnie as much as for Lena."

Vida and I were silent for several moments. "Well." It was Vida who finally spoke, though without her usual decisiveness. "Lena wouldn't have approved of putting a billiard room in the basement, anyway."

"No." I laughed, somewhat halfheartedly. "I'm sure she also got rid of Cornelius's hunting trophies and the elephant-foot umbrella stand and Simone's Parisian furnishings. Of all the family members, Lena's presence remains the strongest."

Vida was staring into her mug. She still wasn't be-
having quite like herself. "Are you going to call your
new friends tonight and reveal all?" There was a trace
of sarcasm in her tone.

I glanced at the kitchen clock. It was not yet eight-
thirty. Paul would still be up, and so, of course, would
Jackie. "I'll probably wait until tomorrow," I said. "The
rates will be down since it's Saturday. I should take a
look at this week's edition of *The Advocate* before I do
anything else."

Vida perked up. "Yes, you should. You won't be
pleased, but at least you'll be able to see the problems
we had for yourself."

I suppressed a smile. *Vida was jealous. Never mind
that the trip to the Olympic Peninsula had been her
idea. She hadn't liked my new friendships, she resented
the time I'd invested in the mystery instead of the paper,
and she definitely didn't care for being left out of my
life. I was touched. But I didn't dare say so. Vida, in her
own words, would have a cat fit.*

I started out into the living room where I'd left the
mail and the newspapers. "I'm still amazed that you
knew some of these people," I remarked, pausing in the
doorway. "Really, Vida, you astound me." It was as
close as I could come to voicing my affection.

Vida shrugged her wide shoulders. "It helped, I
guess. You found out what happened to Simone and
Armand Nievalle. And Aunt Julia. You know that Julia
didn't run off with some half-baked teenager. Claudia
Cameron might like to know that part. I suppose you'll
call her, too."

"I might." And I might not. Claudia had preserved
the image of her sister sneaking off to meet a young
man. It was more romantic than the reality about the
visits to Simone. Enlightening Claudia about the real
reason Julia had run away would only open the door to

other, more sinister revelations. In her old age Claudia didn't need to learn the truth about her mother. No one outside of those of us who had worked on the Melcher mystery needed to know. There would be no feature story for the state wire service and no IRS write-off. My considerable expenses of the past four days were completely down the drain.

"By the way," I said, taking a step back into the kitchen, "you never said what happened to young Charles. Did he eventually leave Alpine, too?"

Suddenly, Vida was again exhibiting distress signals. "No." She fidgeted with her mug, then stood up and rinsed it out in the sink. Her back was turned to me. "Charles stayed here. He would never leave. He couldn't live anywhere else." She looked at me over her shoulder, and to my surprise she actually blushed. "You see, Charles Nievalle is Crazy Eights Neffel."

Fortunately, I didn't laugh. Crazy Eights, Alpine's resident loony, had been raised by Vida's aunt and uncle. Vida and Crazy Eights were practically related. I gave myself a good shake. "That's . . . remarkable. How did Nievalle become Neffel?" I asked, hoping to soothe Vida with a mundane question.

Vida turned to face me, her presence somehow majestic. She took a deep breath. "Charles wasn't very good at spelling. Also he tended to mumble. Somewhere along the line he went from Nievalle to Neffel. French names were quite exotic in a basically Scandinavian community like Alpine. I suppose Neffel sounded more . . . ordinary. The nickname of Crazy Eights was from some sort of game the children played. I don't remember it. We had hopscotch and chuck-the-wicket." The blush had faded and Vida was speaking with dignity.

It would have been unkind to tease Vida about her

connection to Crazy Eights Neffel. "At least he's not a murderer or a rapist or a bigamist," I remarked. "The best news for the Melchers is that they're not related to any of those people. They were all Rowleys and Malones."

When I returned to the kitchen, Vida seemed more at ease. I opened *The Advocate* and immediately cringed. The press work was definitely not up to par and the layout was sloppy. Vida's makeshift job on the hardware and shoe store ads was adequate, if uninspired. I would wait until later to read all of the copy. However, I couldn't resist asking Vida to point out the typo on Darla Puckett's name.

"Page seven," she answered promptly. "It's terrible. When you see it, you'll know why Darla was wild."

I saw it, third column, middle of the page. Now I had to laugh. Carla Steinmetz had erred, all right. Darla Puckett's name was misprinted as *Carla Puckett.*

It could have been worse. Maybe.

After Vida went home around nine, I listened to the rest of my messages. None was urgent. Adam's list of wants included another couple of items, neither of which he would receive before coming to Alpine. My son didn't realize that his mother was unexpectedly broke. The window was closed. But Adam's final, seemingly casual, remarks caught me off-guard.

"It's really great down here, Mom. No rain, no snow. I'm thinking about switching to Arizona or Arizona State this fall. See you."

I could never remember if Tuba City was on daylight savings time. It seemed to me that Arizona was capricious, with individual towns and areas following the local whim. On the chance that it might be after ten o'clock for Ben and Adam, I decided to call them before I unpacked.

Ben's crackling voice on the answering machine caused me to smile. "This is the San Martin de Braga rectory. We're unable to answer your call, but we'll get back to you as soon as we can. Daily Mass is at eight A.M., Sundays and Holy Days at nine A.M. and seven P.M. Confessions are heard starting at four P.M. before the Saturday Mass at five." The message was repeated in Ben's grammatically correct if egregiously accented Spanish. Then he spoke what I presumed was Navajo. I trusted it was better than his Spanish. There was a faint pause. "If this is Hector calling, we'll be at the dig around three. Don't drop that polychrome bowl on your foot. It sounds like a world-class find."

It also sounded as if Ben and Adam were off and running, making momentous discoveries in the fourteenth-century sandstone of Arizona. Their excavations were more uplifting than the one I'd left behind in Port Angeles. I hoped they would bring along pictures of their summer's work. My brief message informed them that I'd call back in the morning. Maybe by then Adam would have forgotten about trying to hold me up. Again. Maybe he would also have forgotten about changing colleges. Again. Neither was likely. My son's memory was often faulty, but rarely when it came to his own wants and needs.

Still gripping the receiver, I decided to go ahead and phone Jackie and Paul. Having assuaged Vida by putting *The Advocate* at the top of my priorities, I felt no need to postpone calling Port Angeles.

Jackie answered on the third ring. "Emma! I just wrapped the bracelet! What about the earrings? I'm sending you a check, but I don't know the amount. How much were the groceries you bought?"

"Skip the check." I grimaced, thinking of my dwindling money reserves and my ascending bank-card statement. "That's my treat as a houseguest. If you mail

it, I'll tear it up. Keep the earrings. I'd never get around
to converting them into clips. But I wouldn't mind having the bracelet."

At my request, Jackie sent Paul upstairs to join us on
the extension. "It's too bad we don't have three-way
calling," Jackie said while we waited for Paul to pick
up the bedroom phone. "We could get Mike and have
him listen, too."

I murmured halfhearted agreement, then heard Paul
come on the line. Not wanting to make my phone bill
any larger than it already was, I tried to keep my sum-
mation brief. Jackie shrieked when I confirmed that
Minnie Burke, not Carrie Rowley, was the real Mrs.
James Malone. She howled when I revealed that their
skeleton was Minnie Burke, not Carrie Rowley. Jackie
was utterly silent when I announced that Carrie had
killed Minnie and impersonated her for most of the next
half-century.

It was Paul who spoke up at the other end of the line.
"I guess I should be relieved. I guess I am. The police
took the remains away this afternoon. We'll have her
buried just the same. I wonder if there's any room in the
family plot at Ocean View?"

Jackie found her voice. "We can't do that! She
wasn't family! Not even by a stretch!" Apparently
Jackie had finally let go. Maybe it was my departure,
not Minnie's, that she'd dreaded. New brides often
missed their mothers, and I had been subbing for Mavis.

I waited for Paul's response. Obviously, he was considering his wife's words. "No, Sweets, I don't agree
that we should exclude Minnie. She lived here, she took
care of the kids, she worked for the family. After the
last few days I feel as if I know her as well as any of
the rest of the ones who died before I was born. We
owe her something. Besides," he added with a weak
chuckle, "maybe it'll put the ghost to rest."

"The ghost!" exclaimed Jackie. "I forgot about the ghost! Oh, Lamb-love, do you think the ghost was Minnie? She might have had dark hair, too, like Simone! The Irish do, you know. They aren't all red-heads."

"I wonder who saw that ghost," Paul said in a musing voice. "I don't suppose we'll ever know."

"Aunt Sara might remember," Jackie said, and I could sense from her tone that she was warming up for another trip into the past. "We could call her and ask if—"

I felt like a third wheel, and it was costing me money. "Hey, Jackie, when your mother gets back from her trip, tell her she owes me a letter. Meanwhile, you two take care. And thanks for the mystery."

"What?" Jackie sounded startled, and I could see her face wreathed with confusion. "Oh! Sure, I'll tell her. Oh, poopy!" In her typical style, Jackie's mood changed abruptly. "Now we've got to find another name for a girl! We were going to call her Carrie! That won't do, will it?" Before I could respond, she went off on another tangent. "But what if it turns out to be twins? Then I could call them Minnie and—"

"Jackie . . ." Paul's voice was gently reproving. "Jimmy was kind of a skunk."

"Not Jimmy!" Jackie cried. "Minnie and *Jimmy*? That's awful. I mean Minnie and *Mickey*. What do you think?"

I didn't. Softly, I hung up the phone. Jackie and Paul Melcher didn't need me. They had each other and the baby to come. I was needed here at home, at *The Advocate,* in the community of Alpine. I was also needed, to some extent, by Adam and Ben, and, I had just discovered, by Vida. So what if there was no husband who needed me? Maybe I didn't need him, either.

I still had to unpack, but I felt obliged to flip through

the mail. There were two letters buried among the bills and circulars. One was from my old high school chum, Ursula Guy Wilcox in Houston. The other was from Tom Cavanaugh. Nervously, I ripped open Tom's letter first.

"Dear Emma," he began, as I noted the date from last Sunday . . .

I've been meaning to write ever since I got back from the conference at Lake Chelan. As usual, the crises piled up in my absence, on both the newspaper and the home front. I won't bore you with the details of the former, since you're all too familiar with what can go wrong with a weekly. Let's just say that I've got a couple of local publishers here in northern California who think they have no responsibility to their community.

As for the domestic side, Sandra started taking a new medication the first of this month and the side effects have been horrific. Her doctors are trying to find something else that will help, not hinder, but so far, no luck. She's become very withdrawn and refuses to leave the house. Given some of her previous escapades, I suppose I should be thankful. But she doesn't want me to go anywhere, either. She clings, but doesn't communicate. As I may have mentioned, we planned a two-week trip to Italy in September, but unless she improves, there's no way I'll be able to get her on a plane.

Enough of gloom. I feel as if I'm taking out all my frustrations on you in this letter. Maybe part of it is that I felt so terrific after our weekend in Chelan. Except for seeing Adam on his way to Arizona, the summer hasn't been much fun.

My original intention was to write you a long, soulful letter about my reactions to our get-together (hey, love those euphemisms!), but to be honest, I haven't had much time for soul-searching. All I know is that I haven't been so happy in twenty years. Really. I also know it's not fair to say so.

One of these days, I'll find a few spare hours to think about us. Don't be angry or hurt because I haven't done it yet. You're always on my mind, a 8vivid presence that helps me get through the rest of the daily grind (right, I said *vivid*—stop making faces—you're always so alive, and you're almost never nuts). Yes, I love you. I love Adam, too. I've got to go now—Sandra just woke up from her fourth nap of the day. Take care, let me hear from you, write when you get a chance.

By the way, one of my publishers in the L.A. area had to fire the ad manager of the weekly I own out in the San Fernando Valley. I've known him for years, and he's basically a good guy and a hard worker who's been through some rough times. I'm told he was heading up to the Pacific Northwest to look for a job. I know you've got Ed Bronsky (who I hope is still taking his energy injections or whatever perked him up), but I thought you might have heard of some other openings through the grapevine. If you know of anybody who's interested, have the contact write to Leo Fulton Walsh, P.O. Box 534, Culver City, California 90255.

Love, Tom

In Alpine, murder always seems to occur
in alphabetical order . . .

. . . and you can be sure Emma Lord,
editor and publisher of *The Alpine Advocate*,
is there to report every detail.

THE EMMA LORD MYSTERIES

by Mary Daheim
Published by Ballantine Books.
Available wherever books are sold.